Toxic Treacle

By

Echo Freer

Best wishes,
Echo Freer

G✦P

First published in the UK by G-Press Fiction, an imprint of
Golden Guides Press Ltd.

10 8 6 4 2 1 3 5 7 9

A CIP catalogue record for this book is available from the
British Library.

ISBN 978-1-78095-005-1

Typeset in 9.5pt Palatino by Mac Style, Beverley, East Yorkshire.
Cover design by Ian Hughes.
Cover illustration by Bethany Straker.
Printed and Bound in the UK.

Golden Guides Press Ltd
P.O. Box 171
Newhaven
E. Sussex
BN9 1AZ
admin@goldenguidespress.com
www.goldenguidespress.com

Dedication

For my gorgeous girl,
Lyra Lily

Contents

Chapter 1

Boys Out on the Town

MICKEY Gibbon, better known as Monkey on the streets, slipped the hood of his jacket over his head and pulled up a blue and white chequered scarf to cover his nose and mouth.

'Who is it?' his friend Trevor, aka Tragic, whispered. They had reached The Plaza in the centre of town: the meeting point of several brotherhood turfs and always an area to be treated with caution.

'Dunno. Can't catch the vocals,' Monkey replied, stuffing the football he'd been carrying, up the front of his hoodie. Their dark clothing could easily go unnoticed in the shadows but the white of the football would attract attention – if not from rival brotherhoods, then from Security.

Monkey craned his neck to try to catch a glimpse of something that could identify the group occupying the town centre. He dodged back against the wall quickly as the sound of a gunshot resonated round The Plaza.

'Shiltz!' Tragic muttered. 'Were they aiming at us?' The use of profane language by pre-breeders had been outlawed by The Assembly on the grounds that: *a foul mouth was the sign of a foul mind.* But most of the adolescent males had developed their own expletives for use in times of extreme stress and Tragic was no exception.

Monkey shrugged. 'Can't tell.' He wrapped his fingers round the knife in his pocket. He carried it for protection – not that it would be much use against a gun. 'Wait there,' he whispered, moving slowly out of the shadows.

An electric billboard above their heads was buzzing erratically. It showed two smiling females with their babies and bore the slogan: *NURTURERS KNOW BEST*. Next to it, a recently posted flyer supporting The Unity Party in the forthcoming General Election had been pasted over the top of several missing persons' posters. It was torn and flapped annoyingly in the icy breeze. Monkey ripped off the bottom of the poster and tossed it aside impatiently, before peering round the corner to spy on the action in the square.

A gang of about a dozen pre-breeders was gathered on the steps of the town clock, their faces concealed beneath dark scarves. It was crucial that Monkey identified the colour of the scarves. In the unlikely event that they were wearing blue and white chequered like he and Tragic, the brotherhood in the square would be Mooners: pre-breeders from Moonstone Park, the Professional Nurturing Zone to the north-east of town, and the boys would be safe to cross. If not, they would have to go home by a circuitous but equally dangerous route, crossing several other brotherhood territories.

Monkey screwed up his eyes to focus on the figures silhouetted against the large illuminated plasma-boards that flashed constant images across The Plaza. Images of mothers and children; their slogans preaching the post-war ideals that Monkey and Tragic had grown up with:

> *SOW THE SEEDS OF LOVE TODAY –*
> *AND REAP THE HARVEST OF*
> *COMPASSION TOMORROW;*
> *RESPECT BREEDS RESPECT;*
> *LOVE CAN HEAL THE WORLD;*
> *A HAPPY CHILD MAKES A HAPPY SOCIETY.*

A loud jeer went up from the square as another shot rang out and sparks flew from the largest screen before it flickered and died. Monkey indicated for Tragic to back away. He thought he'd caught a glimpse of a red scarf, although he couldn't be sure. In the dim light, it could've been brown. Either way, it wasn't a chequered one that would have signalled safety.

'What we gonna do?' Tragic asked.

Monkey's state-of-the-art ring-cam flashed up. It was Vivian, his nurturer. 'Off!' he whispered quickly and the light dimmed on Vivian's image. The last thing he wanted was her applying anguish. 'We'll cut through the Muni and across the bridge.'

Tragic glanced at his own ring-cam, dark and silent. 'I'll just let Jane know that I'll be late,' he said, almost apologetically. He flicked the side of the ring and spoke his nurturer's name gently. Her face flashed up on the screen and, drawing the back of his hand closer to his mouth, he began to whisper, 'Sorry, but I'm going to be a bit late.'

'Where are you? Why have you turned down the visual?' Monkey heard her say.

'I haven't,' Tragic lied. 'It's just very dark.'

'Don't try to fool me, Trevor.'

Monkey shook his head: no way would he let *his* nurturer talk to him like that. Who did Jane think she was? Tradge had practically graduated and she was still treating him like a bub.

Both boys were approaching 16, the age when they would graduate from the care of their nurturers, the females who had bred and nurtured them, to the Breeders' Zone: the specially segregated area where males between the ages of 16 and 20 lived while they fathered children.

'I'm telling the truth,' Tragic lied again. 'It's just that Monkey and I went out to see a vid…'

'A vid? At this time of night?' There was a pause, then, 'Is Mickey with you?'

'Yes.'

'I need you back as soon as you can.' Jane was clearly fretting about her son. 'Do you understand?'

'I know, I know,' Tragic spluttered. 'We just got talking and forgot about the time. I'll be back soon, OK?'

'And be careful,' his nurturer warned.

Monkey shook his head and smiled. He worried for Tragic. It was only six days until he graduated. What would he do then? How was he going to cope when his only contact with

Jane would be by ring-cam or meeting in public? It wasn't that Monkey hated his own nurturer, Vivian, but she was a presidential pain in the butt and he would have to wait another two months before his own graduation. After that, the weekly cam-talks with her would suit him just fine. But Tragic seemed to be terminally attached to Jane – and Monkey didn't need to be a psyche to know that that was a recipe for severe severance trauma.

Monkey punched him on the arm and smiled. 'They don't call you Tragic for nothing, do they, Tradge?'

The heavy sigh of hydraulic brakes startled them.

'Stealth!' Monkey whispered urgently, pushing his friend along the delivery duct behind the mall. 'Keep outta sight.'

Tragic pulled at Monkey's sleeve. 'Come on, Monk. Let's get outta here. We don't want any trouble – not at this stage.' He was aware that, not only were they out of their zone, but they'd also been playing football which was against Health and Safety Laws. It was illegal to kick a ball anywhere except on a State pitch and only then for the purposes of exhibitions or skill practice.

They ducked into a doorway as the armoured stealth bus cruised silently past the end of the alley, its overhead searchlights and infrared scanners sweeping the road in its path. It was crucial that they kept out of its range. To be caught by Security meant a stint on The Farm and none of the pre-breeders Monkey knew who'd been sentenced to cultivation therapy had ever returned to their zone. There'd been Pinto, who'd been found brewing illegal keg and selling it to pre-breeders. He went to The Farm nearly a year ago and he was younger than Monkey so, by rights, he wasn't old enough to graduate yet, but he'd never been heard of again. Then there was Raz, the one time leader of the Mooners, caught in Eastway while he was tasking after curfew, and Jumpy, the hyperactive pre-breeder who was caught with that pretty pre-nurturer from Uplands; Edge and Raffe and Riddler – all gone; erased from the cam-database; untraceable the minute they were transported to The Farm. The rumour was that they'd gone straight from The Farm to the Breeders' Zone and Monkey was sure that, once he graduated, all of his old mates would be there to welcome him. Life was going to be all right once he got to the Breeders' Zone.

'Have they gone?' Tragic whispered.

Monkey leant forward and looked along the length of the passage. The flashes of the receding lights could be seen reflected in the metal shutters across the way. The vehicle had passed.

'It's safe.' Monkey gave Tragic a friendly punch on the arm as they made their way along the delivery duct behind the town centre. 'Look at you, you wuzzle!'

'Am not a wuzzle!' Tragic protested. Monkey grabbed him in a headlock as a playful gesture, but Tragic shrugged him away. 'Leave it out!'

'What is your problem, Tradge?' Monkey couldn't wait to graduate. Tragic, however, seemed less keen and Monkey was at a loss to understand why. 'Graduation's gonna be fridge – I'm telling you – I can't wait. Get my own place; finally doing the business.' He nudged Tragic. 'I mean, can you imagine it? We gonna have the freedom to do what we want, when we want; drink decent keg – legally! I'm gonna be a pro-footballer and, you and me, we can get places next to each other and we can…'

'I keep telling you – it's not like that.' Tragic thrust his hands in his pockets and kicked at a stone. 'You don't get to choose. And you've still got to go to college and work and everything.'

'So?'

'You don't always get to do what you want to do either. It depends what The Assembly thinks you're good at for a start. '

'Yeah, right! And how do you know?'

Tragic hesitated. 'I just heard – that's all.'

'Well, that's not what they told us at T.R.E.A.C.L.E.,' Monkey countered.

T.R.E.A.C.L.E. or 'Training and Resources for the Education of Adolescent Children in a Loving Environment' was compulsory for all pre-nurturers and pre-breeders from the age of 12 until they graduated at 16. The weekly meetings were in addition to formal schooling and focused on basic citizenship, civil duties and parenting, through games, activities and rewards. Few of the pre-breeders of Monkey and Tragic's age still attended as they approached graduation – although it was a brave leader who reported truants: most were content to welcome the peace that their absence afforded. Tonight, however, despite believing that he had outgrown T.R.E.A.C.L.E., Monkey was happy to cite their teachings to support his own argument.

'Trust me, Tradge, when we graduate, we are going to paradise, my old chum. And there's centres where pre-nurturers come and you can... you know.'

'I know. And I know what they told us too, but...'

Monkey gave him another nudge. 'Hey, lighten up, mate. You do want to do it, right?'

'Yeah, of course I want to do it. Only...'

'Only what? I've been dreaming of this for years.'

'I keep telling you – it's not like that. For a start, what if Angel doesn't choose you for breeding?'

Angel Ellison was a pre-nurturer in their division at school. Monkey really liked her and was hoping, once she'd also turned 16, she would select him as her breeder. Then, once he'd bred a couple of bubs for her, he'd progress to the Providers' Zone where he'd spend his days playing footie, watching vids and drinking decent keg until it was time to retire to The Pastures. What more could any full-blooded male want? He really couldn't understand Tragic's problem.

'You know as well as I do, she'd be mad not to,' he laughed trying to conceal the niggling doubt that Angel might not choose him to breed with. 'But, even so, there are others. I mean, Jeanie's OK, or Becca.'

'Yeah, but what if Moni Morrison gets in there first and chooses you?'

Monkey grimaced. 'That T.R.E.A.C.L.E. tart? No way!'

'That's my point,' Tragic said. 'It's not your shout.'

Monkey hesitated, then shrugged. 'Neh! You're just getting cold feet!' he rationalised. Then, adopting a lighter tone, he put a comforting arm round his friend. 'Poor little Tradge – snatched away from his mov and the warmth of the Nurturing Zone. How will he cope?'

They walked on laughing and teasing as they made their way through the Municipal Leisure Zone. At that time of night, it was almost deserted and they walked quickly, skirting the shopping mall and eateries of the town, most of which were closed for the evening. A male-only snug near the western side of town was just closing up, its shutters only partially down. Monkey peered through the door to try and catch a glimpse of the interior. He'd been past during the day many times and been intrigued by its eating alcoves and alcohol areas; all dimly lit and mysterious and, even better, all to be accessible to him in just eight weeks. Tonight though, a couple of lone providers were sitting over their pints of keg. Although the curfew only applied to pres – pre-breeders and pre-nurturers under 16 – most adults rarely ventured out after dark. The risk of meeting the brotherhoods was too great. The two in the snug were staring at the info-screen above the bar and Monkey could just make out a female newsreader relating the story of an artisan nurturer who had just given birth to quads.

One of the providers shook his head and slurred, 'I hope it was your last breeding, mate! Otherwise, the poor bloke's out for a duck!' The other man concurred and they both took a sip of their beer before sinking down on their stools again.

The newsreader moved on to an item about some young pro-footballer giving an exhibition over the border in Cymru – all news was good news under The Assembly, with the sole exception of the missing persons' roll call at the end of each bulletin.

'Look at it, Tradge,' Monkey started up the conversation again. 'How stupe is that?'

'If you like that sort of thing,' Tragic agreed, half-heartedly.

'That could be you and me in a few months; just dawdlin', watching the game, having a few kegs.' Monkey seemed enraptured with the image of male independence before him.

The provider behind the bar looked up and eyed them suspiciously. He said nothing: it was never a good idea to tackle a pre single-handed; you never knew where the rest of their hood might be and no one wanted to invite trouble. As the info-screen flicked on to a Party Election Broadcast, they noticed him raise his ring-cam to his lips. It didn't take a genius to work out that he was calling Security.

'Come on, I need to get back: I promised Jane,' Tragic said.

They walked on, all the time on their guard for hoods or stealths. The plasma-screens along the way, as well as promoting the messages of peace from The Assembly and election information, flashed up advertisements for local services and requests for the whereabouts of missing persons. An accountant beaming over his books and offering reduced fees for those about to move on to The Pastures, merged into a photo of a missing nurturer smiling with her offspring and the promise of a reward for information, faded into a lawyer staring sternly into the eyes of the onlooker. The boys took little notice of the screens as they made their way through the town: they needed to stay alert. Every junction required the utmost caution; every corner was approached with self-preservation as a priority. Monkey took the lead, checking that the way was clear before leading Tragic over the Lower Bridge towards the male zones.

The town was bisected by the river as it meandered its way westwards to the coast. The main part of the town had expanded on the northern side of the river with the south bank being largely marshland and flood plain. Towards the end of the last century though, the south bank had been drained and developed as high-rise affordable housing. And, after the Oil Wars, when the balance of power changed, the layout lent itself very well to the new Segregation Laws. The males, both the teenage breeders and, once they had produced a maximum of three offspring, the post-20-year-old providers, lived in their own zones on the south bank, separated from the nurturers and their offspring. The main residential areas of the town were now solely allocated to females; nurturers and their extended families in zones according to their status, as well as some zones designated for 'spins': those females either unable, or unwilling, to bear children.

Monkey had, for years, been fascinated by the vast estates to the south of the town, now gated and secure. He couldn't understand the need for such security; was it to keep the breeders and providers in, or to keep prying pre-breeders like himself out? As he and Tragic passed the high metal gates of the Providers' Zone, Monkey's awe could not be concealed.

'Just think, Tradge, a few more years and we could be in there.'

Tragic sighed. 'You just don't get it, do you?'

'Get what?'

'You think it's going to be some sort of Utopia and we'll be free once we graduate, but we won't – I'm telling you!'

'I think you've been at the mov-love too much. Jane doesn't want you graduating, so she's filled your head with all sorts of garbage. I mean, look.' They had reached the next area, the one into which they would both be graduating shortly: the Breeders' Zone. 'Hold up!' Monkey said, running down the towpath between the high walls of the Breeders' Zone and the river. 'Give me a leg up.'

In a well-practised manoeuvre, Tragic clasped his hands together and Monkey quickly stepped on them to be pushed upwards, trying to catch a glimpse of what lay behind the security fence. But it had been designed specifically to avoid all such attempts at snooping. Even the bridge had had its parapets dismantled so that prying eyes could not infiltrate the male zones.

'Aw, man!' Monkey teased. 'It is so unjust that you're going to see it before…' He stopped short.

They had both heard it; the breaking of glass followed by the muted footsteps of a group trying to move quietly.

Security usually travelled in stealths for safety so, the chances were, it was a brotherhood.

'Quick!' Monkey whispered urgently, jumping down to the ground and grabbing Tragic's sleeve.

He dragged his friend down the slippery bank of the river and pushed him under the vaulted stonework of the Upper Bridge. They backed away from the open air until they were several metres in from the edge, balancing on a narrow ledge of brickwork that was barely more than a foot's width wide. It ran along the underside of the bridge about 30 centimetres above the fast-flowing water and was slippery with mud from the recent spring floods. Monkey pulled his hood down as low as he could over his face and pushed his chequered scarf down inside his jacket out of sight – he didn't want anything light-coloured to give away their presence.

They could hear voices on the towpath; probably about a dozen of them.

'Where'd they go?' a voice echoed from the riverbank.

'Dunno,' replied another. 'Reckon they're Villagers?'

'Neh, Mooners or Elders judging by the flag,' said the first voice.

Tragic poked Monkey as though reprimanding him for allowing his scarf to be seen. Eldridge Way brotherhood also wore chequers, in green rather than blue but, still, easy to mistake in the dark.

Monkey was annoyed with himself. He was hanging on to the metal struts under the bridge and trying to steady his breathing as he listened to the dialogue above them.

'They gotta come back this way – 'less they're gonna swim home. So, if we stay here, we'll cut 'em off,' he heard another voice remark.

'Cut 'em off, then cut 'em up!' There was the sound of laughter and Tragic shot Monkey a look of terror.

Monkey's mouth was dry and, despite the cold, his palms were sweating. Or were they? Carefully, he let go of the metal struts and wiped them, one at a time, down his jacket. He flinched as he pushed his right hand down the fabric and, peering through the dark, saw a deep stain. It was blood where he'd pressed his palm into his own blade so hard that he'd cut himself. The last thing he wanted was to be leaving a trail of blood. Still, no point worrying about that just yet; he had to get himself and Tragic out of there first.

He beckoned Tragic to follow him as he slowly began to edge his way along the ledge, away from the towpath side of the bridge, back towards the road they'd just come along. He knew he wasn't leading his friend to safety, but at least they would stand more chance of escape if they doubled back on themselves and legged it through a built-up area. If they'd tried to run out along the towpath into the hinters, there was nothing but the turbine park and a bio-fuel depot. Tentatively, he pushed one foot forward then slid the other after it, inching forwards, his fingers clinging to the ironwork above his head, his back pressed against the damp stone. Every few steps, he turned his head, checking that Tragic was keeping up.

The voices overhead were getting further and further away and the lights of the town, glimmering on the river, grew closer. If they could make it back to town, there was a delivery duct just metres from the Lower Bridge; they could dodge into it and make their way back towards The Plaza, then up through the village – it shouldn't be too bad at this time of night. Villagers weren't much of a threat. The town lights were still on, so Monkey knew it must still be before midnight. Suddenly, a piece of stonework gave way under Monkey's foot and he slithered off the ledge sending fragments of stone into the river.

'Hey!' A cry went up from the hood. 'They're there!'

Tragic swore. 'We've got to get out of here!'

Monkey's leg was dangling in the water, icy from recently melted snow. His slashed hand was sore but he clung to the metalwork above his head to save himself from slipping into the swollen river. Just then, the football that had been concealed under his jacket, slipped out and hit the water with a splash before being carried away downstream. He cursed under his breath.

'Over there! Get 'em!' someone from the brotherhood cried out.

'Just run for it!' Monkey hoisted himself back on to the ledge and they shuffled, as quickly as they could, towards the eastern side. The footsteps of the brotherhood running across the road above them reverberated through the fabric of the bridge. They were overtaking them. There was a flash of light and a gunshot echoed deafeningly around the arched underbelly of the structure as a bullet ricocheted off the pillars that supported it.

Monkey and Tragic both ducked instinctively but it was hard to manoeuvre in such a confined space. Monkey could make out the silhouettes of their pursuers at the eastern side of the bridge, waiting for them. He clenched his teeth in exasperation; they'd been too slow! He looked back from where they'd come, but the outlines of the rest of the hood told him that they'd got them in a pincer movement – both exits blocked. There was nothing else for it.

'Into the water,' he whispered. 'Quietly as you can. Don't make a splash.'

'Are you raggin' me?' Tragic asked in shock.

'Just do it!'

'I can't swim in that.'

'You won't have to,' Monkey said, lowering himself off the ledge and gasping as the cold water hit him. 'Well, not very far anyway! Look where the footie's gone.' He pointed to the white ball bobbing westward away from town and drifting across the river towards the north bank. 'Take a deep breath and keep your head down until I get us out of range, then all you've gotta do is float. The current'll do the rest.'

'No wa…!' Another shot echoed round the underneath of the bridge, instantly prompting Tragic to slither into the swollen river. 'Crap!'

'Hold on to me – and don't struggle!' With that, Monkey pushed off from the side.

'There they are!' shouted one of the hood from the bank.

Monkey braced himself for the shot that he was sure was going to follow, then felt relief course through him as the whole town was plunged into darkness. Midnight! Saved by the Energy Conservation Shut Down.

'You're doing fine,' he reassured Tragic. 'We'll have you home in no time.'

With one arm held firmly on to his friend and the other acting as a rudder, he steered them diagonally across to the Nurturing Zones. Monkey was an excellent swimmer but negotiating a seething mass of water was tougher than he'd realised. Tragic had done exactly as he'd been told and his compliance had been a huge part of their success. Together, they'd half-drifted, half-swum until they were out of sight of both the bridge and the brotherhood.

'Jack-heads!' Monkey laughed as he helped Tragic out of the river. 'They're probably still looking for us back there. Stupid buffs!' They'd come ashore by the Lunar Park in the hinter of Uplands; about a mile out of their way. But they were safe – cold and wet, but safe.

'I just want to get back,' Tragic said, shaking the water off his ring-cam and pressing it.

'Leave it,' Monkey warned. 'We're in for enough anguish when we get home. No point in inviting it already.'

The pair walked home in silence. Uplands was a district mainly allocated to young nurturers with pre-schoolers. Its own brotherhood was young and, by and large, adhered to the curfew so the chances of meeting another hood were slight. They were grateful for the chance to relax their vigilance. By the time they parted company, it was almost two in the morning. Monkey's hand was throbbing but the buzz of adrenaline pulsed through him. Tragic was shivering and seemed drained.

'See you tomorrow,' Monkey called as they went their separate ways. 'Usual place – OK?'

Tragic nodded slowly. He turned towards his home, then stopped and called after his friend, 'You've been a good mate

18

to me, you know, Monk. I want you to know that, whatever happens, you're the best.'

Monkey shook his head again and laughed. 'Less of the tragic, Tragic! We came out of it all right didn't we?'

'Yeah, yeah,' Tragic said. 'It's not that; I meant what we were talking about earlier…'

'You'll be fine. I've told you, stop being a wuz.'

Tragic gave a half smile and nodded sadly. 'Check you later.' Then he walked down the hill to his home.

Drama queen! Monkey chuckled to himself; anyone would think he was going to his death rather than his graduation the way he went on. He broke into a jog – he was going to get some macro anguish from Vivian about tonight, but what did he care? He'd only got two more months of her in his face all the time and then graduation. He couldn't wait!

Chapter 2

The Tragic Disappearance of Tragic

THE FOLLOWING morning, Monkey kicked his heels against a clump of grass that had broken through the concrete of the road as he waited by the disused loco bridge.

'Time,' he said to his clenched fist.

'O-8:45,' an automated voice replied from the ring on his left hand.

He looked round impatiently. The street was deserted. Most mornings, he and Tragic tried to time their journey to school to casually coincide with that of Angel Ellison but he knew that, by now, she'd be long gone. Almost everyone of school age would be in class and most of the nurturers would be at work. The only people left on the streets at this time would be the young nurturers with their bubbies and post-nurturers with their pets; the feral pre-breeders of the hoods looking for a rush, and the special security squads sent out to round up any brotherhood members too slow to evade the school patrollers – staff sent out to hurry along tardy students. If he didn't get to school soon, Monkey would find himself arrested, hauled off in a stealth van and shipped off to The Farm.

'Tragic,' he said into his ring-cam, then waited for it to light up. But it didn't.

Monkey sighed. He wished his mate would get a move on. It wasn't like Tragic to be late. Jane, his nurturer, was always up at six to make sure that her son was awake and fed before she left for the studio. Jane certainly took her role seriously – not like Vivian. Sure, she'd been there for him when he was younger but, for the last couple of years, she'd practically washed her hands of him. Not that it bothered Monkey.

He spoke to his ring-cam again, 'Tragic?' But still nothing.

Where was he? Maybe he'd caught a chill last night? Monkey speculated. Their little escapade had certainly put the wind up him. That, coupled with his stupid fretting about graduation, might have been enough to make him ill. But, although sickness would explain his friend's absence, it wouldn't account for the fact that Tragic wasn't answering. Even if he was in bed, he would still be able to speak, wouldn't he?

Monkey looked round anxiously checking for patrollers or catchers. It was no good; he couldn't wait around any longer; he needed to get to school himself before the electronic register alerted the school to his absence and they came round looking for him. It was imperative that he made it through the next few weeks with a clean slate. If Tragic didn't show up later, he'd go round to his house after school and find out the score face to face.

He pulled up the collar of his jacket and winced as he pushed his hands deep into his pockets. Vivian had thrown a frenz last night when she'd seen his hand. Still, it paid to have a nurturer who was a doctor. She'd stitched him up and dressed it and, although it still throbbed, he knew it would earn him max kude at school. He wouldn't tell them it was self-inflicted of course, he'd just say he got it in a jar last night.

There'd been some extreme anguish when she'd seen the blade. But he'd refused to give it up. He wrapped his bandaged hand around it now; it was his security as he walked to school alone. Monkey knew, though, that he'd have to find somewhere to ditch it before he reached the gates. He didn't want the detectors going off the minute he passed the scanners. He'd be in enough bother today just for being late.

The houses of Moonstone Park were secluded and detached. Built in the early part of the previous century, they denoted the status of the nurturers who lived there. Most were surrounded by large sustenance patches and screened from the road by hedges and walls. As a doctor, Vivian's family warranted a house in a professional zone, but Tragic and his mov were there almost by default: Jane was an artist and 'creatives' were normally allocated houses in The Village. But, as Jane did commissioned work for The Assembly, she'd managed to acquire a house just inside the much sought after Moonstone Park boundary; one of two converted gatehouses to a larger mansion that was now a pre-school. Vivian was forever telling Monkey that he should be grateful for where he lived, but Monkey wasn't impressed. Mooners had a rep for being wuzzles – not quite in the same league as Villagers, but not far off – and as such, were often the target of anguish when they went into town. If Monkey's mov had lived in an artisan or manual zone, he'd get more 'spect and less angst and life would be easier all round.

Moonstone Academy was of a more recent design than the other buildings in the zone. It had been built at the end of the last century, just before the war and was one of the more affluent, academic and, consequently, 'soft' educational institutions in town, a reflection of its catchment area. It also had a male head teacher, Professor Reed, one of the few providers to rise to a position of authority in post-war society. And, although physical punishment had not been allowed for half a century, Professor Reed had an air of authority that, despite the law, suggested it was always a possibility. As a result, there was little trouble at Moonstone Academy compared to some of the other schools in town. But still, Monkey was reassured to know that he'd got his weapon for the journey – it only took a few restless hoods to decide to go looking for trouble and that would be the end of his dream – and no way was Monkey risking that.

In his head, Monkey had his life all planned out. He wasn't one of those materialistic pre-breeders like Piers Fielding, who wanted a penthouse and a pool and a boring job on the exchange buying and selling commodities such as wood or apples or electrics. Once Monkey had graduated, he was going to enrol for soccer school and become a pro.

But, in order to ensure that that happened, he had to keep clean for two more months. As he approached the enormous metal gates of the school, he checked that there were no cameras watching, then bent down, as though refastening his shoe, and carefully slid his blade into a tight gap between the walls of two sustenance patches, a couple of houses down from the gates. He stood up, pushed his hood from his head and walked leisurely up to the iris recognition scanner at the entrance to Moonstone Academy. Once he'd been checked, the single metal barrier swung open allowing him to enter the grounds. He made his way across the forecourt, only vaguely aware of the cameras whirring, tracking his progress to the double doors at the front of the building.

The lobby was deserted. Instruction had started and he was going to be in big angst. He placed his ring-cam against a second scanner and began to walk past, but a siren sounded. Shiltz! He'd thought he might have got away with it.

A stocky patroller came out of the office, one of the many providers brought in by stealth vans to work in the school. 'Michael Gibbon?'

'You must be new, geez,' Monkey said, cheekily. 'It's Mickey to my friends.'

'I'm no friend of yours. Now, get inside!' the provider ordered. Monkey shrugged and did as he'd been told. 'Wait there until Professor Reed calls you.'

'Or?' Monkey laughed.

The burly man approached him with a look of menace in his eye. 'There is no "or". You wait there like I told you. End.'

Monkey's bravado faded and he put up his hands as a sign of capitulation. 'Hey! Easy!' He leant back against the wall.

'Stand up straight!' the patroller barked.

Monkey slowly pulled himself upright and gazed at the poster on the opposite wall: *Hug the hood to make them good.* Couldn't this guy read? He was supposed to be being nice to Monkey, not shouting at him! Everyone knew that *shouting bred resentment and resentment was hatred – and the only antidote to hatred was loving kindness.* So, why was this new bloke intent on breeding resentment and hatred? Professor Reed ran a clean school; he never needed to shout. Sure, he doled out punishments – like sweeping the yard, scrubbing the hall floor or washing down the walls of the sports hall – but he would never shout.

With that, the Professor opened an inner door. 'Come in, Mickey.'

Monkey eyed the patroller with a look as if to say, You see! *He* knows how to show respect. Then, he followed the head teacher into his room. One wall was dominated by an enormous screen showing dozens of images from all round the school. Every room, every corridor, every open space was relayed live into the head's office.

'My data tells me that you were 15 minutes late this morning. I'd like you to explain yourself,' he said.

'Erm…' What could he say? He looked down and saw the bandage on his hand. 'I cut myself at breakfast and my mov had to stitch me up.' It wasn't a total lie – only the bit about it happening at breakfast.

'And if I contact Doctor Mov Gibbon and ask her, will she verify your story?' the Professor asked, looking him straight in the eye.

'Of course!' Monkey feigned offence. 'But she's in clinic this morning.'

'And your sister?'

'Ask her yourself,' Monkey challenged.

Penny was OK. At 13, she was just becoming a pre-nurturer, so she wasn't allowed to play with Monkey the way she used to when they were younger; most of her time had to go on domestics these days. But, even so, he'd spun her the line that he'd cut it on a kitchen knife, so he felt confident that she wouldn't let him down.

The teacher spoke into a small mic above the plasma-board on the wall and an image of Penny's division came forward on the screen. A provider was teaching maths but the Professor interrupted.

'I'd like to speak to Penny Gibbon.' The lens swivelled round until Penny's face was centre screen. 'Penny, I'd like you to tell me how your brother cut his hand.'.

Without hesitation, Penny replied, 'He cut it on a kitchen knife, Professor. Mov Vivian had to suture and dress it.'

'Thank you.' The screen returned to the multi-image again and Monkey stifled a grin. Nice one! But his relief was premature. 'Now, perhaps you can explain the security report placing you and Trevor Patterson out of zone after curfew last night?'

Oh crud! There was nothing else for it, he was going to have to use his old favourite. 'Wasn't us, Professor. Must be mistaken identity. You know what these old security cams are like.'

'Credit me with some intelligence, Mickey,' the head teacher said. 'If I refer this back to Security, you know what that would mean, don't you?'

Monkey nodded, suddenly sober with the realisation of how close he was to losing everything.

'You are a bright boy, Mickey and, after your graduation in a few weeks, I think you should seriously consider applying for university.' Monkey rolled his eyes but the Professor was not finished. 'I've seen many a pre-breeder like you waste his intellect once he graduates, and then end up in some menial job, regretting it. You could easily follow in your nurturer's footsteps and become a doctor. Or, you could do worse than becoming a teacher like myself…' Monkey raised an eyebrow – he'd rather have been caught by the hood last night than even contemplate a future like the Prof's.

Professor Reed ignored Monkey's silent insult. 'I would like to make you wash the yard with a toothbrush but, obviously, you need to keep your hand dry. Therefore, you will cut all the grass pathways in the school sustenance patch – with scissors. Now, before you go to your division, perhaps you can throw some light on the whereabouts of Trevor Patterson?'

Monkey shrugged. This, he didn't need to lie about. 'I dunno. He didn't turn up this morning and he's not answering his ring-cam.'

'I'm aware of that,' replied the head.

'So why're you asking me? Ask his nurturer,' Monkey said.

The Professor held him with a contemptuous stare before turning his back on him. 'Dismissed.'

Monkey reckoned he'd got off lightly, considering that they'd actually been clocked last night. It could've been much worse. People had been sent to The Farm for less. They'd only gone out to kick a ball around: it wasn't like they'd set out to cause trouble. Anyway, there was no way he was cutting any grass or scrubbing any yards or anything else in his own time: he would truck off Art to carry out his punishment – go through the motions to satisfy the Prof and Security.

He left the office with a bounce in his step and a smirk to the new patroller sitting in the foyer, then tried Tragic again. But there was still no response. He didn't know what Tragic was playing at and he was annoyed with him, so he closed down his own ring-cam and strode into class, holding up his bandaged hand like a war wound.

Chapter 3

Absent Friends

MONKEY couldn't wait to get to class so that he could impress Angel with his battle injury. Mov Felton, the I.D.H.C. teacher, had tried to get large with him. She'd accused him of being late and then disrupting the instruction by bragging about his injured hand. Monkey had just laughed at her. He was one of the oldest in the class and just killing time. Apart from Tragic, who would be leaving at the end of the week anyway, the only pre-breeders left in his division were Jordan Grainger, Mark Watts, Leon McRae – tags: Danger, Fuse and Kraze – and Monkey himself.

Kraze had been the leader of the Mooners since Raz had gone to The Farm. It had been a toss up between him and Monkey but Monkey had let Kraze have the role. Kraze knew that Monkey had relinquished his claim to leadership and, in a strange way, that gave Monkey the upper hand. Kraze might be the front man, but Monkey was the power behind the hood. What Monkey said, went – regardless of Kraze's opinion. If Monkey decided to pay attention and work hard, then the rest of the hood paid attention. If, like this morning, Monkey decided to disrupt I.D.H.C., the rest of the pre-breeders followed suit. They talked, they joked, they tossed the key to the plasma-screen around between them and, generally, ignored Mov Felton. She flapped, she ordered, she threatened. But Monkey knew there was a limit to how many times and how many students could be sent out. They were in a win-win situation and, like it or not, Mov Felton had to put up with them.

In fact, Monkey's beef was not with Mov Felton, it was with her subject: Identity, Diversity, History and Citizenship!

What was the point of it? Hadn't he had enough of that at T.R.E.A.C.L.E.? Today, they'd been watching pre-revolution footage of some war crimes trial. An old man was sitting with his arms folded, refusing to answer questions, claiming that he didn't recognise the Court.

Monkey draped himself over his chair with his back to the screen and called out, 'I refuse to recognise this instruction!' Everyone laughed and he enjoyed being the centre of attention, especially where Angel was concerned.

It had not been a personal protest against the instructor, it had been a gesture of disrespect for the tedium of the subject. Now, if Mov Felton had shown them vids like the ones Tragic had acquired a few weeks ago, then I.D.H.C. might not have been such a brain-drain.

Tragic had told Monkey to go round to his house one evening. 'Just you, not the rest of the hood, OK?' he'd insisted. He'd shown Monkey vids, old ones from before the war, of football matches. Matches, the like of which Monkey had never seen. They were proper matches with goals and winners and tournaments and trophies. There were even some international games; one country playing against another. Imagine it – going across the ocean to other lands and cultures just to play football. Monkey had been enthralled.

'Where d'ya get them?' he'd asked Tragic.

'Jane got them for me. She found them.'

Monkey eyed him, unconvinced. Tragic never could lie. 'OK – if you say so.'

Monkey hadn't pushed it. He'd sat back and watched in awe at the skill of those old guys. He knew, of course that *competition was the enemy of co-operation* but, to watch those old footballers working together and scoring goals and winning trophies, it certainly didn't look like competition had spoiled their co-operation – that was real teamwork. And the thrill they'd shown when they'd driven the ball into the net, it was inspirational: like nothing he'd ever seen before.

That's when he and Tragic had started going out to kick a ball around – and score goals – even though it was only against a door or between jumpers. Several times a week, they'd split from the hood, watch the old vids and then go out and play football. It had become their 'thing'. And, that morning, the boring vid of the old geezer with his arms crossed had only served to remind Monkey of Tragic's absence and the fact that, in five days, when Tragic graduated, it would be a permanent situation. It wasn't something he wanted to dwell on.

'Hey, who wants to see some gore?' he pushed back his chair noisily and sauntered across the classroom to the table where Angel was sitting with a group of pre-nurturers. Ignoring Mov Felton's pleas to sit down, pay attention and think of others who wanted to learn, he pulled the bandage away from his palm to reveal the top of the gash on his hand. 'Neat, eh?' he said, smiling at Angel.

Moni Morrison leant across, looked at his hand, then flashed him a smile. 'Quite the wounded soldier, aren't you, Monkey?' Moni, the daughter of a T.R.E.A.C.L.E. trainer, and an enthusiastic assistant at meetings herself, had always had a soft spot for Monkey: a soft spot that was far from reciprocated.

'What's it to you?' Monkey retorted coldly. If Monkey dreamt about being chosen for breeding by Angel, he had nightmares that Moni might get to him first. He was eager to dispel any possible feelings that she might be harbouring in that field.

'You do know that conflict never resolved anything, don't you?' Moni went on. 'It's so pre-war. Civilised societies communicate with empathy.'

Monkey raised his eyebrow and shrugged. 'Guess it must be in my genes.' And he walked from the room, throwing Mov Felton the excuse that he needed to relieve himself.

Later that afternoon, Angel walked home from school with him and expressed no surprise when he retrieved his blade from between the walls.

She pointed to his bandaged hand. 'It must hurt,' she said, keeping a circumspect distance from him as they talked. Any behaviour that smacked of flirting was strictly forbidden outside the Breeding Centres.

'Neh! You should've seen the other geez,' Monkey laughed.

'You could've got caught,' she went on, anxiously. 'Didn't you think of that?'

'We're too clever.' He ducked and dodged, avoiding punches like one of the pre-war boxers Tragic had showed him on vid. 'We're like neenjas.'

Angel smiled. 'So, what happened to Tragic, then? If you two are so clever, why didn't he turn up today? Was he arrested?'

'Neh!' Monkey laughed, as though it was the most ridiculous suggestion in the world. 'He had a meeting about his graduation,' he lied. 'I'm just going to see him now.'

Angel looked at him but said nothing. Monkey averted his eyes guiltily and they walked on in silence until they came to the disused bridge.

'See you tomorrow,' Angel said, giving a slight wave and heading home.

Monkey gave her a nod before turning southwards towards The Village boundary and Tragic's house. He felt uncomfortable about lying to Angel. He liked her; liked her a lot. Tragic was forever telling him that it didn't always work out that they'd be able to breed with the nurturer of their choice, but Monkey hoped, more than anything else in his life (except maybe becoming a pro-footballer) that no one else would choose him for breeding before Angel turned 16 – especially Moni Morrison. He felt his face flush with rage, before putting the thought out of his head and breaking into a jog.

When he arrived at the small lodge that Tragic shared with Jane, far from allaying Monkey's fears about his friend's absence, what he found only served to deepen them. The one thing he could always say about Tragic's home was that it was just that: a home. Jane's artistic temperament had created a welcoming atmosphere. It was hard to explain it but, whenever he went to Tragic's, there was a warmth about the place. It was cosy and friendly – much more so than any of his other mates' houses. Friendlier than his own home, if he was being honest.

As he banged on the door now, though, it wasn't at all welcoming. The shutters were down and there were no lights on inside. He called through the mail-slat but no one answered. There was no sound or movement at all.

Perplexed, he ventured round to the back of the house. The windows at the back were also shuttered and the doors locked. His attention was drawn to the cables from the wind turbine by the side of the sustenance patch; they were draped over the fence and attached to the generator of the other gatehouse next door. That was weird. Why would Tragic's nurturer give away their electricity? Didn't she know it was illegal? All surplus supplies had to be given to The Assembly.

Monkey hoisted himself up on the roof of the bike-house and peered through a damaged slat on the shutters over Tragic's bedroom window.

'Tragic!' Monkey called, banging on the shutter. 'Tradge! Are you in there?'

As his eyes grew accustomed to the darkness inside the house, he could make out several items strewn across the bed and floor: clothes, shoes, backpacks and papers. Tragic, apart from being tragically attached to his nurturer, was also tragically tidy. But today, not only was Tradge missing from school, he was missing from home, too. In other circumstances, it would be natural to assume that the house had been jacked, but Monkey had been all round and there was no sign of entry. Had he been arrested, as Angel suggested? Or maybe he'd done a runner – but to where? There was nowhere to run – Security was everywhere. And, more worryingly, if he had been arrested because of last night, wouldn't they be round looking for Monkey before long?

He slid down from the roof of the lean-to and the door swung open to reveal that it was empty: the bikes had gone. Security didn't take people on their bikes – Monkey knew that much. Perhaps Tragic had graduated early? Maybe he hadn't wanted the whole graduation party thing and had just slipped off to the Breeders' Zone without any fuss? But, then, why would he leave his room in such a mess? Why hadn't he taken his things with him? If he'd graduated, surely Professor Reed would've known and wouldn't have been giving Monkey the third degree as to his whereabouts? And why was Jane giving her power to the post-nurturer next door?

Something was seriously not right about this. Monkey spoke into his ring-cam. 'Angel.' The girl's face flashed on to the screen and his stomach tightened with a frisson of excitement. 'Can I trust you?'

Chapter 4

Searching for Tragic

'YOUR dinner's ready,' Vivian said wearily as Monkey pulled on his jacket. He ignored her and headed for the door. She raised her voice to try and sound authoritative. 'Mickey, you haven't eaten and you need to take your vitamins.'

She held out her hand with two tablets in the palm.

'I told you – I ain't taking no more vitamins. What is it with the vitamins anyway? When I was a bub, you said if we ate a healthy diet we'd get all the nutrients we needed – right? So why, the minute we get to 12, does The Assembly start pumping us full of vitamins? Maybe, instead of sending all the pres to T.R.E.A.C.L.E., they should send all the nurturers to nutrition class, eh?'

'Just take them – please.'

He took the tablets and put them in his pocket. 'I'll take them later.'

Vivian sighed. 'Thank you. But you can't go out, you have homework to do.'

'And?'

She sighed again. 'Just because you're about to graduate, it doesn't mean you can give up on your education. You're out roaming the streets every night. When are you going to knuckle down and start acting like the adult you're going to be in a few weeks?'

Monkey eyed her with contempt. 'What – one of those *adults* you're so fond of downing at every opportunity?'

'Here we go again,' his sister, Penny, groaned.

Instantly, Vivian turned to her daughter and her voice softened. 'It's all right, darling. '

33

'Oh yeah – she's your *darling*! I'm just some fegging piece of crap you can't wait to pack off to the good-riddance heap…'

Vivian slammed her hand down on the table. 'I am sick of you and your foul mouth!' she railed.

His grand-mov, Sarah, piped up, 'We wouldn't have stood for it in our day. Mind you, we weren't trying to be everything to everyone…'

'Thank you – I really don't need this right now!' Vivian snapped at the older woman.

Vivian turned her back on Grand-mov and tried to position herself between her son and the door. 'You are not going out tonight. I forbid it.'

'Forbid it?' Monkey gave an ironic chuckle. 'Really?'

'Yes, really! Now, go to your room and do your homework.'

'Go boil yourself in crap,' Monkey said, calmly pushing her to one side and leaving the house.

It was a ritual they went through most nights and Vivian never won. It was amazing to Monkey that she hadn't given up by now. There'd be anguish again tonight when he got in, but what was new? After all, what could she do? Ground him? Fat chance of that! He'd just go out anyway. Corporal punishment was illegal and, if she even tried to lift a finger to him, she knew he had twice her strength. So, if he retaliated, she'd come off worse – and then have to explain herself to the authorities; probably even lose her job. She was in a no-win situation, whichever way you looked at it.

'How dare you!' Vivian yelled down the path after him. 'Come back this minute!'

Monkey ignored her. He pulled the hood of his jacket over his head, covered his nose with the chequered scarf of the Mooners and tossed the vitamin tablets to the ground. He breathed a sigh of relief to be out of the house and felt for the security of the blade in his pocket. OK – he was ready.

His walk through Moonstone Park was uneventful with the exception of a group of pre-nurturers, whispering and giggling as their skirts swished by, rushing home from

T.R.E.A.C.L.E. before curfew. Monkey recognised a couple of them from a younger division at school but he averted his eyes, pulled his hood lower and tucked his injured hand up his sleeve to conceal any distinguishing feature that might identify him later.

As he approached the disused loco bridge, a lone figure was leaning against the wall, one leg bent, raised foot pressed into the bridge, head bowed. The garb was the same as Monkey's: hood pulled low, nose and mouth covered, hands pushed deep into the pockets.

'Woz happenin'?' Monkey asked.

Angel pulled down the scarf and smiled. 'I've been waiting ages. I was starting to think you weren't coming.'

Monkey stepped back and looked her up and down, approvingly. Although The Assembly had never outlawed trousers for nurturers and pre-nurturers, wearing them was generally frowned upon. Except for the female security officers, of course. Nurturers were not allowed in the security forces; only those females who had either chosen not to breed, or had been unable to. Trousers were deemed to be the garb of providers: harsh, straight and to the point – not at all feminine. Monkey grinned. Seeing Angel standing there in batties and trainers rather than the normal skirts and court shoes of pre-nurturers looked weird. But, to an outsider or, more importantly, to the security cameras, she looked every inch one of the pre-breeders of the brotherhood.

'You look kinda fridge in that.'

'My brother will kill me if he finds out I've borrowed his stuff,' she said.

'Where is he?'

'At home. Sally wanted him to stay in tonight.' Angel's brother, Alex, was three years younger than her and a fledgling Mooner but, at 12, he was still under the influence of his nurturer.

'What about you? What did you tell her?' Monkey asked.

'That I'd got extra gym club tonight.' They both knew that such a clandestine meeting between a pre-breeder and a pre-nurturer would guarantee them both a spell of re-education; Monkey on The Farm and Angel in The Sanctuary.

'What about curfew? How d'ya get round that?'

'Told her I'll be going round to Shanay's afterwards. It's only two doors along, so I'd easily get back without being seen.'

'Any chance she'll check up?'

Angel shook her head. 'She's not that friendly with Shanay's nurturer. But why would she, anyway?' She cocked her head on one side, coquettishly. 'I'm a good girl – remember?'

Monkey felt a jolt of electricity shoot through his abdomen and looked away. 'Come on, then. We'd better make sure your rep stays intact.' He indicated for her to cover her face again. 'Now, if anyone speaks to us, you keep quiet and let me do the talking – OK?' Angel nodded. 'Keep your hood as low as possible and your hands in your pockets.' He pulled at the hips of her loose trousers. 'These need to be lower.'

'Hey!' Angel reprimanded him as the top of her lacy knickers was revealed.

Monkey blushed and swallowed hard. 'Next time, borrow your brother's boxers too, all right? Those are a bit of a giveaway,' he blustered.

'Next time?' she queried, hitching up her brother's trousers. 'I thought this was a one-off to go and see Tragic.'

'Yeah, yeah – course!' Monkey said quickly and began strutting up and down under the loco bridge. 'You'll have to walk differently too if you want to get away with this. So, cop the bowl.'

With each step, he pushed his opposite shoulder forward, giving a rolling motion to his gait that was designed to instil intimidation into anyone in his path. Angel tried to imitate him, bouncing along the footpath with more of a skip than a swagger.

'That'll do,' Monkey said unconvincingly. 'Let's go.'

It was already past curfew when they arrived at Tragic's house and it was just the same as when Monkey had been there earlier in the day, not a sign of life anywhere. Monkey led Angel round to the sustenance patch at the back.

'I thought you said we were coming to see Tragic?' Angel queried. 'What's going on?'

'That's what I want to know,' he said, studying the rear of the lodge for a possible means of entry. 'OK.' He pointed to where the shutters were damaged on the window of Tragic's bedroom. It was just above the lean-to bike house and several of the metal slats were jutting outwards slightly.

Monkey climbed up onto the bike house roof, took the knife from his pocket and, reaching through the rent in the metal, inserted it into the side of the window frame. He moved it carefully backwards and forwards until he felt the resistance of the catch, then gave a sharp flick of the knife and pushed the window inwards away from him. 'OK, that's the window open, now let's work on the shutter. Come on,' he whispered, beckoning Angel to climb up and follow him. 'We need to push both sides together…'

She shook her head. 'No way! You said you wanted me to come with you to talk to Tragic. You didn't mention the fact that he wasn't here and we'd have to break into his house. Have you any idea what will happen if we're caught?'

'Of course! Now, just come with me and I'll explain it all later.'

'No!' Angel stood her ground. 'Actually, Mickey, I don't think you do know what'll happen to me. It's fine for you – you'll go off to The Farm for a while, then straight back to the Breeders' Zone and carry on with your life as normal. Me? I'll be sent to The Sanctuary, banned from uni, probably have to live in an artisan zone away from my family and friends. My children will be artisans too and they could even penalise Sal and confiscate her practice. Being caught breaking curfew's one thing, but breaking and entering? Have you gone insane?'

Monkey hovered uncomfortably. He hadn't envisaged any protest when he'd asked her to come. He was beginning to wish he'd just done it on his own now. He'd thought it would be exciting when he'd suggested it, a way of getting to know her better; building a bond so that she'd remember him and choose him as her breeder when the time came. But now, it didn't seem like such a good idea.

'What's going on?' a voice said from the other side of the bike house. Monkey turned quickly.

'It's OK, Mov Bailey,' Monkey reassured Tragic's neighbour. He'd met her once some time ago when they'd kicked their ball into her sustenance patch. She really should have moved out to The Pastures but Jane kept an eye on her. Monkey doubted if she'd remember him, but he wasn't going to risk it. 'It's me, Marlon Griffiths, Trevor's friend, remember?' he lied, looking down from his elevated position.

'No one's home. They've gone,' she said solemnly. 'Young Trevor graduated a week early and Jane left last night, she did.'

Monkey's eyes flashed down at Angel. He frowned slightly, and moved his eyes towards the wall of the house, warning her to move round the corner and not give away the fact that she was there.

'Yes, I know,' the lies flowed easily, 'but I lent Trevor some of my things and he forgot to give them back before he graduated. I've just come to collect them.'

'Gone off to the rurals, she has,' Mov Bailey continued in a forlorn voice. 'Gave me her electrics – till the Assembly finds out…' She looked up, terrified. 'You're not from The Assembly are you? You've not come to lock me away?'

'No, no, don't worry about that. It's me, Marlon, Trevor's friend. Just come to collect some things I lent him.'

'Gone to stay with an aunt, Jane said, out in the rurals. But she's never mentioned any aunts before. Just up and left she did, her and her sister. Piled everything into a couple of bags and off they went on their bikes. In the middle of the night! I was watching out of my window. Worried for them I was, what with the hoods and all, roaming the streets after curfew. Should've gone in the daylight if you ask me. You won't tell about the electrics will you?'

'Of course not – as long as you don't tell anyone I've been round to pick up my stuff,' he bargained.

Angel stepped out from the corner of the house, looked up at Monkey and folded her arms as though disapproving of the whole business.

'I can let you in, you know,' Mov Bailey said. 'Jane put me on the iris recognition so I can keep an eye on the place.' She chuckled. 'Keep an *eye* on it! I've just seen the funny side.' She was still laughing to herself as she opened the small gate between the two properties and shuffled round. 'You only had to ask, you know.'

Angel dodged back into the shadows quickly and Monkey slid down the roof as the elderly nurturer reached up on tiptoe, placed her eye against the small scanner on the wall and turned the handle on the door. Monkey did his best to stifle a smile of relief. 'Mind you shut it firm when you've done,' she said, shuffling back towards her own house. 'It don't close proper sometimes.' Then added, 'I don't use all her electrics. Only when I'm cold, like now. Mine's one of the early turbines. They're not very efficient, you know. Jane used to let me use hers sometimes when she was at work. It's not stealing, she used to say, more like sharing.'

Once the elderly neighbour had gone back into her own home, Monkey propped open the door, then sought out Angel and led her towards the house, grinning. 'It's not breaking and entering if we've been let in officially!'

'You're despicable!' Angel said as they entered the dark kitchen. 'I don't want any part of this.'

Now that they were in the relative safety of the house, Monkey relaxed a little.

'Look, I'm sorry – OK? I'm really worried about Tradge and I needed someone I trusted to come with me. I should've come clean with you from the start but I didn't think you'd come.'

'Too right I wouldn't have come!' Angel retorted. 'Anyway, now you know that he's graduated early, we can get going.'

She turned towards the door to leave but Monkey caught her hand and pulled her to face him.

'You don't get it, do you? Tragic hasn't graduated early. The school would've known if he had. And Jane hasn't got any aunts either – or a sister. Tragic used to moan about the fact that he never got any presents for his birthdays except from his nurturer because she didn't have any other family – either in town *or* in the rurals. And anyway, who do you know who lives in the rurals these days? Unless they're geriatric or been sent to The Farm.'

Angel looked confused. 'So what're you saying?'

'I don't know what's going on or why they've left but I'm not giving up until I find out where he is and that he's all right.' He looked her in the eye as he spoke. 'But, if you want...' He stopped mid-sentence.

Flashing along the hallway, through the glass of the front door was the intermittent red searchlights of a stealth. They heard the sigh of the air-brakes as it drew to a halt, then muffled voices and footsteps headed down the path towards the house.

'Shiltz!' Monkey whispered urgently.

Suddenly, a loud banging noise echoed down the hallway. He could make out the silhouettes of at least four Security officers through the glazed front door.

A female voice boomed through the mail-slot. 'Jane Patterson? Security. Open up!'

Chapter 5

Secrets, Codes and Hiding Places

'QUICK!' Monkey grabbed Angel's hand and pulled her towards a door that opened off the kitchen. There was a padlock near the top, but it was hanging open and the door was slightly ajar. 'Down here!'

There was a cellar under the house that Monkey remembered from a few years earlier. When he and Tragic had been younger, they'd gone down there once to play hide and seek. It was the only time he recalled Jane being angry with Tragic. 'Don't you ever – EVER – go down there again!' the normally placid Jane had shouted, slamming the door and bolting it firmly. Shortly after that, the bolt had been removed and the padlock had appeared. The cellar had been firmly out of bounds from then on. Jane had told them it was because the rickety old steps were too dangerous. They could have fallen and been injured, she'd said, once more reverting to her gentle, caring self and Tragic never questioned her.

As Monkey and Angel made their way down the wooden steps now, Monkey realised that they were firm and relatively new – certainly not as old as the house. They'd probably been replaced within the last 10 years, so would have been quite safe at the time that he and Tragic had played down there. As they descended the steps, Angel's hood caught on a nail. She stumbled and gasped but Monkey put out a hand to steady her, then raised a finger to his lips warning her to be quiet. A frisson of excitement shot through him at the physical contact but she pulled her hand away from his sharply; irritated.

When his feet touched the floor of the underground room, he narrowed his eyes, scouring the cellar for suitable hiding places. It was pitch-dark apart from the spasmodic red glare that flashed through a ventilation grille at the front. A cobweb caught Monkey in the face and he brushed it away impatiently.

As his eyes became accustomed to the dark he could make out dozens of large canvases lining two of the walls, some covered with cloth, others displaying Jane's weird paintings. They were abstract and Monkey had never been able to understand them. Shelves laden with pots and paints, tools and tins were along another wall. There were piles of what looked like old clothes and shoes – no doubt Jane's working clothes, kept down here because they were dirty. But he could see nowhere to hide two people.

'They're bound to come down here,' Angel whispered.

'Don't worry,' Monkey reassured her; although he wished he felt as confident as he was trying to sound. Outside, they could hear the rumble of feet running down the side of the house.

'The back door's open!' a voice called and more feet thundered towards the rear of the house.

Monkey groaned and mentally gave himself a kick for not shutting the door properly as Mov Bailey had advised him to do. He would have expected a patroller to come looking for a school-dodger but was confused as to why there would be this level of security looking for Tragic – or, more to the point, Jane. At least Angel had closed the cellar door after them. Hopefully, that would allow them some time.

Angel tugged at Monkey's sleeve and pointed to the corner at the back of the cellar. He could just make out two large chest freezers against the back wall. Monkey knew that Jane had always been keen on homegrown food. Tragic had told him she'd even taken on a public sustenance patch to boost their food quota. No wonder she needed two freezers.

They crept over to them and Monkey lifted the lid of the first one. It was full of bags and boxes of food arranged in wire baskets, all going soggy through lack of electricity. Angel opened the second. It also appeared full. Monkey was about to lower the lid despondently, when Angel stopped him.

'It's different,' she whispered. 'Give me a hand.' Monkey didn't know what she meant by *different*. He looked at her questioningly as she felt round the rim of the freezer. There were none of the baskets and bags of vegetables like the other freezer. As far as he could make out, the food in the second, larger one was mainly pre-packed, manufactured foods stored in what appeared to be five shallow wooden trays. Angel prised her fingers under the lip of one of the trays and raised it up to reveal a totally empty freezer beneath. 'Come on,' she said, impatiently, lifting the trays and stacking them on top of one another at one side. Monkey picked up one of the boxes of burgers and shook it. It was empty; a shell. So was the box of chicken pieces – and the fish fillets.

'Dummies,' Angel said quietly. 'Now get in.'

'We can't hide in here.' He was alarmed. 'We'll suffocate.'

Angel shrugged. 'Well, someone's been hiding in here.' She pointed to the interior of the freezer. Three of the sides were the metallic casing that Monkey would have expected. The fourth, the one that was up against the wall, had a large rectangle cut out so that the brickwork was showing through.

They could hear footsteps above them, marching purposefully round the house instilling a sense of urgency in them. Carefully, without making a sound, Angel stepped into the huge freezer. She pulled the cord from the hood of her brother's jacket and tied it round the lock of the lid, then crouched down and began pulling the trays of empty boxes back over her head. 'Get in,' she told him.

Monkey followed. He slid two more trays of dummy food into place, leaving a space in the centre so that he could reach up and grab the cord that Angel had attached to the lid. It was a tricky manoeuvre. He had to pull the lid to the point where gravity would finish the job, then remove the cord from the lock, slip his arm down, push the final tray into place and wait for the lid to close itself – all in a matter of seconds; all in the pitch-dark of the cellar. As he pulled the last tray over his head and sank down next to Angel, he had a fleeting moment of satisfaction at how he had acquitted himself, before the freezer top crashed down so loudly, the whole road must have heard it!

Monkey froze. He could feel his heart thumping against his rib cage and throbbing in his ears. His breathing seemed as loud as a loco in the silence of the freezer. He closed his eyes, waiting for the repercussions and swallowed hard, trying to steady the fear that was threatening to overwhelm him. He could feel Angel next to him, smell her. She smelt clean; of soap and shampoo. Wonderful! But what if Security had brought dogs with them? Crap! He hadn't thought of that. He couldn't bear it if they'd gone through all this just to be sniffed out. Angel's hair was so close to his face, it brushed against his skin and her breath was warm against his cheek. God, he fancied her! If she didn't choose him for breeding, he didn't know what he'd do.

He could hear the footsteps descend the stairs into the cellar through the hole that had been cut in the back of the freezer. He sensed Angel tense; holding her breath. Monkey did the same. In the all-encompassing blackness of the freezer, there was a shadow of grey at the back where the hole was. What if Security had thermal imaging? What if their body heat escaped through the hole and cast a bloom against the wall? What if it picked up their footprints on the cellar floor? What if one of them moved? Or sneezed? All these terrors ran through Monkey's mind as the footsteps came to a halt at the bottom of the steps.

He heard some shuffling and banging; obviously whoever was down there was going through the paintings.

'Nothing here,' he heard one voice say; a male voice. 'Must have been next door.'

'Maybe,' a female replied. Then, 'Wait! What's that over there?'

Monkey felt a looseness in his abdomen; a churning. He was going to crap himself. He squeezed his eyes even tighter, as though that could shut out his fear. He'd never felt so scared; not even when he was being chased by the hood. But it wasn't fear for himself, it was for Angel. He'd got her into this. If he stuffed up now, he'd ruin her life forever.

A diffused yellow light flashed across the brickwork at the back of the freezer. Monkey felt easier; they'd got sulphur torches rather than heat-seeking equipment. That was one weight off his mind. And he couldn't hear any dogs either. He started to relax a little.

'Just some old clothes,' the male said.

'They look like providers' clothes to me,' remarked the female. 'Best take them with us.'

The male didn't sound convinced. 'Could be the pre's. Or maybe they're hers; she's an artist apparently. You know what those Bohemians are like.'

'You're not paid to make decisions. Just take them!' the female ordered, and Monkey could hear the sound of scraping as though something was being picked up from the floor. 'And check out those freezers at the back,' she barked.

'Yes, Ma'am,' the male voice acquiesced.

Monkey went rigid. There was a creak as the lid of the other freezer was raised. He heard rustling, then a thud as it closed again. The footsteps grew closer and stopped next to their hiding place. The air in the freezer was warm now, almost stale with their breath. He felt Angel's fingers creep across his hand and wrap themselves around it. He squeezed hers in return by way of reassurance and tried not to flinch as a bolt of pain shot through the wound on his palm. The lid of the freezer groaned upwards. Monkey couldn't bear it. He wanted to jump up and shout, "found us!" like he did with Tragic when they were young. But he didn't.

'Anything?' the female voice shouted.

The lid seemed to be raised for an eternity. They held their breaths.

'Just food,' the male voice said eventually and the lid crashed down again.

Monkey let out his breath and felt relief flood through him. He gave Angel's hand another squeeze and allowed himself a smile as he listened to the conversation between the two Security officers from the basement and what sounded like two more on the ground floor.

'Anything upstairs?' the female asked.

'The back bedroom window's ajar and there's a load of the pre's schoolwork on the bed in there. The nurturer's room's empty.'

'No propaganda of any sort?'

'No, Ma'am.'

'Does the window look like forced entry?'

'Hard to tell in this light.'

'Very well.'

'Do you want us to take in the schoolwork?'

'No. We've found what looks like providers' clothing in the cellar; we'll take that to forensics and send a team out in the morning to collect the rest. Do we know how the door came to be open?'

A fourth voice spoke, 'Yes, Ma'am. The post-nurturer next door says a pre-breeder came round earlier and she let him in. And we've also issued her with a summons for misappropriation of electricity.'

'Good.' There was a pause, then the female continued. 'Bring her in for questioning; she probably knows more than she's letting on. You – find out who the pre-breeder was that was snooping round. And, you, stand guard at the front until we've cleared the house and checked for prints in the morning.'

There was a muttering of "Yes, Ma'ams" before they heard the door at the top of the steps close, then the distant sound of the back door slamming. After a while, the brakes of the stealth hissed and it went silently on its way.

The house was quiet. Monkey and Angel stayed still; listening.

When he was certain that the house was empty, Monkey whispered, 'You OK?'

'Yeah,' Angel said. 'Now what do we do?'

Monkey shuffled round until his back was against the front of the freezer and his feet could extend out through the hole at the back. He pressed them against the wall and slowly stretched his legs, pushing the freezer away from the brickwork and creating a space for them to escape. Still cautious, the two of them tiptoed up the steps and out into the relative light of the kitchen.

'Phew!' breathed Angel, looking from the back door to the front. 'Now, how do we get out of here?'

'We go out the back, through the pre-school grounds and over the fences,' Monkey replied. 'But first,' his eyes scanned the kitchen, 'we find what we came for.'

Angel's face set. 'Which is?'

'Evidence of where Tradge has gone.'

She folded her arms and glared at him. 'Are you mocking me?'

'Nuh-huh,' said Monkey, distractedly. 'What's the point of surviving all that if we just give up and go home?'

Angel turned on her ring-cam. 'Have you any idea what time it is?'

'Nope.' Monkey was already halfway up the stairs. 'Sometime between curfew and shutdown, I'd guess.' When Angel didn't follow him, he returned to the top of the stairs and looked down at her. 'Give me 10 minutes – OK? If I haven't found anything in that time, we'll leave. Deal?'

Angel sighed and followed him reluctantly. 'Fine.'

He went straight into Tragic's bedroom. There on the bed, as the Security officer had said, were e-screens and books, along with some papers. Angel began going though the drawers and cupboards while Monkey tipped out Tragic's backpack and began rummaging through the debris of his friend's life.

'This is weird,' Angel commented. 'It doesn't feel right to be going through his stuff like this.'

Monkey agreed with her but was not going to admit as such. 'Has to be done,' he said, rather more harshly than he'd intended. He was annoyed with himself. It had been an act of lunacy bringing her here. He'd endangered her life – and her freedom. And why? Because he'd got the hots for her! What had started as a ploy to make a bond and try to ensure that she chose him after he'd graduated, had almost got them both arrested and had practically guaranteed that she'd never look at him again.

He gave an almost imperceptible shake as though trying to rid himself of such thoughts and focus on the more burning questions: what had his friend got himself involved in? Why was there a dummy freezer in the cellar? Who had it been designed to hide? And, more worryingly: why was Security trying to find Tragic and Jane and what sort of propaganda had they been looking for in Tragic's room? None of it made any sense. Monkey had thought that Tragic had simply been trying to evade graduation, but there was something more sinister going on, of that he was sure.

'Look at this.' Angel was holding up a piece of paper she'd found in one of the drawers in Tragic's desk. It had a drawing of a baboon hanging by its tail in the top corner and the words: King of Kongs in the centre. King of Kongs was a name Tragic called Monkey sometimes as a joke. He stared at the sheet of paper in her hand. A series of numbers were written in the form of a mathematical equation. The bottom of the paper was torn so that it appeared that the last line was incomplete.

$$98499 \times 9952 = 1258554398$$
$$57 \times 54 = 5882933$$
$$69697 \div 8984 = 7979$$
$$7366 \div 0188 = 995$$
$$7298 - 343 = 3509$$
$$4$$
$$\neg 9769 + 75$$

Angel looked at the paper and shook her head. 'Either your mate's rubbish at maths, or that's some sort of secret message,' she commented.

But, before Monkey had the chance to say more, he heard a sound that filled him with dread. A yelp; distant but distinct. Monkey's heart sank: they'd brought in a dog unit already.

He looked at Angel. 'You reckon you're good at gymnastics?' She nodded. 'Well, you're gonna have to be!'

She stuffed the paper into her pocket as Monkey grabbed her hand and pulled her out of the room. He ran, half dragging her, down the stairs and out of the back door. Monkey jumped over the fence at the back and Angel followed. Together, they ran across the grounds of the pre-school and neighbouring sustenance patches, vaulting fence after fence. Monkey was surprised that Angel's agility made her a match for his superior speed. He'd assumed that having her in tow would slow him down but, on the contrary, she was easily able to keep up with him and in no way jeopardised their escape. Finally, they slowed to a walk and, once more, adopted the swagger of the hood as they reached the bottom of Angel's road. Outside her gate, Monkey nodded, as he would have done to any other member of the Mooners.

'Check you later,' he said.

Angel held him with a glare. 'If there are any repercussions from this, you'd better be ready to take the rap.' She walked down the path towards the house.

He watched her slip into the outbuilding that had once been a garage and emerge in the normal skirt and top of a pre-nurturer. She pressed her eye against the scanner on the door and went in without looking back.

The street lights clunked into darkness and Monkey wandered home, feeling heavy and very much alone.

Chapter 6

Angel or Devil in Disguise?

THE NEXT day, Monkey was keen to speak to Angel about the previous evening but a curt nod as she pressed the scrap of paper bearing the code into his hand was the only indication that she even knew him, let alone had been huddled in a freezer with him, squeezing his hand for reassurance. If he caught her eye, she looked away; if he approached her in the corridor, she changed direction. She was making it very clear that she wanted to put as much distance between herself and Monkey as possible. Much as he'd expected her to give him a wide berth at school, he was, nevertheless, disappointed and frustrated that she did so.

The code itself had been simple enough to break. He and Tragic had devised a system of communication when they were younger so that they could send secret but innocent messages in school; where to meet up, what time they would play football, whose house they would go to. They used mathematical base ten, starting the alphabet with their favourite number. Monkey's favourite number was nine, but Tragic's was five; therefore, in all his notes, A went under five, B under six; C under seven – right up to Z under zero. Of course, this also meant that K and U were also under number five, so a certain degree of reasoning needed to be applied. Mathematical signs were the spaces between words so that, to anyone finding the notes, they looked like obscure mathematical equations.

When he'd got home, Monkey had lost no time in sitting down and working out what Tragic had written to him.

Enjoy your graduation.
am at address
below don't come
will find you
when its safe
t
ombe mag

Monkey stared at the deciphered code. It made little sense and it certainly didn't answer any of the questions that were running through his head; in fact, it posed more questions than it answered. What did Tragic mean: *will find you when it's safe*? What address below? And what was the last line that had been torn at both ends? He ran through the alphabet for possibilities: bombe, combe, dombe, fombe – tombe, perhaps? And what was this *mag*? Magazine? Magnum? Magnet? Could *that* be the 'address below' that Tragic referred to? And, if so, was it a house, an estate or a town? And where was it?

He was preoccupied with the meaning behind the message and could think of nothing else, spending as much time as he could, without arousing suspicion, on the school info-web and, after school, going into town to the Central Resource Centre. He desperately wanted to talk to Angel but, as the week rolled on, she became even cooler. Instruction after instruction, he sat at the back of room, watching her from behind and silently cursing himself for blowing it.

Both at home and at school, he was quizzed about his missing friend. He'd been interrogated by Security as to his whereabouts on the night and whether or not he knew one Marlon Griffiths – the false name he'd given old Mov Bailey – but they'd seemed satisfied with his answers. He knew Professor Reed suspected that he knew more about the whereabouts of the Pattersons than he was letting on, but he couldn't prove anything.

The other Mooners also plied him with questions about their mate, to which Monkey could, in all honesty, shrug and say, 'Dunno.' But, outside school, they were becoming increasingly irritated with his lack of participation in their forays into other hoods.

'We're storming Eastway tonight. You up?' Kraze asked him on the Friday evening as they walked home from school.

Monkey gave a casual shrug. 'Neh. I'm fridge.'

'So, what's happenin' with you, Monk?' the hood leader challenged. 'This has been, like, every night for a week you've bottled.'

Monkey eyeballed him, affronted. 'I haven't *bottled*,' he said evenly, determined not to show that he was rattled by the inference that he was afraid to accompany them into enemy hoods. 'I have other stuff to deal with.'

'What *other stuff*?' Kraze was smirking but Monkey knew that, inside, he would be bricking it. He wasn't confident as leader and needed Monkey's backing when they went out of their zone. 'You still frettin' over Tradge?' He gave a laugh and turned round to the rest of the hood, ridiculing Monkey to gain their respect.

'Just stuff,' Monkey stated firmly, standing his ground; aware that a small crowd had gathered.

The tension was almost palpable.

'You snakin' on us?' Kraze had his hands in his pockets and was fumbling with something – possibly a blade, Monkey thought. He needed to be careful: the last thing he wanted was to alienate his own and, if Kraze convinced the others that Monkey was a turncoat, he'd be watching his back even on his own turf. The rest of the Mooners moved closer. Monkey looked round. With less than eight weeks until he turned 16, he was easily the eldest. Some of them, like Angel's brother, Alex, were still practically bubs. But he also knew that there was strength in numbers: he knew he had to play it fridge.

Monkey held out both hands as a gesture of openness showing that he had no weapon. He spoke lightly, almost teasingly. 'Hey, cuz, what's with the screw face? This is me you're scanting. I don't *do* snakin', you know that. I'm a Mooner till I grad. But, right now, I've got some anguish going on that's personal – sav?' He forced himself to breathe evenly as he waited for Kraze's response, never lowering his stare.

Kraze drew the blade from his pocket and spun it in his fingers, watching it glint in the pale afternoon sunlight. He nodded slowly, as though mulling over Monkey's words. 'That's good, cuz – 'cos I'd hate to think you'd been raggin' me. You know what I mean?'

Still maintaining eye contact, Monkey nodded. 'I'm glad we understand each other.' He held out his hand and Kraze brushed it briefly. 'Take it easy, all right?'

With a nonchalance belying the anxiety he was feeling, Monkey turned and walked away. No sooner had he left the rest of the hood, than his ring-cam flashed on and Angel's face appeared on the screen.

'That was impressive,' she said.

Monkey was puzzled. 'Where are you?' He looked round but could see no sign of her.

'By the wall.'

Again Monkey looked round but could only see someone in Mooners' garb leaning against a high wall at the other side of the road, hood pulled low and scarf high to obscure any facial features.

Looking back to the face on the ring-cam, he saw that she had covered her face. 'Nice touch. How d'you get away with it?' he said.

'Where do you hide an elephant?' Angel replied.

'Huh?'

'In a jungle,' she said, answering her own riddle. 'So, how did I infiltrate the hood? Dress like them.'

Monkey smiled to himself. 'But Alex is here.' He looked back to where the rest of the hood had congregated.

Angel shook her head. 'Even my brother has a change of clothes, you know.' Then her voice turned serious. 'Follow me. I've got some information for you. I think I've cracked the code.'

Monkey followed her at a discreet distance to the disused loco bridge. They went to the far end and climbed up the embankment so that they were in a blind spot, obscured from both the road and the security cameras.

'Go on,' Monkey said, wanting to find out how much she'd discovered before he disclosed his hand.

'Well,' Angel began, 'it's a code that uses base 10 but starts at number five…'

'I know what the code says,' Monkey interrupted; irritated that she should have cracked it so easily. 'What else do you know?'

Angel seemed disappointed that he wasn't more grateful, but went on, 'I'm pretty sure that the last line, ombe mag, is a reference to a small hamlet about 15K out of town called Combe Magna.'

'And?' Monkey asked.

'Well, before the fossil fuels ran out, it was a satellite village for commuters. Prior to that, at the beginning of the last century, it was a rural community of smallholders and arable farmers.'

Angel gave Monkey a potted history of rural life before the revolution. When farming was no longer viable, the farmers moved out and the commuters moved in, travelling into town daily in their motor vehicles to go to work. With the abolition of private ownership of cars after the Oil Wars, the commuters moved back into town, and the villages, including Combe Magna, fell into disrepair. With the exception of a few seniors who were too able-bodied for The Pastures and who preferred to run their own self-sufficient communes rather than move into the towns, many of the houses in the once thriving rural communities were almost derelict.

'So, why would Tragic and Jane have gone there?' Monkey asked. 'And how did you find out all this?'

Angel shrugged. 'In answer to question one: I have no idea. But I got all the other stuff from Sally's info-web. Don't forget, she's a solicitor so she has a higher level clearance than the school or even the CRC. She went downstairs yesterday and I snuck into her room while she was logged on.' Monkey raised an eyebrow. So much for Angel being a good girl! 'Apparently, Combe Magna was one of the villages in contention for a Farm development, but The Assembly decided against it.'

'Why?'

'It was too close to town and there was always a danger of escape. Look.' She drew a printout of an old map from her pocket. 'See, it's just north of here. We could walk it in two and a half hours – or cycle in less.'

'We?' Monkey looked at her and shook his head. 'No way!'

'Fine!' she said, purposefully folding up the map and putting it back in her pocket. She stood up to leave. 'Let me know how you get on.'

'Wait!' Monkey put out a hand and grabbed her arm to stop her leaving. 'Why're you doing this?'

Angel smiled. 'Because it's exciting.' She sat down again. 'You have no idea how boring it is just studying and going to gym club and chatting about nurturing and clothes and cooking and stuff.' She groaned and dropped her head forwards, then sat up and looked Monkey in the eye. 'I got a real buzz the other night. OK, so I was terrified but, once my heart rate slowed down again, I'd enjoyed doing something un-nurturey. And, I agree with you: I do think there's something sinister going on and I want to find out what.'

Monkey thought for a moment – but only for a moment. In fact, it was a no-brainer really: she was clever, athletic, brave – and hot as hell. 'When shall we go?' he asked.

'No time like the present,' replied Angel.

Chapter 7

Into the Rurals

THEY had both gone home to eat and collect some food to take with them. Angel fabricated a story of staying over at her friend, Moni Morrison's, house, while Monkey and Vivian went through their usual evening routine: Vivian banning him from leaving, Monkey swearing at her, Vivian shouting, Grand-mov intervening, Vivian turning on her own nurturer, and Monkey taking the opportunity to walk out.

As he pulled up his scarf to cover his face, he sighed in relief to be out of the house. Vivian never used to be like this. When he was a bub, she was fine; you never heard her so much as raise her voice. She played with him and Penny; took them places; they laughed more and she would even sit with him on her lap and cuddle him – not that he wanted that now. But some sort of respect would be nice. The last couple of years, she'd turned into psycho-mov. Most nurturers went that way, from what he could see – except Jane. She seemed to be the exception as far as the nurturers in his hood were concerned. In fact, he felt sorry for the younger Mooners like Alex; they didn't know what they were in for! As for himself, he was just counting the days until all this would be history.

Then he stopped himself: living in the Breeders' Zone wouldn't be the same without Tragic. They'd known each other since alpha-school; grown up together. Tragic might act like an oversensitive wuzzle, but Monkey was nothing without his sidekick. A heaviness descended on him with this realisation. His friend was in danger and he was not going to stop until he found out what was going on.

He met Angel under the bridge at 19:00. It was already dark but the infrared cameras would still be able to make out their presence, so, once again, they climbed up the embankment out of view.

'Look,' Angel said, unfolding the map and frantically winding the handle on the side of her torch until it shone a pinprick beam on to the crumpled paper. 'I've been thinking, this loco line used to go to Mercia and it runs within about a couple of Ks of Combe Magna.'

'Too exposed,' Monkey said quickly, knowing immediately what she was going to suggest. 'The roads'll be safer.'

'Well, it would be more direct to go along the line so it would be quicker and there'll be less chance of being spotted by stealth patrols.'

Monkey was uneasy. 'I dunno. What about cameras? If we're spotted on the track, we're like sitting ducks.'

'No, it's OK. I asked Sally about that…'

'Whoa! Whoa! Whoa!' Monkey was shocked. He couldn't believe she'd discussed this with her nurturer. 'You talked to Sally about this? What the fegg do you think you were doing?'

Angel stood up. 'Hey! I might be dressed like one of your hood but I'm not one of them – OK! So don't even start with me like that.' She tossed the map at him. 'You want to do this on your own, then go ahead.'

'OK. OK.' Monkey capitulated. He was beginning to think that, hot or not, she was going to be hard work. 'I just don't want any of this getting out.'

'I'm not stupid, you know.' Angel sat back down on the bank. Then muttered, just loud enough so that Monkey could hear, 'I cracked your code easily enough.' Monkey eyed her but said nothing. Right now, it wasn't so much that he needed her, although he must admit, he was impressed with the amount of information she'd discovered, but he *wanted* her company. 'Anyway,' she went on, 'I was asking Sal about her work…subtly,' she said pointedly, giving Monkey a sideways glance. 'You know, as if I was thinking about my own future career.'

'Go on,' Monkey said.

'Well, turns out, she had a client who was accused of stealing from the house of this post-nurturer who's in The Assembly. She lives in a massive mansion about three Ks east of Beauchamp Park, outside town, and Security claimed that they had footage of Sal's client entering and leaving the property. But Sal discovered that it was a fit up. And she proved it because none of the cameras work once you get out of the street light zone.'

'What?'

'It's true. The cameras outside town are dummies; the cost of electricity would be too much to run them, so they're just there as a deterrent.'

Monkey's mind went into overdrive. 'Have you any idea what this information would do if it got out?'

'Exactly,' Angel said. 'It mustn't get out. As a solicitor, Sal had to sign an Official Confidentiality Order. She only let it slip because we were talking one night after Alex had gone to bed and she'd had a couple of kegs. She'd lose her job if they knew.' Angel looked at him anxiously. 'Promise me, this is between you and me. You won't tell the hood?'

Monkey nodded slowly, taking in the information she'd just told him. 'So, it doesn't matter whether we go on the roads or the track.' He smiled. 'Whaled! Let's take the direct route, then.'

Most of the sleepers and train tracks had long since been removed from the embankment, leaving it overgrown and stony but, nevertheless, straight. Angel and Monkey kept up a brisk pace, sometimes chatting about people at school; staff and students, and their hopes for their futures, sometimes maintaining an easy silence. It was cold but the constant movement kept them warm. Monkey found it eerily quiet once they left the street-lit suburbs of town. From their elevated position, they could look down on the largely overgrown roads. There was no street lighting out in the rurals and they saw no State vehicles, either Security or official Assembly limos, to cast their headlights on the roads and offer some illumination. The moonless night afforded them plenty of cover but also made their progress slower than they'd hoped. It was pitch-dark but it was too risky to use the torch out in the open and they both stumbled on stones and potholes along the way.

They'd been walking for just over half an hour when Angel's ring-cam lit up; it was her nurturer. Angel dodged down into one of the bushes that had sprouted up along the track and answered.

'Sorry, darling, I'm going to need you to come home tonight,' Sally said. 'I've got a big case that's in court on Monday and I need to work late tonight.'

'Sal!' Angel couldn't hide her disappointment. 'Alex is 12 now, he doesn't need me to be there.'

'Yes, he does. Now, don't argue. You can stay over at Moni's tomorrow night. Make sure you're home by nine.' The dial went blank.

Angel kicked at a stone in frustration. Monkey felt sorry for her; that was the difference between being a pre-breeder and a pre-nurturer he supposed. There was no way he'd go home just because Vivian told him to but, then, his nurturer had no jurisdiction over him; in a few weeks he'd be a free agent and she knew it. Angel, on the other hand would be under Sal's thumb for years, probably decades. Even when Angel was a nurturer in her own right, Sal would still be the head of the family, just as his grand-mov was (in theory, anyway) the matriarch in Vivian's little kingdom.

'Come on, let's go back,' he said with resignation.

Angel shook her head. 'No, you go on. Take the torch and the map.' She opened the paper and shone the thin beam of light onto it. 'See this bridge here?' She pointed to a spot where the loco line went over the road next to a disused smallholding. 'When you get to that, you need to come down and follow the road. Take a left at the first junction and that'll bring you into Combe Magna.' She checked her ring-cam. 'You should do it in about an hour.'

Monkey tried to argue but Angel was adamant. It would be a waste of time and energy, she said, if neither of them went. 'Good luck. Let me know how you get on.' Then, she did the unthinkable: she leant forward and gave him a peck on the cheek.

Physical contact between pres was a crime more heinous than breaking curfew *and* drinking illegal keg – at the same time. In fact, fraternising with the opposite gender outside school hours was worse than almost anything else, apart from murder. Yet, Angel had done it. Her lips had actually made contact with his skin. And his mind was in turmoil. What had she meant by it? Was she letting him know that she would select him for breeding? And if so, shouldn't he go after her?

His mind went round and round while his feet stayed put until Angel merged with the night and her kiss was no more than a shadow on his memory.

How long he'd remained still he didn't know, but it was long enough for the cold to penetrate the soles of his shoes and seep up the muscles in his calves. He was startled back to consciousness by a crunching noise below and the sudden awareness that an armoured stealth was driving along the road that ran alongside the loco track. Monkey dodged down into the bushes and watched it rumble silently back towards town, squashing any fallen branches or broken concrete that lay in its path. A routine patrol no doubt but, nevertheless, a timely reminder to stay on his guard. He gave one last look along the track the way Angel had headed, then turned and walked in the other direction, out towards the rurals.

By the time he reached the village, Monkey's fingers were so numb with cold that they could barely turn the handle of the clockwork torch. He fumbled with his ring-cam to flash up the time: 22:15. It had taken far longer than Angel had anticipated. He wandered along the deserted street looking for… Looking for what? A sign saying, *Tragic is here*? Like that was going to happen! He shivered as he walked slowly through the silence. A jumble of cottages huddled round a dark, open space. He had a distant memory of learning about the feudal system at alpha-school and thought it was probably a village green. It was clear that the place was inhabited from the lights glowing through the curtains of some of the houses, but by whom? And, if Tragic was here, which one was his? Now Monkey had found the place, how the hell did he go about finding his friend? He could hardly just knock on doors, asking. And that was even supposing that Angel had correctly guessed at the missing letters on the note. What if she'd been wrong? And, even if she'd been correct, perhaps Jane had told Tragic that they were going to Combe Magna as a decoy.

Then another, more sinister, doubt bore its way into his mind, multiplying until it consumed everything else: what if he'd been set up? Wasn't it just too convenient that she hadn't spoken to him for days, then suddenly turned up the whereabouts of Tragic with reasoning powers bordering on genius? And, there was nothing weird about accompanying him halfway there, then suddenly having to turn back, was there? A pre-nurturer, daughter of a solicitor, friend of an assistant T.R.E.A.C.L.E. trainer, destined for The Assembly if she played her cards right, risking her entire future to mix with a hood, steal information and break curfew? He felt sick!

His eyes flashed round the ramshackle houses, no longer warm and welcoming with their flickering glow but, now, potential traps. He scoured the hazy outlines of the cottages looking for signs of Security. Every dark shadow between them seemed to be filled with lurking terror. Standing in the road, Monkey felt exposed; vulnerable, yet afraid to seek refuge. There were no street lights here, even though it was two hours before Shut Down. It was quiet too; scarily quiet – as though no humans inhabited the place. Although some lights were on, he could hear no chatter from the cottages; no laughter, no doors closing, or info-screens blaring out. He didn't like it. He was beginning to wish he hadn't come.

There was a rustle behind him. He jumped, then froze; waiting. He breathed again as a fox leapt over a gate and loped down the middle of the street, dragging a dead chicken in its jaws. Monkey's heart was beating rapidly and his tongue felt as though it was stuck to the roof of his mouth with fear. Funny how brave he could be in the face of an enemy hood but, here he was, crapping himself over a fox! He tried to smile at the irony but it felt as though his mouth was set in concrete. This was stupid, he told himself. He needed to get out of here. He didn't know why he'd come in the first place. If Tragic wanted to disappear, that was his lookout.

At that moment, the door of a cottage, slightly ahead of him on the other side of the street, opened and a group of nurturers came out of the house. He moved away from the road, into the shadows of a gateway and watched. There were four of them and, as they stood in the doorway, the yellow light from the cottage lit up their faces. They were nodding. The one facing him looked very serious. As the door closed, one nurturer went back inside while two walked off towards the village green, but the one who had had her back to Monkey turned and headed towards him. He gasped when he saw her. It was Jane.

Chapter 8

Friends Reunited

RELIEF coursed through him and he ran towards her but stopped when he saw the look on her face. It wasn't the warm, welcoming expression he was used to. In fact, it was nothing short of terror.

'Mickey?' Jane whispered, her eyes darting from side to side, scouring the darkness around him. 'Are you alone?'

'Yes.' He saw the tension ease in her eyes.

'What are you doing here? How did you find us?'

But, before he could answer, she put a finger to his lips, took his arm and led him towards one of the smaller cottages down a side lane. She let herself in and Monkey noticed that there was no iris scanner on this door, just a simple, old-fashioned keypad to open it. Once inside, Jane indicated for Monkey to wait in the narrow hallway that led straight to the staircase while she lifted the latch and entered a room to the side. A warm glow spread out into the hall and he could hear whispering. Then Tragic came to the door.

'Monkey!' He put his arms out and patted Monkey on the back. 'Good to see you. Good to see you.' There was something odd about Tragic's manner. He did look genuinely pleased to see his friend but he was cagey, too. Monkey couldn't quite make him out. 'So, how d'ya find us?' he went on in a stilted tone, only giving half his attention to Monkey, as though he was listening to something else, or *for* something else.

'I got your note,' Monkey replied.

'Good, good.'

And then, as though Tragic and his nurturer had been up to something, Jane appeared and Tragic visibly relaxed and ushered Monkey into the room with the fire.

'Come and get yourself warm. Do you want something to eat? How d'ya get here?'

The room was sparsely furnished with a cooking range and a sink at one end and a couple of Jane's paintings on the wall. In the main body of the room, were three simple wooden chairs and a table in front of a large, open fire that was more than welcoming to Monkey's frozen hands and feet. Sometimes Vivian lit a fire at home but wood was in short supply, so it was usually only on special occasions. Mickey accepted a bowl of homemade soup and some bread. He desperately wanted to talk to Tragic in private, but it was clear from Jane's hovering presence and pursed lips that she had no intention of leaving them alone.

'So, you coming back?' Monkey asked when he finished his soup.

Tragic shook his head.

'What about graduation?' Monkey asked. 'And the two of us in the Breeders' Zone? You know, like we planned.'

'Like *you* planned, Monk,' Tragic corrected. 'I never planned to graduate.'

Monkey was stunned. 'What... You mean you always planned to run away?'

'I haven't run away!' Tragic denied emphatically, but Jane put a hand on his arm as though warning him not to say too much.

'We've just decided to opt out of the system,' she said, calmly. 'Now, I'm sure you need to be getting back. Did you cycle or walk?'

It was clear that Monkey was being given his marching orders but he wasn't going until he had some answers.

'So how d'ya get here? When I left you that night, you never said anything.'

Tragic's eyes flitted from his friend to his nurturer. Again, it was Jane who intervened.

'It's lovely to see you, Mickey, and I know Trevor appreciates you coming all this way, but it really is best if you go back now.' She stood up as an added hint for Monkey to leave but he remained seated.

'I want to know what's going on.'

Jane was clearly becoming exasperated. 'Trust me, Mickey, the less you know the better for everyone.'

'The better for you, you mean!' Monkey challenged.

'No! The better for you, too!'

She stared at him, and Monkey had never seen Jane looking so authoritative – not since the day she found they'd been in the basement. Slowly, things began to make sense.

'Something weird's going down here,' Monkey said. 'I've been in your cellar. I've seen the freezer with the back cut out. And Security were there too – looking for you.' He saw her start at the news. 'And they took away some providers' clothes that were down there to have them tested by forensics.' He looked from Jane to Tragic. ' I've risked The Farm to find you, so the least you can do is give me some sort of explanation.'

The fire crackled, and the distant hooting of an owl could be heard outside, but there was no other sound. Monkey looked from Tragic to Jane, waiting for one of them to speak. Finally, Tragic spoke.

'I'll be 16 tomorrow,' he said. 'If we'd stayed, I'd have been having my graduation party, then that would've been it. I'd have been off to the Breeders' Zone on Sunday and just sucked into the whole world of breeding and providing. That would've been my connection with my family gone; ended…' He clicked his fingers. 'Forever.'

'We've been through this…' Monkey began, but Tragic shook his head.

'Hear me out. Mum and I didn't want that.' Monkey's eyes opened wide at the word *Mum*. It was archaic. No one called their nurturers *mum*. Tragic was sounding practically prehistoric. But Monkey let him continue. 'So, we made some enquiries and found this community of people who've opted out.' He looked Monkey in the eye and shrugged apologetically. 'I'm sorry I couldn't say anything before. We couldn't risk it getting out and…'

'So, why'd you leave a note?' Monkey challenged.

Tragic shrugged. 'I was going to send it to you, but then I changed my mind. I didn't think you'd go to the house.'

Jane looked anxiously at her son. 'You wrote a note? With our whereabouts in it?'

'Yeah – sorry. I didn't think…'

She turned to Monkey. 'Where is it? You didn't leave it there, did you?'

'No. I took it with me.' He noticed mother and son relax visibly. 'Well?' he asked. 'Are you gonna tell me what's really going on?'

'It's like I said,' Tragic said, unconvincingly.

Jane put her hand on her son's knee and smiled. 'It's OK, I'm sure Mickey understands.'

But Monkey far from understood. 'So, in this "*community*" you've joined,' he said, sarcastically, 'how're you gonna finish your education?' Monkey couldn't believe he was asking such questions. He sounded like Professor Reed – or, worse – Vivian. 'What you gonna do for a job, Tradge? And what about…you know…' He shot an embarrassed look in Jane's direction. '…breeding and stuff?'

Tragic cleared his throat and blushed. 'It'll be OK,' he said, directing his gaze to the floor.

Jane came to his rescue. 'We're pretty self-sufficient here. Don't worry about Trevor – he'll be fine. We grow all our own food and make our own furniture.'

Monkey snorted, louder than he'd intended. 'So what, you've turned Amish, now?' He stood up abruptly. 'You know what – something weird's going on. I don't know what it is, but maybe next time I come…'

'No!' Tragic and Jane interrupted together.

'I'm sorry, Mickey but you mustn't come again,' Jane said urgently. 'It was really kind of you to find Trevor but, for everyone's sake – yours *and* ours – you mustn't come back.' She paused, then asked anxiously, 'Does anyone else know you're here?'

'Only…' Monkey was going to say *only Angel Ellison*. Tragic knew how he felt about Angel – he'd be rapt to know that they'd got together. But he changed his mind. Better keep her out of it. 'Only me,' he answered. 'No one else.'

'Good. And can we rely on you to keep it that way – *please*?' she implored. Monkey nodded. 'And it would be best if you turned off your ring-cam until you're back in town,' Jane said.

Monkey reluctantly did as she had asked, then held out his hand to his friend. 'So this is it, is it – the big adios?'

Tragic stood up and Monkey realised that he'd grown somehow in the few days since he'd seen him; not in height, but in maturity. 'I'll be fridge, mate. Trust me.'

Jane walked Monkey to the edge of the village, making sure that he and Tragic had no time alone together. She stood in the road watching as he walked out into the night and back towards the loco track. The visit had left him with even more questions than when he'd arrived. None of it made sense. Was he seriously expected to believe that Tragic was willing to drop out of society, give up on his education, his career, his breeding rights, to live on homemade soup for the rest of his life – with his nurturer? He knew Tragic was tragic, but he wasn't a head case.

As soon as he was out of sight, Monkey switched on his ring-cam again.

'Time?' he whispered. It was almost midnight. His limbs felt like lead and his eyes struggled to stay open. The hope that had sustained him on his way out to the village was gone; replaced by a sense of despair that he would never see his friend again. It weighed on him as heavily as a bereavement, and unfamiliar tears pricked his eyes. He blinked them back furiously as he trudged the long lane back to the main road.

And then he heard it: a noise he'd only previously heard emanating from the snug in town or from the sports ground behind the fence of the Providers' Zone. It was the sound of male laughter; deep and throaty and it resonated across the countryside. Monkey looked round. There was a five-barred gate leading to a field and there, not 30 metres from him, walking across the bare earth, was a group of three providers, their silhouettes barely visible against the black of the night as he peered through the gate. He slipped off the road and ducked down into the hedge, watching the men coming towards him. As they got closer, he could see that they each carried tools, sledgehammers, slung on their shoulders, and one had a coil of wire looped over the other arm. Their jovial camaraderie was obvious even from where Monkey was hiding. This was what he yearned for – that raw masculinity of the providers. Tragic was mad to have given up the prospect.

The men tossed their sledgehammers over the gate onto the grass verge, then released the catch, opened the gate and stepped out onto the lane. They couldn't have been more than four metres from him. Who were they? he wondered. Prisoners from The Farm? Although Angel's research said that Combe Magna had been rejected as a site for a Farm development. Maybe they were working for The Assembly? After all, the food couldn't all come from The Farms, could it? There must be other arable sites that grew crops for the nurturers and their families. He'd never really thought about it before.

'I'll get Laura to drop some more fence posts off at the north end in the morning, then this is secure,' said one of the providers.

'Yeah, give this hedge a couple of years and it'll thicken up nicely. Won't need to be fencing it. I had enough fencing for a lifetime when I was on The Farm.' The voice behind the laughter sounded much younger than the first provider and, Monkey thought, vaguely familiar.

'Come on, then,' said the first man. 'Let's get this lot back and pick up those seed potatoes. Try and get all the early crop in before morning, shall we?'

'I'd like to get finished a bit early if I can,' said a third as they picked up their tools and headed back towards the village. 'Big day tomorrow.'

'Aye. We'll have to get him down the snug for his first keg – well, *legal* keg, anyway,' laughed the first voice and the others joined in the laughter as they disappeared into the night.

Monkey crept out of the hedge bottom and stood in the middle of the lane staring into the inky blackness as though he could still see the men. He didn't know who they were, or why they were there, or even if they had anything to do with Tragic's sudden liking for vegetable soup and primitive carpentry. What he did know was that, whether Jane liked it or not, he was coming back – and, next time, he wanted answers.

Chapter 9

Uninvited Guests

THE FOLLOWING day was Saturday and Monkey slept late. By the time his ring-cam penetrated his consciousness, it was already early afternoon. He flicked it on, realised it was Angel, so immediately turned down the visuals. No way did he want her seeing him looking like an extra from some monster horror-vid.

Her disembodied voice came from the blank screen, 'I've been ringing you all morning. How d'you get on last night?'

Monkey hesitated; torn between hope for his future breeding with her, and suspicion that she might, in some way, be setting him up with The Assembly. He gave her a skeleton account of the previous night, as he rubbed his eyes and combed his hair, making himself presentable for the ring-cam: he preferred speaking with eye contact; you got an insight into a person's sincerity. He leant out of bed so that he could check his reflection in the mirror over his desk, then pressed the button for visuals.

'That's better,' Angel remarked. 'So, what's your next move?'

Monkey sighed. He didn't know what his next move was – and if he did, should he tell her? 'How do I know I can trust you?' he said before he'd realised that his thoughts had formulated into words.

Angel looked surprised. 'You don't.' There was an uncomfortable silence. 'I came in on this because you asked me to. I'll back off if that's what you want?'

Monkey pondered her response; she'd sounded genuine and her eyes hadn't flickered when she'd spoken. He sighed. 'I think whatever Tragic's got into, he's in too deep,' he said simply. 'There's Security and The Assembly – they're all involved. And I think Criminal Justice might have some interest, too. This is big league. And…' he paused. 'Your nurturer is a solicitor. We need to be careful: she's establishment.'

'Listen, Monkey…' There was something about the way she used his tag; he loved it. '…Sal's…' she paused, choosing her words carefully, '…well, let's just say that not all nurturers are pro-Assembly. Sal doesn't like this regime any more than the providers do…'

'Whoa!' Monkey had been lying back in bed but he sat up abruptly. 'What d'you mean *regime*? And what are you going on about; *any more than the providers do*? Is Sal a provider? I don't think so! How does she know what they like and don't like?'

He didn't know why he'd reacted so fiercely, but there was something about the way she'd had a sly dig at the system that had annoyed him. He noticed her expression on his ring-cam as she blinked, clearly nonplussed by his response.

'Meet me by the loco bridge in an hour,' she said. 'We need to talk.'

Five minutes later, she rang back. 'Come disguised as a nurturer – and bring Vivian's bike.' Then she added with a nervous laugh, 'And don't forget to shave your legs.'

* * *

This had better not be a fit-up, Monkey railed inwardly as he pedalled towards the bridge on his nurturer's bike. He was doing his best to emulate the sedate cycling style of a female more than twice his age. The wind whipped up the plaid skirt that he'd sneaked out of his nurturer's wardrobe while she and Penny were in town and Grand-mov was dozing in her chair. He pushed it down again with one hand to try and protect his knees – and other parts – and swore under his breath: shiltz – it was cold! And the stupidly thin hose that nurturers wore did nothing to protect his privates! A fine drizzle penetrated the cardigan he'd pulled over the top of his T-shirt and flattened the silky strands of Penny's dressing-up wig to his face. He was just grateful that it was a Saturday and most people would be in the municipal leisure centre or just cruising the streets round

The Plaza. He prayed that none of the hood was lingering on home turf and caught sight of him.

When he arrived, she was already waiting. A wide grin spread across her face as she eyed him up and down. 'Good job breeders can't say no,' she teased.

'Lose it!' he snapped, embarrassed. 'This had better be worth it.'

'Come on.' She got onto her own bike and indicated for him to follow her. 'We'll talk as we ride.'

'Where are we going?'

'Combe Magna.'

Monkey stopped. 'No way! In broad daylight? Are you insane?'

Angel eyed him and sighed. 'We are two nurturers out for a cycle. Who's going to question us?' She grinned again. 'Although Security might be interested in that hair – it is criminally bad.'

Monkey feigned laughter; then his face set. 'I'm serious, Angel; this is ranged.'

'What was it that the old mov said – "Jane just up and left with her sister"?'

'And?'

'Only, you said that there is no sister.'

'Your point?'

'Haven't you worked out who it was yet?

Monkey narrowed his eyes. 'You're not going to tell me it was Tragic?'

Angel shrugged. 'That would be my guess, but we can ask him ourselves later. Come on.' And, once more, she set off on her bike.

On the ride out into the rurals, Angel told Monkey the information she had gleaned about an underground organisation, P.A.R.E.N.T. – Partners Advocating Rearing, Educating and Nurturing Together. They were dissatisfied with the current system whereby nurturers were solely responsible for the child-rearing, and wanted providers also to have a say in the upbringing of their offspring.

Monkey snorted. 'Who the hell are these people? I mean, Who on Earth wants that?'

'You'd be surprised. They're from across the board – providers who want to know their children and see them grow up, some nurturers who really liked the person they bred with and want to work in partnership with them and other nurturers who just want to share the responsibility.'

'So? They can meet up with them in town. There are mixed snugs, aren't there?'

'Yes – for networking and business deals; but not for socialising.'

Monkey shook his head. 'But why would any self-respecting provider want to be part of a nurturing unit anyway?'

'It's not necessarily about being part of a nurturing unit: it's about taking responsibility for the children you've created.' Angel sounded terse.

'Responsibility!' Monkey sneered. 'That's a nurturer's job!'

Angel skidded to a halt and Monkey almost went over the handlebars as he slammed on the brakes of Vivian's bike. She looked him in the eye. 'You're telling me that you'd be happy to breed and just walk away? That it would never cross your mind what your bub looked like? And you wouldn't be interested in its education or health or future career – or even if it was alive or dead?'

Monkey shrugged. 'I've never thought about it.'

'So you've never wondered what *your* provider's like?' Angel sounded shocked.

Monkey thought for a moment. 'I remember Grand-mov telling me he was a law student or something. It was when I was little and Vivian got into a right frenz about it. Said she wasn't allowed to talk about him again…'

The reality of what Angel was saying began to make sense: if Angel selected him for breeding, once she'd had two bubs – or three at most – he'd be moved up to the Providers' Zone, never to see either her or his offspring again. He had never questioned the scenario before but, now, the enormity of the situation dawned on him. That would be the end of his friendship with her. His contribution to the National Maintenance Fund would be deducted at source, dependent upon his salary, and that would be his only input into her life and theirs. That was, of course, provided that Angel *did* select him and no one else, such as Moni Morrison, chose him first. He felt a sudden contraction in his gut, as though he was going to be sick. Suddenly, the lifestyle that had, only recently, appeared so attractive, was beginning to look significantly less so.

'How come you know all this rebel stuff anyway?' he challenged.

'Since Monday, when you took me to Tragic's, I've made it my business to find out what's going on. What do you think I've been doing all week?'

Monkey shook his head. 'At first, I thought you'd been scared off and didn't want anything to do with me. Then, when you came up with the map, I thought you'd just been trying to crack our code…'

Angel raised her eyes upwards and smiled at the irony. 'Your code was hardly Enigma!' she laughed. 'I cracked it in no time.' Her tone became serious. 'Last week, I kept my distance because I didn't want to arouse suspicion. I've been doing research; eavesdropping, keeping my eyes and ears open – learning everything I can about The Assembly. And I don't like what I've discovered.' She leant forward, intently. 'Monkey, in a few weeks, you'll go off to the Breeders' Zone, breed a few times and that'll be your job done. But, for me,' she shook her head, pleading with him to understand the full connotations of her future, 'my job will just be beginning. For the next 20 years, it'll be my responsibility to bring up my offs – on my own.'

'But that's what nurturers wanted, isn't it?' he queried. 'Wasn't that the whole point of the revolution?'

'Revolutions always happen for a reason but I wasn't there, I don't know what the point of it was: only what they tell us in T.R.E.A.C.L.E.,' she said, 'And I'm starting to think that that's not the whole truth.'

Monkey looked round, anxiously checking that there was no one around to overhear them – this was dangerous talk.

'Stop it,' he said quickly. 'What's got into you?' This wasn't turning out the way he'd planned when he'd first invited her along to find Tragic. He was the bad boy; she was the angelic Angel. He was supposed to impress her but she was taking over. He turned on her, defensively. 'Nurturers and providers both get what they want. ' He wasn't sure if he was trying to convince her or himself. 'You get to raise the bubs your way, and we get to live our lives our way: it's a win: win situation.'

Angel shook her head. 'Who's winning, Monkey? Open your eyes!'

Monkey shivered and straightened the wig that had worked its way forward. The conversation was becoming uncomfortable. 'Let's get going.'

They continued cycling but Angel was not to be silenced.

'I've discovered a lot about how people used to raise kids and it wasn't all bad, you know. It wasn't like we've been taught to believe.' Monkey groaned; she was starting to sound like Tragic. 'When I have bubs, I want to make sure that they've got the best possible chance in the world. I don't want to be one of those nurturers who indulges their offs as long as they're little but, as soon as they get to be pres, opts out and lets them run loose.'

Monkey suspected that there was an implied slur on himself and Vivian. 'Look who's talking. You and Alex are no different.'

'That's my point. Sal was great when we were bubs, but she's struggling now – not so much with me, but Alex is only 12 and already he's starting to backchat. I don't want that if I have male offs. I want them to grow up responsible and contributing.'

'Breeders and providers are responsible and they do contribute,' Monkey argued.

'I mean they should contribute more than sperm and money,' she retorted flatly.

Monkey felt affronted. He rode on in silence; confused. The Angel he thought he knew was turning out to be someone very different. This wasn't the placid, compliant Angel who was in his division looking sweet and the epitome of her name; this was some counter-revolutionary with no respect for providers and, from some of her recent antics, what looked like a death wish. He was beginning to think that Tragic wasn't the only one who'd got in too deep.

The rain had eased but the wind had got up and Vivian's skirt clung to Monkey's legs like an icy rag. They were using the roads rather than the track, partly because the surface would be easier on bikes but also so as not to draw attention to themselves. Two nurturers cycling on the road in the rain might look silly, but cycling on a disused loco track would look downright suspicious. They saw no one else other than an official limo, obviously one of The Assembly visiting an outlying constituency in the run-up to the election, but its occupant drove on, paying them no attention.

Their progress was slow and it was almost dark when they arrived in Combe Magna. As they approached the cottage where Tragic and Jane were living, they stowed their bikes in an outbuilding and Monkey led Angel down the narrow lane. They were disappointed to find that the cottage was in darkness. Monkey knocked but there was no reply.

'Now what?' Angel asked. 'Shall we wait?'

Monkey thought for a moment. 'No,' he said. 'Let's have a look round.'

Still disguised as adult nurturers, the two of them wandered along the main street of the village and past the green. The smell of wood smoke filled the damp air. Lights flickered in the windows of some of the cottages. A large building at the far end of the village caught their attention. It had lights illuminating every window and, as they approached, they could hear the sound of people talking inside. There was laughter, too, and what sounded like singing. A large wooden sign hung above the door with a picture of a figure with two faces, one male, one female and the words 'The Volte Face' written underneath.

'Looks like some sort of snug,' Monkey whispered. He beckoned Angel to follow him down a narrow alley along the side, leading towards the back of the building. There were two windows that shone light onto the overgrown footpath. Monkey waved Angel to stay behind him, then carefully leant forward to peer in through the first window.

He narrowed his eyes, trying to understand the scene in front of him. There were nurturers, providers and pres, all sitting around a roaring fire with glasses of keg in their hands and singing. Jane was there and a provider was sitting next to her – with his arm round her shoulder! Monkey gasped. He turned away from the window, shocked at the brazenness of his friend's nurturer. He'd always thought of her as kind, caring and upright – not one of those charity-spins he'd heard about to whom providers went when they felt the need for comfort, long after their official breeding days were over.

'What is it?' Angel whispered and leant forward to see for herself.

But Monkey restrained her. 'Don't look,' he warned. 'I don't want you to think badly of Tragic's nurturer.' He returned to the window and stared at Jane. The provider reached over and kissed her full on the lips, then pulled away, laughing. Jane was laughing too; her head thrown back in joy. Monkey had never seen her looking so relaxed – and beautiful.

A roar went up and Tragic strode into the crowd. His eyes sparkled in the firelight and he looked happier than Monkey had ever seen him. Everyone raised their glasses and began singing *Happy Birthday* as though he was a bub again. No one sang at graduation parties – and no one drank keg either; they were just about wishing your friends well and giving them a gift to see them on their way on the next stage of their life. But then, Monkey witnessed the most shocking spectacle of all; a pre-nurturer, no older than Tragic, went up to him and kissed him – on the mouth! In front of everybody! And everyone cheered.

Monkey moved away from the window and leant back against the wall, trying to make sense of it all.

'What's happening?' Angel asked, urgently.

Before Monkey could reply, a deep male voice boomed along the footpath behind them, 'That's what I want to know!'

Chapter 10

The State of the Nation

THE LAUGHTER and singing ceased and an uneasy silence descended on the birthday celebrations. Apart from the pain in his upper arm where a burly male was holding him tightly, Monkey was acutely aware that he was standing in the midst of a group of people wearing his nurturer's skirt and his sister's childhood dressing-up wig. It was hardly the first impression he might have hoped to make. With his free hand, he snatched the wig from his head and glowered balefully at the provider who held him captive.

'Monkey! Angel?' Tragic was standing with one arm round the shoulder of a pre-nurturer and a glass of keg in his other hand. 'What are you doing here?'

Monkey scanned the assembled crowd then shook himself free of the provider's grip. ''Flecting back, cuz.'

Tragic dropped his arm from the girl's shoulder and his eyes darted to Jane and the provider whom Monkey had seen kissing her earlier. It was the male who broke the tension.

'You must be Mickey; Jane and Trevor have told me a lot about you.' He turned to Angel. 'And, if I'm not mistaken, you'll be Angelina?'

Angel stepped forward and cocked her head enquiringly. 'How did you…'

'I recognise the description,' he gave her a disarming smile. 'I'm Tom – Trevor's father.'

Monkey recognised his voice immediately; he was one of the providers who had been working in the field the previous night when Monkey had been on his way home: the one who'd been talking about having a 'big day' and taking someone down the snug for his first legal keg. Then came another voice that was familiar to Monkey, only, when he'd heard it the previous evening out in the field, he'd been unable to place it.

'Mickey, man! Wozzapp'nin'? What you doin' here?' It was Jumpy, the hyperactive Mooner who'd been sentenced to a spell on The Farm for being caught with a pre-nurturer before he'd graduated.

'Jumpy?' Monkey was shocked.

'They call me Noel here. And guess what? I ain't jumpy no more, neither!' he grinned, raising his glass and taking a sip of keg. 'Edge and Riddler are over there too – only we call 'em Edward and Roger. We don't do tags here. Good to see you, mate.' He walked off towards the back of the snug where several pre-breeders and pre-nurturers were gathered round a table. One or two of them raised their glasses when they saw Monkey, as though toasting his welcome to the community.

'They think you've joined us,' Tragic commented.

'What're they doing here? I thought they went straight from The Farm to the Breeders' Zone?'

Tragic shook his head. 'There's quite a few Farm escapees in the rurals. They hear what the zones are like from some of the older farm workers and there's no way they're going there. So they make a run for it.'

Monkey was struggling to take it all in. 'And who's...' he looked at the pre-nurturer who had kissed Tragic but had now moved slightly away from him.

'Oh, this is Zoë – she's my girlfriend.' He shot Zoë a sideways glance, blushed, then looked at his feet, grinning widely.

'Girlfriend?' Monkey shook his head in disbelief. 'First, you're calling Jane, *Mum*, and then some guy introduces himself as your father – now you've got yourself a *girlfriend*. What's going on here, Tradge? You've only been away a week and it's like you've turned back time 50 years.'

Tragic shrugged. 'Well, maybe that's not such a bad thing.'

Monkey slapped his head with his hand. 'You have got to be raggin' me!'

Tom interrupted and suggested they go somewhere quiet so that Monkey could be offered some explanations. Tragic said his goodbyes to the crowd in the snug, kissed Zoë and told her he'd see her later, then Tom and Jane led them back to the cottage. Jane could barely conceal her consternation that Monkey had returned, so it was Tom who spoke.

He explained that all the adult males in the snug had once been residents of the state zones. They'd started out just like Monkey and Tragic, attending the local school, eager for graduation; many had been in brotherhoods, some had the scars to show for it. Once in the Breeders' Zone, some had continued their education but many had dropped out, doing menial jobs just for the money until they'd bred their offspring and moved on to the Providers' Zone. Here, they spent their days working, evenings watching vids or drinking down the snug and weekends playing sports. They ate, they slept, they drank – a few took solace with the charity-spins – but a substantial number of providers found themselves bored after a while. The old rivalries of the hoods reared their heads from time to time to add spice and excitement but, for many, life lacked any purpose or meaning.

'Basically, we were all just waiting to move on to The Pastures – and die,' he said.

'That's what I kept trying to tell you,' Tragic chipped in. 'It wasn't this Utopia that T.R.E.A.C.L.E. wanted us to believe.'

Monkey looked at Tom, 'And you're telling me it took 16 years for the coin to drop?'

Tom smiled. 'No – about five, actually – and then another couple to get out.' Monkey raised his eyebrows as though to say, *go on*. 'I was one of the ones who did carry on with my education…'

'Now, why doesn't that surprise me,' Monkey sneered, trying not to show his disillusionment that everything he'd believed in; had hoped for all his life, was a sham.

Tom went on, 'I became a teacher…'

'Figures!' Monkey interjected.

'…and, seeing the students growing up and moving on, touched something in me. I got to wondering about my own child.' He looked across the room at Jane; there was softness in his expression. 'And his nurturer.' Tom turned back to Monkey. 'I wanted to know what they were doing, what my son looked like. I knew Jane had miscarried a couple of times but I didn't know if she'd chosen someone else to breed with after I went on to the Providers' Zone, and it started to eat away at me.' Monkey shook his head as though dismissing Tom as a wuzzle and silently thinking that he could now see where Tragic got it from. 'One evening, I was playing racquetball with another guy and he told me he felt the same way. And it started from there.'

The men had made contact with the nurturers of their children, publicly at first to avoid suspicion then, when it was clear that there was still attraction between some of them – like Tom and Jane – they continued to meet in secret, Tom going to the house several times a week.

'So, they were your clothes in the cellar,' Angel observed.

'Yes, and when Security started to snoop around, we had to get an extra freezer and cut it open so that I could hide down there in case there was a raid.'

'Whoa! Whoa! Whoa!' Monkey stood up and began pacing the floor. 'You're telling me this has been going on for years?' He turned to his friend. 'And you didn't think to mention this?'

Tragic looked away guiltily. 'I didn't know until recently,' he pleaded. 'But then, when I did find out, I couldn't say anything. Like Dad says, Security was hot and I couldn't risk you letting it slip.'

Monkey snorted. 'Cheers for the vote of confidence.'

Three clear knocks sounded from the front door of the cottage and the room fell silent. Tragic, Tom and Jane looked at each other anxiously. Tom made a gesture for the others to remain quiet and Jane, clearly agitated, indicated for him to take Tragic, Monkey and Angel to the back of the room behind the screen that separated the kitchen area. Two distinct knocks followed and Jane relaxed slightly and, when a further three knocks were heard, she breathed deeply and went to answer the door.

'What's going on, Tradge?' Monkey whispered from behind the sheet of fabric that had been strung across the back of the room.

Tom peered round the edge of the screen then, visibly relieved, went out to meet the two males who had entered the cramped room, one wearing women's clothing.

Tragic replied, 'We're expecting an escapee but you can't be too careful. You never know who might be kosher and who's a spy.'

Monkey heard one of the newcomers speak. 'Evening, Tom; Jane. This is Karl. We were hoping to find you down The Volte Face, but they said you'd gone. Had you forgotten he was coming out tonight?'

The three pres emerged from behind the screen, startling the two men.

Tom reassured them. 'It's OK. They can be trusted.'

The man in the skirt and headscarf, who had been introduced as Karl, looked at Monkey's female apparel and shot a look of betrayal at the others. 'You didn't tell me anyone else was coming out tonight.'

Tom beckoned the three forward. 'This is Trevor, my son – and these are some friends of his,' he hedged. 'They are all 100 percent trustworthy.' He looked directly at Monkey as though daring him to breach his trust. He turned back to Karl. 'Now, let's get you something to eat and find you a bed. I hope you don't mind sharing with Trevor.'

Karl smiled, relieved. 'No. It's only for tonight. I'm on my way north to join my kid and his nurturer. Told The Assembly I was transferring to Anglia,' he laughed. 'That should give me a few days to go to ground before they're on to me.'

Tom smiled. 'They think I went to Deira: probably still looking for me up there.'

During the course of the evening, Monkey and Angel listened to the others discussing the political situation. With the help of the rebels, providers were leaving their zones in ones and twos; applying for transfers to far-flung towns across the country, then joining the network of underground communities that were springing up in the rurals. Females were allowed to move around freely, so many of the providers and pre-breeders fleeing the regime did so undercover of female garb, much as Monkey and Karl had done that day. Local road traffic barely existed – unless it was by bike or donkey cart. And inter-city travel was by state coach on the motorways, or loco via the capital. The by-roads had long since fallen into disrepair, making travel through the countryside slower but safer than the State-controlled routes.

And, from what the adults were saying, it wasn't just the providers who were turning their backs on the system: nurturers too, tired of raising their offspring alone, were finding obscure, and sometimes manufactured, relatives to go and live with, away from the hood violence that terrorised the towns. The security forces, already stretched, had neither the time nor the personnel to follow up everyone reported missing; many were simply presumed dead, caught up in the crossfire of rival zones and disposed of after shut down. From what Monkey could gather, once a community had been established, the males worked under cover of night so that, should Security or representatives of The Assembly decide to do a random check, the villages were, ostensibly, self-sufficient co-operatives run by nurturers, for nurturers. In the privacy of their communities, however, nurturers and providers worked in partnership to raise their offspring with a balance of both male and female role models and some, like Jane and Tom, even lived together.

As the adults talked, Monkey looked around the room and reflected on his situation. If the hood could see him now, sitting there in a skirt, listening to a provider who must be over two metres tall and weigh nearly 100 kilos – who was also wearing a skirt, he'd be mocked until he graduated. He didn't know what to make of all this political intrigue he was hearing about. Angel was quite clearly devouring every word, nodding and shaking her head in, what seemed to Monkey, appropriate places. But Monkey's mind was in turmoil. What he was hearing conflicted with everything he'd been brought up to understand and believe. His head felt like a box that was so crammed full to bursting, it hurt with the effort of trying to make sense of it all.

Karl was talking again, alternately wringing his hands and clenching his fists. 'The nurturer of my lad already had a male bub before we bred. He'd be 15 now if he was still alive.' He shook his head. 'Got into a turf war and was mauled to death by dogs. Rotties, Staffs, Dobermans – used them as weapons – a whole pack of them. Didn't stand a chance.' He looked round the group gathered by the fire. 'No way is that going to happen to my kid. He's 10 and she says he's already hankering after revenge.' He dropped his head into his hands. 'I've got to get to him: talk sense into him before…'

Tom put a consoling hand on his shoulder. 'We'll get you out, no worries.' He let out an explosive sigh. 'This madness has to stop – and the sooner the better.'

Karl turned to Jane, the only adult female present, his voice suddenly bitter. 'All this *let-'em-do-as-they-like* crap that The Assembly advocates! Can't they see it doesn't work? *Love the hood and make them good*? All this sickly-sweet philosophy is poisoning society. It's like anything: balance it with a bit of savoury and it's fine but too much and it becomes toxic. Love isn't just about saying *darling* at the end of every sentence: it's about guidance and balance and being there – day and night – even when it's tough. And it's about boundaries and consistency…'

'It's OK – I'm on your side,' Jane interrupted, clearly taken aback by the way Karl appeared to be making her personally responsible for how the matriarchal society had descended into anarchy.

'Sorry,' he apologised. 'I get so frustrated. I've been hearing for years that there was a movement underway to repeal the Segregation Laws but I don't see any changes – not for the better anyway. Do you know,' Karl scanned the room, 'last week, on my way to work, I saw a provider beaten and kicked to the ground just for looking at some of the hood that were hanging round The Plaza. A grown man! In broad daylight! Forked out every month into the National Maintenance Fund to provide for those ... those...' Karl broke down. The rest of them watched him, uncomfortable in their impotence. Slowly, he straightened up, shook his head and whispered shamefully, 'And I was too scared to go and help him.'

Monkey lowered his eyes guiltily; aware that, although he and the Mooners had never set dogs on anyone or beaten an innocent passer-by, he was not entirely blameless when it came to inter-hood warfare. But it was just part of life, wasn't it? Tom himself had said that most of the providers in the village had once been in hoods. It was a means of survival. Hoods carried weapons to protect themselves. There was no such thing as a unilateral amnesty: it was tantamount to certain death. The only person he'd known to walk out without a weapon had been Tragic, but he'd done so under Monkey's protection, so that didn't count. It was mean out there but it was also part of the initiation into manhood and anyone who thought otherwise didn't understand.

Tom was sympathising with Karl on the futility of the violence and the unfairness of having to support the perpetrators when providers had no idea where – or even who – their own offspring were.

'You know they want to lower the age of graduation for pre-breeders?' Tom told Karl. 'Bring it down to 12 to try and get the hoods off the street.'

Karl shook his head. 'Won't work. What are they going to do with them all, send them all off to The Farm? They're fully stretched as it is.'

'Some sort of boot camp idea, according to our intelligence.'

Karl eyed Tom. 'Is your source reliable?'

Tom nodded. 'A member of The Assembly. Apparently, they want to bring it in straight after the election.'

Karl gave an ironic snort. 'Isn't that what the revolution was about in the first place: getting away from that whole militaristic thing? And that was when they recruited at 18! Now they want children hardly older than bubs being trained in the very thing they objected to!'

The group continued discussing the forthcoming election and as they talked, Monkey watched Tom and Jane with interest bordering on suspicion. They sat close, fingers interlinked, Tom's thumb rubbing the palm of her hand. Jane sighed, resting her head on Tom's shoulder and Tom acknowledged the gesture with a reassuring kiss to the top of her head. Monkey had never witnessed such overt inter-gender affection before. Even in such tense and depressing circumstances, there was an air of contentment about them. He switched his attention to Angel, sitting by the fire, her knees bent, arms wrapped round her legs, the firelight playing on her cheek. He wondered what it would be like for him to have a full-on Tom and Jane-style relationship with her and felt a swell of emotion. He looked away quickly and watched Tragic instead. It seemed weird still calling him Tragic, because he was no longer as his tag implied. He'd changed. He was stronger: whole somehow – definitely more Trev than Tradge. And Monkey noticed how he hung on every word Tom said with admiration and pride.

Monkey was unsettled. He couldn't put his finger on it but he didn't like it. It was the same feeling he got when Vivian spent hours on end with Penny, leaving him to do his own thing. He'd felt it too when he'd seen Angel laughing with Danger one day in school. There was a bitter taste in his mouth. He watched Trevor, Jane and Tom now, saw the looks they gave each other: felt the bond between them. And his stomach knotted up.

He snatched Penny's wig from where he'd stashed it under his jumper, and pressed it on to his head.

'Come on,' he said to Angel. 'We're going!' And he stood up, abruptly taking his leave.

Chapter 11

Snake in the Grass

OVER the next week, Monkey kept his distance from Angel, ignoring her in school and refusing to answer her calls. The visit to the village had confused him. Everything he'd been taught, everything he'd believed in had been called into question. He no longer knew whom to trust. There was too much to take in, so he tried to shut it out; once more immersing himself in the hood, coching with them after school and storming other hoods in the evening. He had only a few weeks until his graduation. If he could get through that, he'd be OK. Everything would be just as he'd planned: he'd show Tragic and those other losers that they'd got it wrong.

On the Friday evening, he was preparing to join Danger, Kraze and the others in The Plaza. The word was that someone from Broadwalk had dissed one of the Mooners and they were going to have beef with them tonight. A frisson of excitement shot through him as he retrieved the shank from under his mattress and tucked it into the waistband of his riders. He took the chequered neckerchief from his chest of drawers, folded it into a triangle and tied it round his neck with the apex to the front. He checked himself in the mirror but froze when, in the glass he caught the reflection of Penny staring through the partially open door. He turned to face her.

'What's up, sis?' he said, amiably.

Penny shrugged. 'You tell me.' She pushed the door wider and nodded to where the knife was concealed under his clothing. 'I saw you.'

Monkey tried to laugh. 'So you're turned spy now, are you?'

Penny did not return the laughter. 'Moni told us at T.R.E.A.C.L.E. that we should dob anyone in if we saw them doing anti-social stuff.'

Monkey feigned a smile. 'What's anti-social about protecting yourself? You know as well as I do, there are dangerous people out there. I'm just making sure I don't get hurt, that's all. I'm not gonna use it.'

Penny shook her head. 'I'm not buying it. You think I'm just some fudgy little pre who hasn't a scoob.'

Monkey dropped the smile. 'So what you saying, sis? You're gonna rat on me? Have me sent off to The Farm when I've only got a few weeks 'till I'm out of yours and Vivian's hair for good? Is that it?'

Penny folded her arms and leant against the door frame. 'Could do.' She held his gaze. 'But I won't.' Monkey relaxed slightly. She entered his room and put her arms round his waist, cuddling him as she used to do when she was a bub. 'I want to hug you and make you good, Mickey. I want you to graduate and be happy. I don't want you to be fighting and arguing all the time. Love cures everything.'

Monkey raised his eyes and sighed. 'Yeah, I know,' he said impatiently. 'And I love you, sis, but, right now, I'm outta here.'

Deftly, Penny snatched the knife from his waist band and stepped away, holding the weapon behind her.

'Give it back!' Monkey ordered.

She shook her head. 'If you weren't going to use it anyway, you can go out without it.'

'Don't mess with me, sis.'

'Who's messing? Leave it behind or I'll call Moni and have you arrested.' Monkey glared at her, but Penny would not be cowed. 'Vivian's been too soft with you,' she went on. 'I bet you didn't really cut yourself on a kitchen knife the other week – I bet you were out fighting with the hood, weren't you? I wouldn't be surprised if Tragic was stabbed and that's why he's disappeared. Vivian should've dobbed you in ages ago, 'stead of covering for you and mollycoddling you.'

'What!' Monkey was shocked. 'You are seriously ranged – you know that! Anyway, what happened to all your *love the hood and make 'em good* crap?'

'I could have you arrested just for saying that,' Penny threatened. 'But it's all going to change soon anyway. A nurturer from The Assembly came and talked to us at T.R.E.A.C.L.E. and she says that we've got to tell our nurturers and grand-movs to vote for the Distaff Party because, if they win the election again, they're going to introduce a pre-breeder zone so that all adolescent males can be re-educated.'

Monkey drew in his breath sharply. Hadn't he heard Tom talking about leaked plans to send all pre-breeders to boot camp at the age of 12? Was this what The Assembly had dressed up as *re-education*?

Penny continued, 'It's too late for you, but at least *my* children will learn how to be kind and loving. They won't even *want* to carry weapons, because they'll be happy and at peace with the world.' She delivered the last line with a victorious flick of her hair.

They glared at each other, much as they had done when they were younger, staring each other out – but, this time, it was no childish game: it was a power struggle and Monkey knew that, if he lost, he would lose more than his dignity: he could lose his freedom and his chance to graduate too. The sound of the info-screen downstairs filtered through the silence between brother and sister – the volume was always turned up to accommodate Grand-mov's failing hearing. Monkey could just make out the words: Party Political Broadcast... Distaff... re-education... re-alignment with society...

It was as though the pieces of the past week had suddenly fallen into place; all the doubts he'd had, all the questions and confusion cleared in one moment of realisation. If Tom had been right about the boot camps, then the chances were, he and the other rebels were right about other things – the lack of freedom for breeders and providers, the latter fleeing in droves to be with their children, the nurturers struggling to cope on their own and desperate to work in partnership.

It was all starting to make sense. He needed to go back to the village. He needed to speak to Tragic. But first, he needed to see Angel.

Monkey held out his hands in a gesture of capitulation. 'It's fine, sis. Keep the blade.'

Penny narrowed her eyes dubiously. 'Just like that?'

'Just like that,' he said, walking past her and down the stairs.

'I'm watching you,' she called after him. 'Moni's told us we need to keep alert for anything untoward.'

'Of course, you do,' he replied. Then added, under his breath, 'We all do.'

As he passed the sitting room, he saw Vivian and Sarah sitting in front of the info-screen. Images of teenage males flashed into view: playing football; laughing together like old men in a snug; working in teams building model vehicles – all happy; all co-operating.

A seductive female voice almost sang the commentary:

'…*instil the old values of respect and consideration. Your pre-breeders will once again be offspring to be proud of. They will be taught co-operation and teamwork; kindness and humanity; diligence and commitment. In an environment of love and compassion, the disillusioned and frightened young pre-breeders of today will be rehabilitated to become fine upstanding providers of tomorrow. Vote Distaff!*'

Distaff! Monkey snorted his disgust as he headed towards the door. They didn't need to broadcast their policies: they'd already got it sewn up. Last year, he'd attended a T.R.E.A.C.L.E. session where they'd been taught about elections. One of the ruling Distaff Assembly members had explained that nurturers and spins had the right to vote the minute they reached 16 – because, as everyone knew, females matured more quickly than males. And, for the same reason, breeders were denied the vote until they reached 20 or had graduated to the Providers' Zone: only then would they be deemed capable of knowing their own minds. At the time, Tragic had been incensed: 'We're mature enough to breed but not mature enough to put an X in a box?' Monkey had shrugged. 'Who gives a shiltz about politics? It's boring.' It was only now that he was beginning to appreciate the injustice of a regime that automatically allocated more votes to its own supporters.

He put his hand on the door knob, then hesitated, overwhelmed by a feeling of fury at his, and millions of other males', situation. What Tom and Jane had said was making more and more sense to him. The village community had got it right. It was fine for the females: Vivian was sitting there with her nurturer, just as, in years to come, Penny would sit with Vivian – but what about him? What about the others? They'd be sent off to breed like the cattle he'd seen on history vids, then left to fester in their zone until it was time to die. Who would sit with him when he was old? A flash of Tragic's family sitting by the fire came into his head. He wanted a chance at a life like that.

'They can say what they like,' he heard his grand-mov say, 'I'm voting Unity; they might bring back a bit of sanity.'

'Oh, for heaven's sake!' Vivian chastised. 'They're not even credible as an opposition party.'

'Only because of a system that keeps them as the opposition,' Sarah argued.

Vivian let out an exasperated sigh. 'I've got some notes to write up.' She left the room and started at seeing Monkey in the hallway. 'I thought you'd gone out,' she challenged.

'Can I ask you something?' he said.

Vivian looked suspicious at the relatively benign demeanour of her son. 'What is it?'

'Doesn't it interest you what happened to the guy you bred with?' he asked. Vivian groaned. He ignored her. 'What if I want to trace him when I graduate? How will I recognise him? At least give me a name.'

Vivian turned away and headed towards the kitchen. 'I've really had enough of all this nonsense.'

Monkey entered the sitting room and approached his grand-mov. Sarah was more sympathetic. 'All I know is that he was studying law when Vivian was doing medicine. Eric someone – she never did tell me his name but she was quite taken with him, from what I recall. They used to meet up in the university snug and talk about books, philosophy and suchlike.'

Monkey went and sat on the arm of her chair. 'The other thing that bothers me is, what about when I have bubs?'

His grand-mov shrugged. 'Don't ask me, Mickey, love. I don't know what it must be like not to know where your children are, what they look like, how they're doing in life. It would cut me up something rotten.'

'So tell me how to find this Eric,' Monkey pleaded.

'I wish I could, love. But I can't help you. I think there are records at the Breeding Centre – you know, so that they can keep a check on how many children men have sired...' Monkey loved the old-fashioned way his grand-mov spoke; using words like men and sired: it was so quaint. '...but, any more than that, I can't say.'

Vivian re-entered the room, and banged down a mug of coffee on the low table in front of Sarah.

'This conversation is closed.' It was a statement of fact rather than a request. 'Now,' she turned to her son, 'are you going out, or are we to be graced with your presence this evening?'

'Don't you ever wonder what he's doing, or if he had any more bubs with anyone else?'

Vivian started. 'He didn't,' she said, quietly.

Monkey smelt victory. 'There you go! You chose him twice – you must've liked him to have chosen the same guy again! And he must've liked you, or he'd have gone with someone else when you didn't take up your option a third time. Wouldn't you like to see him again? Have him around a bit more?'

Vivian spun round, her fury barely concealed. 'Families are better off on their own. Women are the nurturers; we can manage. All we need is the financial provision. And you'll be no different. Once you've bred, you won't want to be bothered with your children; all you'll want to do is to be off with your mates, drinking and watching sport.'

'It seemed to work all right for my generation and hundreds of generations before that,' Sarah interjected.

But Vivian cut her off, 'You only say that because you've forgotten what it was like.'

Sarah shook her head with disdain. 'Forgotten? How could I forget 20 years of my life? Your father might not have won Dad of the Year, but he did his bit. The trouble with your lot is you won't give and take. You want it all your own way.'

'Did his bit?' Vivian questioned.

'He put food on the table, didn't he? And he kept you and your brother in check. Specially when Gordon got to his age,' she nodded at Monkey, 'and started to get too big for his boots; flexed his muscles, like all young bucks!'

'What's going on?' Penny had come downstairs.

'Nothing, darling,' Vivian purred, stifling her retort and pulling her daughter to her. She ran a hand down the back of Penny's head, stroking her hair soothingly. 'Your grand-mov was talking about the olden days – again! And Mickey's just going out.'

Penny peered out from the comfort of her nurturer's bosom and held her brother in a steely gaze.

'Be careful,' she said.

There was a chill in her voice and Monkey heeded the warning: his little sister was no longer someone to be underestimated.

Chapter 12

Screaming Blue Murders

ANGEL had already made plans but she agreed to meet him the following morning. Monkey was restless. He'd wanted to talk to her – she and Trevor were the only ones in whom he could confide and patience was not his strong point.

He felt anxious as he cycled down the road to meet the rest of the hood. The absence of his blade made him edgy. By the time he reached the corner of Moonstone Park, the others had already gone. He kicked the wall in frustration, then set off towards The Plaza. He was alone and unarmed – not a situation to be encouraged for a pre-breeder – and his anxiety increased as he neared the centre of town. He pulled the scarf up high and his hood down low.

It was still early and the last remnants of workers were on their way home ready for the weekend. As he rounded the corner of an office building, Monkey heard a jeer and whooping noise from The Plaza. He braked cautiously and scanned the road for any piece of wood or metal that he might be able to use as a weapon. A row of refuse bins, lined up in a delivery duct, drew his attention and he wheeled his bike into the darkness of the alley. To his relief, he saw a broken stake sticking out of one of the bins. He retrieved it, balanced it across the handlebars of his bike, and rode warily towards The Plaza.

'Hey! Monkey!' several of the hood called as he threw his cycle on top of the tangle of bikes that lay in the centre of the square. The large advertising screen was now mended and, once again, flashing images of serene happy children and their nurturers across the centre of town.

'Took your time,' Kraze challenged.

'I'm here, aren't I?'

Monkey noticed Alex, Angel's brother, standing on the steps of the clock tower. He scanned the group and his heart sank; he was shocked to see that, like Alex, they were mostly novices. Apart from himself, Kraze, Danger and Fuse, there were only five other Mooners approaching graduation age: a grand total of nine 15-year-olds. There were a few from the year below, but the majority were only just out of alpha-school. Broadwalk, on the other hand, was a manual zone. Its hood were hard and, as the housing was mainly low-rise apartments or rows of close-packed terraced houses, it had a much larger population than Moonstone Park and, consequently, a much larger hood. Tonight's mission was supposed to be retribution but, with a force so small – and so young – Monkey was getting a bad feeling about it.

He pulled down his scarf and drew Kraze to one side. 'Woz happenin' with the novs?'

Kraze looked Monkey in the eye and squared his shoulders. 'We need numbers.'

Monkey stood his ground. ' We need experience. Send 'em home.'

Without lowering his gaze, Kraze called over his shoulder, 'Hey, Danger – get everyone on their bikes. We're heading over to Broadwalk.' Addressing Monkey again, he lowered his voice and allowed himself a slight curl of the lip. 'Looks like my call.' With a contemptuous gob to Monkey's feet, he walked slowly back to the group.

Monkey hung back. This was suicide. He didn't know whether to leave them to it and go home, risking their taunts of bottling, or try to work on Kraze to see sense. He saw Angel's brother cycling out into the middle of The Plaza, standing up on his bike, lifting the front wheel and spinning it. Idiot! Didn't he know that stragglers got picked off first?

'Yo! Alex!' Monkey beckoned him over.

'Raisa!' Angel's brother corrected. 'Not Alex.'

'Raisa.' Monkey nodded respect. 'Coch with me – OK? And keep to the middle of the group. No limbing it when you're storming.'

Before the younger boy could respond, a deafening crack split the night, followed by a yowl and an outburst of laugher. Monkey pulled Alex back by the sleeve and went across to where a handgun was lying on the ground. Fuse was dancing up and down, holding his right hand with his left and swearing, while the rest of the hood ridiculed his ineptitude.

'Where the fegg d'you get that?' Monkey asked, kicking the gun away from Fuse.

'Some breeder my brother knows got it for me.' Fuse had two older brothers, both of whom had already graduated.

'You're playing outta your league, cuz. Get rid of it.'

Kraze strolled over to join them and the laughter subsided. 'Pick it up, Fuse. We need it against Broadwalk.'

Monkey bent down and picked up the gun but did not hand it back to Fuse. 'You can't go over there blazin',' he said to Kraze. 'It's ranged.' Kraze held out his hand for the gun, but Monkey shook his head. 'Do us all a favour and call this off before it's too late.'

'You know something?' Kraze said, pacing the square; aware that his leadership was being called into question. 'I've been wondering about you, for a long time.' He circled Monkey, like a lion stalking its prey. 'There's something…' He spun round and, drawing a shank from his pocket, held the blade against Monkey's cheek. '…not quite koshe about you.'

Monkey reared away, shocked at the unexpected turn of events. He'd always thought that if, by some unfortunate accident, he was one of the pre-breeders to die in The Plaza, it would be at the hands of another hood – not his own. He held out the gun in a gesture of capitulation; if Kraze needed it in order to boost his confidence, let him take it. Fuse took the firearm gingerly, but Kraze did not release his knife from Monkey's face.

'I don't know what it is,' he went on, menacingly. 'Something in my gut. What d'ya say, Raisa?'

Angel's brother stepped forward. 'S'right, Kraze. Monk and my sis have been jaunting outta town.'

Monkey felt his stomach knot up. They'd been sussed. His face flushed as he struggled to keep his eyes fixed on Kraze. Slowly, he tried to move his head backwards, in an attempt to relieve the pressure of the knife against his cheek. His mind was in turmoil. His chest barely moved as his breathing became more and more shallow. He knew he had to stay calm; not give anything away. How was he going to get out of this one? And, more importantly, how was he going to get Angel out of it? A warm trickle ran from his cheekbone, where the blade rested, to his jaw.

Still holding the knife in place, Kraze moved forwards until Monkey could feel his breath against his upper lip.

'So where've you been jauntin', Monk?' Suddenly, he lowered his knife. As he stepped away, his tone became taunting, 'All dolled up in a nurturer's dress with a little bow in your hair, eh, cuz?'

Monkey fixed Alex with a look of betrayal. How much more did he know, he wondered, and why had he left it until now to say anything?

Feigning nonchalance, he grinned at his tormentor. 'You know what it's like.' He raised his eyebrows and gave a suggestive smirk. 'Waiting 'till we're in the zone's a mug's game. Me and Angel's got a thing going on – it's no big deal.'

He held his breath, hoping that Alex hadn't actually followed them to the village and that his own quick thinking had got him out of a potentially lethal situation. He would deal with the consequences of his explanation later but, right now, he needed to come out of this alive.

No one spoke. The rest of the hood waited; a pack poised to pounce. Monkey scoured his leader's face for some sign that his story had been believed. Eventually, Kraze tucked his shank back into his waistband and Monkey let out a barely perceptible sigh of relief.

Still holding his stare, Kraze issued a warning, 'Don't scant me, Monk. 'Cos if I 'scover you bin snaking' on us…'

Before he could voice the threat, a second shot split the air. A loud whoop reverberated across The Plaza. Monkey looked to the direction of the shot and saw a group of pre-breeders, at least 50 strong, cycling in random formation at the southerly side of the square.

'Broadwalk!' he yelled at Kraze. 'Get 'em outta here!'

A third shot rang out, then a fourth. Instinctively, Monkey ducked. The younger members ran for cover. Some stumbled, some fell; others crashed into the mountain of bikes in their panic.

Fuse raised his own gun to retaliate.

'Get down!' Monkey yelled.

Another crack echoed round the town centre. Fuse lurched. He staggered a couple of steps, then crumpled onto Monkey.

'Quick!' Monkey hissed at the others, trying to drag Fuse out of the firing line. 'Help me!' he shouted to Danger. Fuse was cradled in his arms, a look of abject terror in his eyes. Monkey tried to reassure him. ''S OK, cuz. You gonna be OK.'

Fuse opened his mouth. No sound came, so he shut it again. His eyelids flickered and closed. A brief tremor ran the length of his body, then he slumped, limp and heavy, against Monkey's chest.

'Fuse!' Monkey shook him. 'Fuse! Stay with us!'

Another shot ricocheted across the now deserted square. Monkey beckoned to Danger for assistance.

'Get outta there!' Danger shouted. 'Leave him!'

A victorious taunt echoed round the empty square, interspersed with gunfire. This time, into the air.

Monkey tried, in vain, to pull the lifeless form of Fuse to one side, but he had been big for his age and his dead weight was too much for Monkey. As an intermittent red light flashed a warning of an approaching stealth, Monkey reluctantly left the body of his friend on the steps of the clock tower and headed for safety.

Most of the other Mooners, including Kraze, had scattered to regroup on their own turf, but Monkey was too agitated to leave the scene. He paced up and down a delivery duct, trying to get his head together; trying to make sense of what had happened. Fuse was one of the good guys: Mark Watts

– gentle giant; always eager to please. Not the sharpest tool in the box, but not malicious. He'd been due to graduate shortly after Monkey. The youngest of three brothers, all with different providers, his nurturer had worked her way up from the Artisans' Zone to become a manager with a house in Moonstone Park. But Fuse had not inherited her ambition. He would have been content to spend his life doing what The Assembly said providers did best: working, drinking and watching sport.

Monkey unwrapped the scarf from his neck and held it up to stem the flow of blood from the gash on his cheek, aware that his injury was negligible compared to what had just happened to his mate. He kicked the side of an industrial bin in rage and let out a roar of grief and fury.

Tom was right; this had to stop! And he was going to do everything in his power to make that happen. He flicked on his ring-cam.

'What's this about?' Angel asked, aware of the anxiety in his tone.

'Can't say.' There was silence. 'Where are you, anyway?'

'Moni's,' she replied.

'Get outta there.'

'Mick…'

'Now! Just get away.' Monkey could see from her expression that Angel was not happy at being ordered out of her friend's house. 'I mean it – you have to get out of there!'

'I don't *have* to do any…' Angel broke off and gasped as Monkey turned the side of his face to the ring-cam so that she could see the gash on his cheek. 'How…' She bit her bottom lip as Monkey ran his cam the length of his body allowing her to see his bloodstained clothing too.

Monkey raised the ring-cam to his face again. 'Meet me at the usual place in ten. I'll explain everything. But be careful – we've been sussed.' Then he added, urgently, 'And don't say jack to Moni.'

* * *

Monkey paced the disused track above the bridge as he related the events of the evening. Angel sat on a pile of rotting sleepers, listening in silence.

'So, I have to get outta here – now!' He stared at her, willing her to agree to go with him.

As though by telepathy, Angel understood. She lowered her head into her hands. 'It's not that simple.'

'OK – I'll make it simple: my prints are on that gun and Fuse's blood is on my clothes. As soon as Security realise it, I'm on The Farm – for life! I have to get away – tonight.'

'But you didn't shoot him.'

'I know that and everyone there knows it, but do you think Security are interested? They've got a body and a gun – you think they want to know the whys and wherefores?' Monkey countered. 'The Prof already thinks I'm mixed up in Tragic's disappearance. What happens if they dust down Jane's house and match the prints there with the ones on the gun? I'm gonna be interrogated about all that crap, too. And believe me…' He gave an anxious laugh. 'I am no superhero: I'm the sort who'll crack under pressure.'

Angel did not return his laughter. 'My prints are in Tragic's cellar, too.'

Monkey nodded. 'I know.' Serious again, he dropped onto his haunches in front of her and took her hands in his. 'I am so sorry I got you involved with all this.' Angel, Monkey noticed, did not remove her hands from his. They were cold and delicate and he wanted to kiss them. 'Come with me,' he pleaded. 'We can go to the village. We can live there together and have bubs and we'll be happy like Tom and Jane and…'

'It won't work.' Angel pulled her hands free and stood up. 'Running away never works.' It was her turn to pace; mulling over the situation, trying to formulate a plan. 'We can go to Sal!' she said, as though the most obvious solution had been staring them in the face all along.

'No way!'

Ignoring Monkey, her enthusiasm increased. 'Of course! She's a solicitor; she'll understand. She'll get you off. I should've talked to her earlier…'

'Ssssh!' Monkey took Angel's hand and pulled her into the undergrowth behind the pile of timbers.

From the road below, they heard footsteps, followed by voices.

'You say you saw them together?' It was an adult male; weary but abrupt. Monkey put his finger to his lip, indicating for Angel to remain silent.

A younger female voice said something inaudible in reply. 'Well, they're not here now, are they?' said the male.

Monkey strained to hear the response but it was too quiet.

The adult spoke again. 'Consorting with a pre-breeder's a pretty strong accusation, you know. You sure you got your facts straight?' Angel looked at Monkey anxiously. They heard the male's voice soften to an almost teasing tone. 'You wouldn't be the first pre-nurturer to get a touch of the green-eye coming up to graduation and make up a story to get a rival out of the picture.'

'I'm telling you, he called her at my house. She looked upset, so I followed her here. I saw them meet up right there.' Angel started: there was no mistaking Moni's voice as it rose in frustration. She made to rise but Monkey restrained her as they heard Moni continue. 'Check the cameras if you don't believe me!'

A radio crackled and the male voice spoke authoritatively. 'Negative, Ma'am. No sign of them… Affirmative.' Monkey's heart was pounding so hard, he was frightened it might give away their presence. He glanced at Angel; her eyes were wide as they darted wildly in the direction of the disembodied voices, trying to comprehend what had happened and what to do. The adult addressed Moni again, telling her that he would log her complaint and ordering her to go home before curfew.

Neither Monkey nor Angel moved for several minutes. They listened, waiting until they were certain that it was safe. It was Monkey who spoke first.

Gently turning Angel's head to face him, he looked into her eyes. 'I'm going to the village. OK?'

Angel nodded slowly.

'You coming?' he asked.

She bit her bottom lip and shook her head.

Monkey set his jaw, trying to conceal his disappointment. 'Fine!' he said, more harshly than he'd intended.

'I'll miss you,' she whispered.

As they stood up, there was the faintest click on the slope down to the road. They spun round. Something moved in the shadows.

'Who is it?' Monkey challenged.

Moni stepped forwards, lowering her ring-cam and grinning with contempt.

'Shame!' she said with mock sympathy. 'I'd always wondered what our bubs would be like, Mickey. Now I guess I'll never know. You do know you're not eligible for breeding after you've been on The Farm?' She cocked her head on one side and grinned. 'Well, it's not so much a case of not being *eligible* – more like not being *able*!' A shudder ran down Monkey's spine. His mind was on turbo. How the hell were they going to get out of this one? Moni turned her attention to Angel and shook her head. 'Such a bright future. I really thought we could be friends you know, Ange – long term. I saw you and me working together in The Assembly; nurturing the cause as well as our bubs. But now, you're going to be cleaning up orphans' poo for the foreseeable future. And for what?' She nodded at Monkey. 'A breeder? Seriously? You're telling me you're willing to jeopardise your future, your freedom, your family – for a *male*?' She tutted. 'I'm disappointed, Angel.'

Monkey watched in astonishment as Angel sprang from the far side of the track where they'd been hiding and, using all her gymnast's agility, executed a near perfect round-off back-flip in Moni's direction. The heel of her shoe caught Moni on the chin and the assistant T.R.E.A.C.L.E. trainer toppled down the embankment knocking her head on a stone.

Monkey scrabbled down the slope to where she lay. Even in the shadows of the embankment, he could see a dark stain spreading down the side of her head.

'Shiltz!' He looked up to where Angel was standing on the disused track, paralysed in horror at the result of her action. 'Don't worry. I'll say I did it,' he called up to her, then let out a low moan of exasperation. Two murders in one night! If Security got him, he was never going to see the light of day again.

Chapter 13

On the Run

IT WAS with a mixture of relief and frustration that Monkey heard Moni groan and saw her eyes flicker open. Relief that she was alive, which meant that there was one less death to worry about, but frustration because the fact that she was alive created another, more pressing, problem: what to do with her?

Moni raised her hand to the cut on her temple and winced. 'You two are so going down for…'

Almost as a reflex action, Monkey pulled off his neckerchief and stuffed it into her mouth. 'I think you've done enough talking for one night.' He looked up the embankment to where Angel remained staring in horror at what was unfolding below. 'Quick!' he said. 'Give me a hand.'

Angel slithered down the bank to Monkey's side and spoke to Moni. 'I'm so sorry – I didn't mean to hurt…'

'Don't worry about that; it was her or us,' Monkey interjected, matter of factly. 'Now, we've got to get her away from here. Gimme your hose.'

Angel started.

'To tie her up,' Monkey explained.

She dodged behind a bush and took off her tights. She shivered as she handed them to Monkey and watched him use them to tie Moni's hands behind her back. Taking Moni's own scarf, he wrapped it round her head to cover her eyes, then hauled her to her feet.

'Jane and Tom'll know what to do,' he said to Angel.

Angel, still shaken from the incident, nodded.

'You'll have to come with me: I can't get her there on my own,' he went on. Noting the look of apprehension in her eyes, he added, 'But you don't have to stay if you don't want.'

The three of them set off along the disused track. Monkey and Angel walked either side of Moni, almost dragging her along the uneven surface. Moni stumbled and struggled, gagging on the scarf that was stuffed into her mouth as they guided her through the night. Monkey and Angel barely spoke; partly to avoid giving away anything that might reveal their destination and also because the events of the evening had shocked them both. Monkey's head felt as though it was oozing with thick mud – there was no clarity about anything; all his thoughts were shrouded in a dark depression. None of this had been in his plan. Sure, when he'd left home that evening, it had been with the intention of going back to the village, but only to learn more about the movement – maybe even to find out how he could help. Now though, everything had changed. Their secret expeditions had been exposed by Alex, and he didn't know who else Angel's brother had seen fit to inform; Fuse was dead and Monkey's prints were on a gun that was by his side. And, to make his situation even worse, now he'd taken hostage a T.R.E.A.C.L.E. assistant trainer.

All he'd wanted was to make it to graduation with a clean record but now he was a wanted criminal. He looked across at Angel and felt sick: her face was pale and pinched in the moonlight and he knew it was his fault. Any hopes he might have harboured about a future with her were gone. She'd be lucky to come out of this and have any sort of life outside The Sanctuary – and it was all down to him! He just hoped Tom and Jane and the rest of the resistance group could come up with some sort of plan.

With Moni in tow, reluctant and resisting, the journey took them far longer than usual. It was the middle of the night when they arrived, but Monkey had no compunction about waking Tragic's family. He gave the coded knock that he'd heard Karl give the previous week and was relieved when Jane opened the door of the cottage. Tom and Tragic were at work, out in the fields, so it was Jane who took control of the situation, and it was clear to Monkey that she was less than pleased to see her night visitors.

She untied the blindfold and used Moni's scarf to bind her feet. Then she carefully removed the ring-cam from Moni's finger, threw it on the flagstone floor and stamped on it.

'You should've done that before you brought her here,' she chastised. 'You have no idea who could be tracking her. You could have jeopardised our whole community.'

Monkey quickly turned off his own ring-cam and indicated for Angel to do the same. 'I didn't know what to do.'

'This isn't a game, you know, Mickey,' Jane said agitated.

Moni writhed and thrashed as she lay on the floor of the cottage. Jane untied the gag and, immediately, Moni screamed, 'I'll get you for this!' She lashed out with her tied feet, aiming at Monkey. 'You are so busted when I get out of here.'

'Be quiet!' Jane spoke sharply. 'You will not be getting out of here, so you can stop threatening – and, if you continue to shout, I will have to gag you again.' Moni glowered at her but remained silent. Jane turned to Monkey and, taking in his slashed cheek and blood-stained appearance, shook her head. 'Oh, Mickey, what on Earth have you done?'

Monkey filled her in on the events of the evening as she bathed his cheek and glued the wound shut. Angel sat, pale and silent throughout, trying to avoid eye contact with Moni. She was shivering with cold and shock.

'We want to stay here… at least, *I* want to stay here,' Monkey corrected. 'Is that OK?'

'I don't know.' Jane ran her hand across her forehead. 'For a while, maybe, then we'll try to find another community away from here that you can go to.' Monkey shot a look at Angel and felt sick. How far away? he wondered. And would he ever see her again? Jane turned to Angel. 'But you must go back tonight.' Angel nodded. 'Pre-breeders disappear all the time, especially ones who're wanted, but a missing pre-nurturer, especially one with such a bright future as you, will cause major repercussions.'

'I know.' Angel, still subdued, stood up to go.

'It's OK, I didn't mean straight away,' Jane said, indicating for her to sit down again. She put some wood on the dying embers of the fire and handed Angel a pair of Tragic's trousers that were hanging from the clothes line that hung across the hearth. 'Put these on; you must be frozen.' She turned to Moni. 'Come on. I'm going to take you to The Volte Face. The landlady there is a friend of mine and I'm sure she'll make you very comfortable in her wine cellars until we can decide what to do with you.'

'You are so going to regr…' Moni began to protest.

But Jane was too quick for her. She wrapped the scarf around Moni's face, once again gagging her.

'We've got quite a few sympathisers in the town,' she said to Angel, taking a scrap of paper and writing something down before pushing it into Angel's hand. 'This is the address of a safe house.' She looked at her earnestly. 'You must not go there except in extreme circumstances. Do you understand? You'll be endangering the lives…' She shot a guilty look at Moni and her voice trailed off, afraid that she might already have said too much. 'I'm sure I don't have to explain.'

Angel nodded and pushed the paper into her pocket.

'Now,' Jane said. 'Mickey, you can sleep in Trevor's room tonight. Angelina, I'll give you a couple of minutes to say your goodbyes but you need to be gone by the time I get back.'

With that, she untied Moni's feet, took her by the upper arm and led her, struggling, out of the door.

Monkey swallowed hard. He didn't know what to say. This would probably be the last time he saw Angel and his chest felt as though it had been filled with lead.

'I'm sorry…' he began, but Angel put her finger across his lips.

'Nothing to be sorry about,' she said. 'I really admire what you're doing.' She lowered her voice and spoke softly. 'It was a privilege to be involved.'

Monkey stared at his feet to avoid meeting her eyes. Tears were welling and the last thing he wanted was for her to see him being weak. 'You know, I really…' The words choked him. 'If things…' he began again, but petered into silence.

Angel took his hand and laced her fingers through his. 'If things had been different,' she continued, as though reading his thoughts, 'we'd have made a great couple.'

Monkey nodded. 'I'll never forget you,' he whispered. He took her other hand and pulled her gently round to face him. Raising his head, he looked down into her eyes, then lowered his lips on to hers. They were so soft, softer than he'd imagined and he felt that familiar tingle of excitement run through his body. To his relief, Angel didn't pull away. She responded, gently at first, then building in passion beyond Monkey's wildest imagination. He moved his hands up her back, until he could feel the contours of her shoulder blades and he drew her closer, clasping her against his body, never wanting to let her go. Their lips moved against each other's, hungrily. Their situation, the surroundings, the danger they were in, all melted away. His lips opened instinctively and he felt an involuntary stirring in his crotch. At T.R.E.A.C.L.E., they'd been given the basics of the breeding process; told how to copulate as though they were factory animals reproducing for the State. No one had explained the overwhelming desire that would course through his entire being. He moved his mouth across hers, pressing harder and harder until his teeth caught her lip and she flinched.

He broke away, blushing awkwardly. 'Sorry. I didn't mean…' he mumbled. Then an uncontrollable grin spread across his face. 'Wow!'

Angel managed a smile. 'It's OK. I enjoyed it.' She looked down again, embarrassed. 'Thank you.'

Despite their circumstances, Monkey couldn't help beaming. He wanted the moment to last forever. More than anything in the world, he wanted her to stay. 'I don't suppose there's any chance…'

She shook her head. 'I have to go,' she said.

His grin faded and Monkey once more felt as though his body was filled with concrete.

Angel opened the latch on the internal door and stood in the small hallway. 'I'll try and get word to you through Tragic.'

Monkey looked away and gave a melancholy nod. 'Yeah. I'll keep in touch. Look after yourself – OK?'

She had just raised her hand to open the front door of the cottage, when they both heard it: a female voice, harsh and clipped as though issuing orders. Monkey put out a hand and pulled Angel back into the hall. The cottage opened onto a side lane, and had no windows with a view of the village main street, so he opened the door slowly and peered out into the darkness.

It was a clear night and, through the gap between the cottages at the end of the lane, he could just make out shadowy figures in military uniform running in the direction of the village green. He went cold. It was a raid.

He dodged back into the cottage and grabbed Angel's hand. 'Come on,' he whispered urgently. 'We've gotta get outta here – fast!'

Together, they crept out into the lane, pulling the door to behind them. A large armoured stealth rumbled past. Monkey led Angel in the opposite direction, away from the main street. Having never seen the village in daylight, he had no idea where he was leading her, or how they were going to get out. They ran past half a dozen cottages until, after about 100 metres, the lane trailed away and became a muddy track.

'If we go across the fields we should be able to make it back to the loco line before dawn,' Monkey assured Angel.

'Monkey,' Angel said, tugging on his hand to make him slow down. 'If we don't make it, I want you to know that everything I've done has been *my* choice. If I'm arrested, it's not your fault. OK?'

'Don't even go there. Neither of us is going to get arrested. Trust me.'

But, before the words had left his lips, they stopped dead. A voice they both recognised drifted down the lane from the main road. 'That's the cottage. They're in there!'

It was Moni. And she was obviously free, ungagged, and directing Security straight to them.

'How the hell did they find her?' Angel whispered.

'Dunno. Probably tracked her ring-cam.' Monkey shook his head. 'How stupid! Why didn't I think to throw it away?'

'No time for that – let's get out of here,' Angel said, climbing a five-barred gate into a field that she hoped would lead them out of the village.

They could hear a commotion from the lane. There were orders and shouts of protest. It sounded like quite a crowd had gathered. Then a younger-sounding voice squealed above the others.

'Moni! You're safe! I rang Security like you told me.'

'You did good, Pen. Real good,' Moni replied.

'Shiltz!' Monkey swore. 'It's Penny – the snake!'

Chapter 14

Danger Aloft!

'THAT must've been who Moni was contacting by the bridge,' Angel said.

'The little traitor!' Monkey banged his hand against the gate in anger. 'How could she?'

'Keep your voice down,' Angel warned, tugging his sleeve. 'Come on.'

They set off across the recently furrowed field, keeping close to the hedge and crouching low so that their heads wouldn't be seen. Clods of earth clung to their feet making it heavy going. Then they heard the sound that they'd both been dreading: dogs!

'Oh for...!' Monkey kicked aimlessly at the earth, exasperated. 'This is pointless! We might as well give ourselves up – we'll never outrun dogs.'

'Listen,' Angel dropped her voice she tried to control her breathing after the exertion of walking through the muddy, rutted soil.

Monkey held his breath and listened. He could hear yelping and, above that, the cries of the dog handlers but farther away, almost at the very edge of his hearing range was something else; faint but clear – running water.

'They can't track us through water,' Angel said. 'When we get to the river, they'll assume we're heading upstream back to town, so if we go the other way, it might throw them.'

Monkey looked at her: the moonlight reflected across her cheeks and the tip of her nose. He thought she was the most beautiful creature he'd ever seen. 'You're...' he started to voice his thoughts, but embarrassment overcame him. '... very clever, aren't you?' he finished, lamely.

'Yes,' she replied, with no hint of conceit. 'Now, come on!'

They made it to the stream and, just as Angel had predicted, the dogs lost the scent and their handlers made the erroneous assumption that they would make their way back to town. They waded through the freezing water, sometimes thigh deep, until dawn broke, grey and hazy. Only then, when they could see their surroundings, did they leave the stream and seek refuge in a disused watermill.

Cold, tired and wet, they collapsed onto a pile of old paper sacks on the floor of the mill. It was too dangerous even to attempt to light a fire and their clothes clung to them, chilling them to the core.

'We should take it in turns to sleep while the other keeps guard,' Monkey said. He put his arm round Angel's shoulder and pulled some of the sacks over her knees. 'You go first.' He put his other arm across her, pulling her to him, protectively and she fell into a deep, immediate sleep with her head on his chest. Try as he might to stop his eyelids from closing, within minutes, Monkey had joined her.

It was dusk again when they woke and their clothes, although still damp, had almost dried from their body heat. Monkey stood up and stretched. His stomach rumbled.

'I'm starving.'

'Me too, but we need to get back.' Angel took the paper Jane had given her from her pocket. It was damp and crumpled but the address of the safe house was still visible – just. 'I know Jane said only to use this in an emergency, but I think this qualifies.'

Monkey agreed and they headed back to town and the safe house Jane had suggested. Under cover of night, they followed the river upstream as it meandered back towards town. A field of late Brussels sprouts and a store of turnips provided them with the worst meal Monkey had ever tasted – or ever hoped to taste again. He consoled himself with the thought that, even if he got caught, the food on The Farm couldn't be any worse than that.

It was still Energy Conservation Shut Down when they entered the town from the west, along the north bank of the river, by the Uplands Lunar Park.

'Where is this safe house, anyway?' Monkey asked.

Angel retrieved the paper and handed it to him. He stopped. 'No way!'

'What's the problem?' There was irritation in her voice. She was tired and anxious, and just wanted to reach safety.

'This is Danger's address.'

'Jordan Grainger?' Angel queried. 'You sure?'

'I should know – I've been there enough times.' He paused, thinking aloud. 'I'm just hoping this isn't some sort of stitch-up. I mean, Danger's hardcore hood. And his nurturer's a teacher – pro-Assembly through and through.'

Angel gnawed at her bottom lip. 'What should we do?'

Monkey sighed. 'What choice do we have? They'll be looking for us at our own homes and there's no way we can go back to the village. Short of living off raw sprouts for the rest of our lives, this is all we've got.'

Angel nodded wearily and, once again, they set off through the suburbs.

The fact that Monkey knew the house made it easier for them to make their way through the rear sustenance patches to the back door, thus avoiding any cameras that might have been trained on Danger's street.

Monkey buzzed the voice-com several times before a sleepy female voice responded.

'I've been given this address by some people in Combe Magna.' Monkey said simply, without identifying himself.

There was silence before the voice replied, 'There are several ways to care for offspring.'

Monkey narrowed his eyes and looked to Angel for some sort of guidance. She moved closer to the grille on the voice-com and spoke quietly. 'Mov Grainger, if that's part of some sort of password, we don't know the rest of it, but we've been given this address by Jane Patterson.'

The voice-com clicked silent, leaving them standing at the back door for several minutes before Danger's nurturer opened the door a fraction and, with the security bar in place, spoke to them through a narrow crack.

'Security has your picture plastered all over town, Mickey.' She looked at Angel. 'And yours too, if you're Angelina.' She was still in her nightclothes and Monkey noticed her pull her dressing gown closer.

'Can we come in – please?' Monkey asked.

Mov Grainger hesitated. 'Why have you come here?'

'We were told this was a safe house,' Angel explained.

The nurturer seemed reluctant. 'I'm not expecting any visitors.'

Monkey was feeling desperate. He could sense Angel's exhaustion and despair. He put his arm round her for comfort and explained to Danger's nurturer about the raid on the village. The shock on her face was evident, even through the narrow gap between the door and the jamb.

'Go on,' she said.

'We've no idea how many were arrested,' he continued. 'They might have got away. We did. We went along the river and then doubled back on ourselves. Moni Morrison was involved and…' he faltered, '…my sister.'

Mov Grainger opened the door and ushered them inside. 'Did anyone follow you?' she asked, urgently peering round the door into the sustenance patch.

'Don't think so,' Monkey said. 'But then, we didn't think anyone had followed us to the village.'

'What's done is done,' the nurturer said, pragmatically. 'Hopefully, you'll have learnt from it. Now, you look as though you need a hot shower and a decent meal. Keep the noise down, my son and daughter are asleep.'

After they had bathed and eaten breakfast, Monkey and Angel were shown upstairs into a spare room where Mov Grainger pulled an old-fashioned wardrobe away from the wall to reveal a staircase that went into the attic.

'You'll stay up here for the time being.' Danger's nurturer showed them a row of mattresses along the eaves and a bucket behind a screen to be used as a toilet. She lit an oil lamp on a small table which also had a variety of playing cards, books and pre-revolution board games on it. There was also a one-way intercom where the occupants of the loft could hear what was going on downstairs so that they would know when to be quiet and when they were safe. And there was a cupboard with bottles of water and packets of biscuits. 'I think you've got everything you'll need.' She held out her hand. 'And I'll take your ring-cams if I may.'

Monkey pulled his hand to his chest, defensively. 'It's turned off – has been since we arrived at the village, the night Fuse…'

'You'll be issued with new ones in good time,' she went on brusquely. 'Ones that have a different encryption. But these must be destroyed.'

Angel handed hers over and nudged Monkey to do the same. 'You know we'd be tempted to use them if we keep them.'

Reluctantly, Monkey pulled his off his finger and placed it in her palm. 'Mov Grainger…'

The woman smiled for the first time since they'd arrived on her doorstep. 'You can call me Pat.'

'Pat,' Monkey went on, 'does Danger know about all this?' He made a sweeping movement, indicating the secret loft room.

'Jordan is like the rest of us – he knows what I, as his next in line, think it advisable for him to know, on a strictly need-to-know basis.'

Monkey looked puzzled. 'But does that mean…'

'What it means is, *you* don't need to know anything more! Now, I'll be going to work at O-7:30 and home again about 18 hundred this evening. You do not come down from here – under any circumstances. Do I make myself clear?'

'Absolutely,' Angel said, flopping down on one of the mattresses.

'Fine,' agreed Monkey, somewhat less wholeheartedly.

He stood at the top of the stairs as Pat left, watching her step back into the spare room and push the wardrobe back into place. As he watched the crack of artificial light slowly disappear, he stared down into the darkness, feeling claustrophobic and frustrated. He had too much to do to be locked in here until Pat got home that evening. He needed to be out there finding out what had happened to Tragic and his family; he wanted to find Penny and give her a piece of his mind and he needed to make sure that Angel's name was cleared of any involvement.

Although he was physically tired, his mind was in overdrive. He picked up the playing cards and tossed them down again in disdain. Then opened the cupboard and shut it again feeling disgruntled and helpless.

'What time is it?' he asked Angel.

'Don't know,' she yawned. 'It was about four when we got here, so probably about five o'clock by now.'

'I'm gonna need more than a few biscuits to keep me going for the next 13 hours,' he said, grumpily. 'I'll see if she can get us any more food – and maybe a games console or something. Do you want anything?'

But Angel didn't answer – she was already asleep.

Stealthily, he took the oil lamp from the table and crept down the stairs. Placing the lamp on the bottom step he pushed the back of the wardrobe that faced him. It didn't move. He pressed his shoulder against it but still nothing. Finally, he turned so that his back was against the wooden panel and, with his feet on the second step, he straightened his legs. Slowly, he felt the wardrobe inch forwards. He moved down slightly and repeated the procedure, edging it out millimetre by millimetre. He turned the other way and sat on the step, putting his feet against the wood and pushing with all his strength. To his horror, he felt it tip forwards beyond its centre of gravity. He tried to grab it and steady it, but it was too heavy for him and it teetered then tumbled forwards, crashing to the floor in the spare room and splintering into pieces.

Lights went on and doors opened. Pat appeared in her nightgown from one room, Danger from another and his older sister, Beth from another. A light flickered on from the ground floor and Monkey heard footsteps running up the stairs.

'It's OK!' Pat called out, through clenched teeth.

A provider appeared from downstairs. He was fully clothed in the uniform of a Security officer. Monkey gasped. It was his head teacher, Professor Reed.

Chapter 15

Best Laid Schemes

DANGER wiped sleep from his eyes and stared at his friend. 'Monk? What're you doing here?'

'Beth, Jordan – go back to bed,' Professor Reed said calmly. 'Pat and I will handle this.'

Beth sighed and kissed Professor Reed on the forehead with a perfunctory, 'Bye, Dad,' before retreating to her room and shutting the door. But Danger hovered on the landing, eager to speak to his former hood member. Monkey looked from his mate to his head teacher and back to Danger again. 'What's happening here? Am I missing something?'

Pat stepped in. 'I told you, Mickey, from now on, everything you are told will be on a need-to-know basis.'

'And you think I don't need to know why someone who pretends to be a straight-down-the-line Party man is in the place I've been told is a safe house – dressed in a Security uniform?'

Pat and Professor Reed looked at each other. Professor Reed spoke.

'You're right. Go back upstairs and Pat will explain everything. Right now, I need to get back to the Providers' Zone before the lights go on.' He tapped his chest. 'This is a disguise that gets me across town without looking suspicious – it's nothing to worry about. I can assure you, this *is* a safe house.' He turned to Pat. 'Don't worry about this mess: I'll sort something out tonight.' He addressed Monkey once again, 'It's even more imperative that you lie low until we get something to conceal the loft access.' He fixed him with a look that told Monkey he would brook no argument. 'I mean it, Mickey. You could endanger the entire movement if you're discovered.'

Professor Reed left and Monkey followed the nurturer back up the loft. She spoke in whispers to avoid waking Angel, who had managed to sleep through the commotion in the bedroom below. She explained that she and Jack, as she referred to Professor Reed, were the parents of Jordan and his older sister, Beth. They were not a couple in the sense that Jane and Tom were a couple but they were friends and had worked in partnership to raise their offspring since Jordan had been born 15 years previously. In fact, they had been part of the counter-revolutionary movement since its inception and had worked undercover, assisting others to parent together. They had helped to sneak out thousands of nurturers and providers and set up dozens of communities in the rurals. All their energies at the moment, Pat told him, were going into canvassing nurturers and spins to vote for The Unity Party, so that they could subvert the election and ensure the downfall of Distaff.

Monkey thought about everything he'd just learnt. 'So, when Tragic first disappeared and the Prof was interrogating me about where he'd gone, he knew all the time?'

Pat nodded. 'He'd arranged their safe passage. He just needed to find out how much you knew.' She looked at him sternly. 'And you almost blew everything with your little escapade that night.'

Monkey shrugged. 'How was I to know?'

Pat smiled, almost affectionately. 'You weren't – and thank goodness for that or you might *really* have let the cat out of the bag.' Monkey's eyes were heavy and he struggled to keep them open. 'You need to get some sleep,' she continued. 'You're going to have to keep your wits about you from now on.'

She left him, and Monkey crawled across to the mattresses beneath the eaves where Angel was curled up under the blankets. He held up the lamp and took a moment to look at her – hair fanned out across the cushion that acted as a pillow, her chest rising and falling gently with each breath. He blew out the flame and lay down next to her, moulding himself into the contours of her body. Angel was warm and clean – and smelt of heaven. He pulled the edge of the blanket across himself and draped his arm over her, drawing her to him until he felt both protective and protected. Within seconds, he was sound asleep.

When he woke, it was to find a cold, empty space next to him. He sat up, disorientated. He felt anxious, but couldn't work out why. The soft glow of the oil lamp illuminated an area ahead of him allowing him to make out the rafters of the roof and the cupboard with the biscuits. He stretched. It was all coming back to him: the escape from the village; the arrival at the safe house; Angel. Angel! Where was she? He looked round for her; patted the blankets to make sure she hadn't snuggled down out of sight, then felt a flood of relief as muted voices filtered through his consciousness and he recognised one of them as hers.

She was sitting at the top of the stairs talking to Danger. They were whispering and, instantly, Monkey felt a knot of jealousy just beneath his sternum.

'Wazzappenin'?' he asked, stumbling over the mattresses to join them.

'Jordan's just been filling me in on the destruction of the wardrobe incident.' Angel smiled, leant forwards and kissed Monkey on the lips. 'I can't believe I slept through it.'

Monkey felt his anxiety ease but he put his arm round her shoulder anyway – just to let Danger know the full nature of their relationship. 'So, when will we get new ring-cams?' he asked, changing the subject.

'Won't be for a while,' Danger answered. 'Dad has to sort it out with the tech guys. They do the encryption.'

There was that word again – *dad*. Monkey felt another pang of jealousy. First Tragic; now Danger. How many more of his friends had secret fathers?

'So, how's this dad thing work, anyway?' he asked. 'How come you never said anything?'

Danger shrugged. 'Dad told me not to.'

Monkey was sceptical. 'And so – what? You just decided that, because he's said not to, you wouldn't?'

Danger thought for a moment, then nodded. 'Yeah, something like that. It was harder when he got appointed to Moonstone Academy. Do you remember that time we nearly moved away?' Monkey nodded. 'That was in case I let slip.'

'I think it's amazing the way you can keep a secret like that,' Angel remarked.

'So, how come you went out storming with the rest of us?' Monkey challenged. 'How come your *dad* didn't step in and stop you?'

'Think about it, Monk. What's the fastest way to raise suspicion?'

'Of course,' Angel said. 'You have to blend in to keep everyone off your case.'

Danger gave an ironic smile. 'And I'll graduate too – go off to the Zone like a good little breeder – do my duty.'

'But why?' Monkey queried, aware that, less than a month ago, he couldn't wait to graduate. 'How can you? I mean, when you know there's an alternative.' He shook his head. It was different when he'd believed all the T.R.E.A.C.L.E. hype but, now that he knew the reality, there was no way he could graduate!

'We need insiders.' Danger said, philosophically. 'Anyway, it might all change after the election.'

'But what if it doesn't? You'll have graduated and you might end up getting chosen by someone you don't…' He looked at Angel and blushed. '…you know …don't *like*.'

Danger grinned sheepishly and slipped into the street talk he and Monkey had used as Mooners. 'Ways and means, cuz, ways and means.' He tapped the side of his nose, knowingly. 'There's ways round everything. Trust me – I ain't doing nothing with no one if the vibe ain't right.'

'How…?'

'If nothing happens, it don't count. So, you just make sure it ain't happening – you get me?'

Angel looked perplexed. 'But doesn't that mess with the nurturer's chance to have offs?'

Danger shook his head. 'Two people book into the Centre; they come out next day, give their report to the clerk on the desk. If everything's fridge it goes on file, if not, the clerk conveniently drops it in the incinerator. Happens all the time. I should know – my sister works at the Breeding Centre.'

Monkey's ears pricked up. 'Your sister?'

'Yeah!'

'Beth?'

'Durr – yeah!'

'The one who lives here?'

'What of it?'

A plan was formulating in Monkey's mind. 'What's her job?'

'She's in the Citizen Resources Department. Why?'

Monkey thought for a moment. 'Does she have access to the records?'

'Is this some quirky quiz or you gonna tell me what's happenin', Monk?'

Monkey ignored Danger and turned to Angel. 'I'm thinking, Beth could go through the records and find out who my breeder was.'

'Whoa, whoa, whoa!' Danger interjected. 'No way!'

Monkey turned on his friend. 'It's OK for you and Tradge – you've got your *fathers*. I haven't got a clue who bred me. I don't even know if he's still alive.' He held his friend with a glare that bordered on hostility. 'I don't think anyone has the right to deny me that information – let alone someone who's supposed to be supporting *the cause!*'

Danger thought for a moment then nodded. 'Let me speak to her – OK?' There was a click on the intercom suggesting that someone had entered the house and closed the door. Quickly, Danger scrambled down the stairs into the spare room. He looked up at Monkey and put his finger to his lips. 'But not a word to Mum or Dad,' he mouthed, before disappearing into his bedroom.

Later that evening, when a new cupboard had been found to block the entrance to the loft, Beth took them some supper. 'Jordan tells me that you want me to get some information for you.'

Monkey fell on the tray of food as though he hadn't eaten in weeks, picking up a leg of chicken and ripping at it with his teeth. 'S'right. Can you do it?' he asked between mouthfuls.

'I can't do it myself. I'm still in training and fully supervised but I know someone who might be able to get you into the Centre out of hours so you can look it up yourself.'

Monkey looked up, astounded. 'Seriously? Break in?'

Beth smiled, 'No so much breaking in as *getting* in.'

Monkey looked at Angel and she shrugged as if to say *it's your call.* He thought for a moment. 'Look at it this way: I'm already in it up to my neck. What's to lose?'

'OK then,' Beth went on. 'If it goes ahead, you'll have to go on the iris scanner and you can get in disguised as cleaners. It'll probably take a day or two to put everything in place.'

'Fridge!' Monkey smiled. A couple of days holed up in the loft with Angel, resting and with all his food provided wasn't so bad. He could live with that.

The following night, Beth came to them with a portable iris and thumb-print scanner and, the next evening, she provided them with false identity papers. Angel was to be an 18-year-old pre-nurturer called Roxanne Spall who lived in de Beauvoir Tower on the Broadwalk Estate: Monkey, a 17-year-old breeder called Aston Holmes. Their uniforms and trolleys would be waiting for them in the janitor's cupboard in the lobby of de Beauvoir Tower the following morning at six and they would have exactly three hours to collect their equipment, walk to the Breeding Centre, find the information they needed and be out of the building before the day staff came on duty at nine.

'How is all this happening if you're so well-supervised?' Angel queried, eyeing the false documents.

'I'm not the one sourcing this. I'm one link in a very large network. I just put it in motion.'

Angel looked sceptical. 'But why would people who don't know us go to all this effort?'

Beth smiled. 'It's what the movement is all about – rebuilding families. The more fathers we can link with their offspring, the more power our organisation has. But secrecy is crucial – that's why I mustn't be directly involved and you mustn't know where this is coming from.'

Angel nodded, seemingly satisfied.

Beth handed them a blueprint. 'This is a plan of the building – the Records Office is in the basement. You'll need both iris and thumb scans to enter the building, after that, it's just iris scans internally.' She handed Monkey a piece of paper. 'This is the password to the info-processors. They're voice-activated but clerks use whichever machine's available, so they're not selective – you can use any one of them. If you need to use the keyboard, make sure you use gloves.' Monkey and Angel both nodded solemnly. 'Keep your heads down when you're moving around – especially in the lifts. Don't let any of the cameras get a full facial shot.' Monkey looked at Angel and offered a reassuring smile. 'If anything goes wrong, you don't know me,' Beth said, looking from one to the other. 'Is that understood?'

They nodded again.

'If Dad's here, he leaves the house at five, so, just to be on the safe side, I'll open up for you at four tomorrow morning.' Beth stood to leave. 'Do not come back here with anything traceable – destroy it as soon as you're out. OK? Oh, and there'll be a tin of spray paint on the trolley, use it to take out the cameras – before you change into the cleaners' outfits.' Then she disappeared down the stairs into the main house and pushed the cupboard against the opening.

'Broadwalk?' Monkey looked at Angel and grimaced. 'Couldn't she have chosen somewhere else? Anywhere else?' Memories of Fuse's death at the hands of the Broadwalk hood came back to him.

'I suppose it's wherever they've got contacts,' Angel reasoned.

Monkey was agitated. 'Yes, but it'll be bad enough going over there during Shut-Down, but it'll be daylight by the time we get out of there. Believe me, being in Broadwalk in the day is no joke.' He paced the floor of the loft. 'Shiltz!' he sighed, then sat down next to Angel. He took her hands in his. 'I'm going to go on my own. It's too dangerous for you…'

'No way!' she moved closer. 'I've been to the village with you; I've evaded Security with you; I've even been chased by dogs with you – twice!' She raised his hand and placed hers against it so that their palms were touching, then laced her fingers through his. 'We are in this together. No arguments!' She kissed him lightly on the lips. 'Anyway, I'd like to know who my father is, too, you know.'

Monkey moved away slightly and looked at her, surprised. 'You've never said you wanted to know who your provider was before.'

Angel shrugged. 'You've never asked. Anyway, all this has got me thinking – that's all.'

The idea that they now had to spend time looking up the details of *two* providers unsettled Monkey. And why had Angel never expressed any interest in finding her father before? He could feel suspicion beginning to grow in his mind again. No – he was being stupid. He'd had doubts about her before, with the code and the map, but she'd always proved herself safe. All this subterfuge was getting to him. He was being paranoid. He leant forward again and returned her kiss but it lacked passion and he broke off quickly when the Professor's voice sounded through the intercom.

'I'll let them know now.' From his tone, he was obviously talking to someone on his ring-cam.

A crack of light broke across the loft as the wardrobe was moved out and they heard footsteps on the stairs. When the Professor appeared, he was carrying a bundle of clothing. He dropped it on the mattresses, then sat down facing the two fugitives.

'We need to move you out of here,' he said, matter of factly. 'It's not safe to stay in one place for too long.'

Monkey felt a band of apprehension grip his chest. 'When? Where to?'

'Tonight,' said the Professor.

'Tonight!' They couldn't go tonight – not when he'd just been given the key to finding his own father.

Angel stroked his arm. 'It's OK,' she said, trying to soothe his sense of panic. Then said to the Professor, 'We just feel very safe here.' Any doubts he might have had about her dissipated and he squeezed her hand.

'I know, but that's why we need to move you on – so that you can stay safe. We have neighbours and not everyone is a sympathiser. It's suspicious enough that I've been here three nights this week. Sooner or later, I could be seen and someone could talk.'

Monkey nodded. His head was spinning, trying to think of a way round this unexpected turn of events. 'Where will we be moved to next?'

'I can't tell you that,' replied Professor Reed, handing them the bundle of clothes. 'These are Security suits and there's ID with each of them. Put them on and familiarise yourselves with your new identities.' Monkey's heart sank; he was only just coming to grips with being Aston Holmes; now he was going to have to be someone totally different. The Professor continued with their instructions, 'We'll need to look like a foot patrol, so we'll jog into town. You'll have to keep in step, so follow me.'

'What – now?' Monkey was shocked at the speed with which things were happening. 'We can't go now – we...' He searched his mind for an excuse to stay. '... haven't got our new ring-cams yet.'

'Your new contact has them.

The professor left them to get changed and Angel turned to Monkey. 'What are we going to do?'

Monkey's head was spinning. He wanted – no, *needed* – a new ring-cam. But he also wanted to find his father. There had to be a way to achieve both.

'I don't know,' he said pensively.

Slowly, he picked up the larger of the two Security uniforms and stepped into it. He pulled it up round his waist, then pushed his arms into the sleeves. Angel did likewise. Monkey zipped up the front of the dark grey, stab-proof garment, then slipped on the flak jacket and fastened it securely.

Once Angel was similarly attired, she spread her arms and gave a twirl. 'What d'you think?'

Monkey caught his breath. He thought she'd look good in anything, but he limited himself to a simple, 'Whaled!'

There was a small plasma-card in his top pocket. He pulled it out and read the ID on the card, then sighed. 'Royston Ashley James – aged 19. I'm getting older by the minute!'

Chapter 16

Identity Crisis

IT WAS almost three in the morning by the time they left the house and ran, military double-march style, along the disused loco track. There had been no goodbye to Danger; no opportunity to let Beth know that the arranged break-in to the Breeding Centre would not take place. Professor Reed had remained in the loft with them until the call came for them to leave.

They jogged towards the centre of town – the opposite direction from their jaunts out to the village. The loco depot was at the far side of Eastway and, as they approached the station, Professor Reed drew them to a halt. Monkey was out of breath. He doubled up with a stitch in his side from the exertion but Professor Reed barked at him to straighten up. Under his breath the provider added, 'We're supposed to be a crack security unit – you mustn't let the cameras pick up on anything suspicious in your behaviour.'

Monkey straightened up again and steadied his breathing. He shot Angel a sideways glance; she was standing to attention, head high, shoulders back like a real security officer. He followed suit to the best of his ability – there was something to be said for all that gymnastic training, he thought.

'Wait here!' the Professor ordered as he looked round the deserted station, then added *sotto voce*, 'Pretend you're searching for something or someone.'

There had been only one loco route into and out of town from the capital since the Oil Wars, so most of the old platforms had long since fallen into disrepair. Monkey and Angel began looking under seating and behind pillars

128

purposefully. It was eerily quiet. The wind whistled through the ornate Victorian brackets that were peeling reminders of the station in its heyday. Discarded paper tumbled along the concrete walkways and a large clock, dating from the last century, creaked precariously on one rusting hinge.

Monkey sidled up to Angel and, trying to be as inconspicuous as possible, whispered through the side of his mouth, 'I've been thinking – soon as we've got the ring-cams, we'll make a dash for it and we can still make it to Broadwalk by six. Once we've got the information from the Centre, we'll take it from there.'

Angel nodded anxiously. She reached down to lift a battered cardboard box as though searching under it, but it moved and she leapt back, startled. 'Aaaggh!' A pigeon fluttered its disapproval at being woken in the middle of the night and Angel jumped again.

Professor Reed appeared from anther part of the station. 'Keep the noise down!'

Angel looked subdued. The cardboard moved again and a filthy knitted hat emerged. Below it, a grimy face with stubble, followed by grubby fingers in worn, partially unravelled fingerless gloves clutching a large duffle bag. A wide grin spread across the vagrant's face as he pushed the box to one side.

'Orright, Monk? Jack?'

Monkey looked startled. He recognised the voice but he screwed up his eyes, trying to match the features to it.

'Daz?' It was the one-time leader of the Mooners, arrested a year previously. 'I thought you'd gone to The Farm.'

'Good – that's what you were supposed to think.' The young male struggled to stand up. 'Now, make like you're arresting me.'

'Are you our contact?' Angel asked.

But Professor Reed cut her off. 'No more questions. Let's get him out of here.'

The group made an elaborate show of arresting and frogmarching Daz from the station. Once outside, they found a disused shed that had previously been identified as being in a blind spot between two cameras.

Professor Reed proffered Monkey a hand. 'Good luck, Mickey. And you, Angelina.' He told them that Daz, or Darren as he was called these days, was to escort Monkey to another safe house before he would be transferred to a community in the north. There, he would be trained as an undercover operative, as Daz had been. 'Angelina, you will lie low for a couple of weeks and then you will return to your family. I'll inform your nurturer that you were coerced into going to the village with Mickey but a short spell in The Sanctuary has allowed you to see the error of your ways.'

Monkey looked at Angel in panic. 'No way!' he clutched her arm. 'We're in this together.'

'Not any more,' the Professor said, curtly. 'Now, Darren, I'll leave these two in your hands. I must get back to the zone before lights-on.' With that, he slipped out of the shed and disappeared into the shadows of a delivery duct, leaving Monkey, Angel and Daz alone.

Monkey turned to his one-time leader. 'Listen up, cuz. And listen up good, 'cos I ain't goin' nowhere without Angel. She's my goody! Sav?'

Angel turned on him, affronted. 'I'm not *your* anything! I am my own person – s*av?*' she added, ferociously.

'Shut it! The both of you,' Daz interrupted. 'You can sort out your little lovers' tiff later. Right now, I gotta get you outta here.' He pulled items of clothing from the duffel bag. 'Ditch the uniforms – we'll burn them later – but keep the IDs. The more identities you can gather, the better.' He produced a couple of ring-cams from his pocket. 'Here – use them sparingly. The Assembly's combing the airways for underground frequencies. They're more so that we can contact you rather than the other way round.'

In the distance, they could hear the clock in The Plaza chime five. Monkey glanced at Angel. They had an hour to make it to Broadwalk if they wanted to break into the Breeding Centre as planned.

'Look, Daz,' Monkey said, as casually as he could manage. 'There's something me and Angel have to do. It won't take long – a few hours max. How 'bout we meet you somewhere, say about ten-ish?'

'Nice try,' laughed the breeder. 'But, right now, I gotta get you to safety before lights-on. Here.' He handed them more identity cards; this time, Monkey was Ricky Kelly, aged 18, a breeder and student of education and Angel: Nigel Chellow, who was studying engineering.

'Jeez!' Monkey grumbled. 'I'm getting younger again, and now I'm a wannabe teacher? How come *she* gets a better job than me?'

Angel raised her eyes and smiled. 'It's not real.'

Monkey sighed, 'I know – but even so…'

'At least you're the right gender,' she pointed out.

'It's only till we get to the holding site,' Daz explained. 'A pre-nurturer on the streets at this time would arouse suspicion. As it is, we're just three of the hood roaming. Once we get to the plant, we'll sort everything out.'

As they adopted the swagger of hood members to walk through the dark streets, Daz continued to fill them in on their futures. 'Like the Prof said, Angel, you'll be staying with us. Monkey, we've got an active cell in Burlington. They're really keen to have you, so we'll make all the arrangements. It might take a couple of days to get you outta town.'

Burlington? Monkey's heart plummeted. That was right up in The Ridings. There was no way he was going that far from Angel. And what was this *plant* Daz was talking about? Was the holding site in some factory somewhere or were they hiding out in the undergrowth of a giant shrubbery? He longed to hold Angel's hand but any indication that she was other than an ordinary pre-breeder looking for trouble would be too dangerous, so he loped alongside her, trying to contain the ache inside.

He'd always liked Angel – everyone knew that – but the feelings he'd had for her since they'd absconded to the village a few days ago, seemed to have exploded. There were times when his feelings were so powerful, they terrified him. He didn't understand. Was this what breeding was all about? Having feelings you could barely control? And, if so, did the females feel the same way? He longed to talk to Tradge about it, find out if he'd experienced the same with that Zoë he'd introduced as his girlfriend, but he couldn't – he didn't even know where he was. He assumed he'd been arrested in the village that night, but he didn't know for sure. There were so many unanswered questions. Angel was his only stability and he would not relinquish her – not under any circumstances.

The threesome strutted along the southerly route of the disused loco track that ran above the deserted streets of Gardener's Grove – the one-time scene of Monkey and Tragic's illicit football escapades that now seemed so insanely innocent – and out towards Broadwalk. Eventually, the track would go across the river in the direction of Wessex and out into the south-westerly rurals. Was that where they were going, Monkey wondered? To another village? He checked his new ring-cam; it was O-5:45. Still time.

Below the track, the low-rise housing of Gardener's Grove, a zone for working pre-movs and spins, became the high-rise towers of Broadwalk, a manual zone and heartland of the hood. Suddenly, Daz veered off the track, slid down the embankment to street level and led them towards the walkways and alleys of the Broadwalk Estate. Monkey tensed. There was no one around that he could see, but that meant nothing. There were footpaths, delivery ducts, maintenance yards and other concealed spaces that, at one time, would have been car parks, where any number of hoods could be lying in wait for such a small, unsuspecting and unprotected group as they were. He looked round, constantly on edge. Visions of Fuse lying dead in his arms flashed into his mind, and he struggled to bite back the bitter taste of bile in his mouth.

It was as he was scouring the desolate urban landscape for any sign of ambush, when he saw it: a sign above the open-plan lobby of one of the blocks: de B a vo r Tow r. This was de Beauvoir Tower; the place where their trolley of cleaning materials and disguises would be left. And there it was – unless Monkey was very much mistaken – standing in the doorway of a maintenance cupboard. It was too good an opportunity to miss.

'I need a pee,' he said to Daz.

'We're nearly there – can't you wait?'

'No.' And he walked purposefully into the entrance lobby.

'Hey, wait!' Daz called in a half-whisper.

But, as he followed Monkey into the building, Monkey turned, pulled Daz's hood down over his eyes and stuffed his neckerchief into his mouth as a gag. Angel quickly unfurled her own scarf and helped Monkey to tie Daz's hands behind his back, whilst using Monkey's scarf to tie his feet.

'We're getting quite good at this,' Monkey said, trying to muster a smile and lighten the enormity of their actions.

'We haven't sprayed the cameras – won't they have seen us?' Angel asked anxiously.

'Just another hood brawl to them,' Monkey reassured her.

When Daz was fully restrained, they pushed him into the cupboard, then, making sure their faces were concealed, sprayed the lenses of the cameras in the lobby. When they were sure they were safe, they quickly changed into the cleaners' uniforms, put the clothes Daz had provided in the duffle bag next to him and pushed the trolley of materials away from the metal door, allowing it to grind shut.

'Sorry, cuz! We'll be back at about nine,' Monkey said through the closing door. 'Nothing personal – this is something we have to do.'

And, with that, Roxanne Spall and Aston Holmes headed towards the Breeding Centre to begin their morning shift as cleaners.

Chapter 17

Clean Sweep

EVEN pushing the trolley, it only took them five minutes to walk from de Beauvoir Tower to the Breeding Centre and, as they approached the service entrance of the enormous building that had once been a hotel, the street lights flickered on, signalling the end of Energy Conservation Shut Down.

Monkey pulled the peak of his cap down over his face and watched as Angel raised herself onto her toes so that her eye was in line with the iris scanner. The small red LCD changed to green and an automated voice instructed her to place her thumb against a panel on the door. As she did so, the back doors of the once opulent building slid open. She hesitated, anxious for Monkey to accompany her.

'Go in,' Monkey encouraged her under his breath. 'You gotta look like you do this every day.'

He stepped forward and went through the identification routine himself, breathing a sigh of relief when he, too, received the green light and could join Angel inside. They made their way to the foyer where the elevators were. Two security guards, one a nurturer in her 40s, the other a much younger male – probably a breeder – were sitting behind the reception desk, chatting idly. An enormous plasma-screen on the wall behind them showed corridor after corridor of the Centre, but not, as far as Monkey could make out, any of the rooms or offices. The guards looked up briefly, but returned to their conversation without a second glance at the two cleaners.

Following Beth's instructions, they made their way to the Records Office in the basement. Their entrance to the room was simple but, once inside, Monkey noticed a camera mounted on the wall above the door. He flicked his eyes in its direction, indicating to Angel the need for caution.

'Pretend to be cleaning,' he muttered, 'until we know if it's operational.'

Angel switched on the floor polisher to drown out any noise they might make and Monkey went through the motions of wiping the flat surfaces while he started up the nearest processor. He kept one eye on the camera as he progressed through the search stages, waiting for the tell-tale whirring of the camera motor that would alert them to the fact that their movements were being monitored. Eventually, the screen in front of him proclaimed the word *WELCOME* and a voice asked whether he was tracing a breeder or a nurturer.

'Nurturer, ' Monkey whispered, but nothing happened. 'Nurturer,' he repeated – again, nothing.' He felt his shoulders slump in disappointment – he hadn't been through all he'd been through in the last couple for weeks, to come away not knowing. He turned to Angel, anxiously. 'It's not working!'

Without stopping cleaning she said, 'Maybe you're speaking too quietly.'

Monkey tried again at normal volume. 'Nurturer.'

'I'm sorry,' the lilting female voice of the computer said, 'I didn't quite catch that.' 'NURTURER!' he almost shouted.

'Ssssh!' Angel warned, turning off the polisher and going over to him. 'Nurturer,' she said.

'Thank you,' the machine responded. 'Now may I have the last name of the nurturer you wish to trace?'

Monkey raised his eyebrow, a nagging feeling of suspicion gnawing away at him again. 'How come it worked for you and it wouldn't for me?'

Angel shrugged. 'It could be the tone of my voice, or maybe it's just that it couldn't make out what was being said over the noise of the polisher. Does it matter?'

'S'pose not,' Monkey conceded, grudgingly, before taking over again.

'Gibbon,' he said and, this time, the machine responded. He went through Vivian's details until, at last, on the screen in front of him he saw a list of dates. They covered a period of six years clearly defined into three batches. It didn't need a genius to work out what some of them meant: there was a cluster of dates in June, the year before his birthday and another cluster in the July: there were five groups – again at monthly intervals – the year before Penny was born. But there were several bunches of dates two years before he'd been born.

Next to the entries before his birth it read:

Pre-mov – Vivian Gibbon.
Occupation: medical student.
Rank: professional.

*   *   *

Breeder – Eric Randall.
Occupation: law student.
Rank: professional.

In a column on the right-hand side of the screen, next to the last date of that batch, it said: *Conception successful – male offspring: Michael Eric Gibbon.*

It was the earlier dates that perplexed him. Again, there were several clusters of dates a month apart but they were two years before he'd been born. Monkey screwed up his eyes trying to make sense of them. Next to the last one, it simply stated: *Sp. Ab.*

'Spontaneous abortion,' Angel helped him out. 'It means that your mother had a miscarriage before you were born.'

Monkey nodded slowly. 'So, my sister was Eric's "three strikes and you're out"?'

'Looks like it.'

Monkey shook his head in disbelief. 'So, my father only got to do it…' he counted up the entries, '…27 times?' He looked at Angel, then lowered his eyes and blushed, embarrassed that he'd spoken to her about this. This sort of stuff was pre-breeder talk. 'Sorry,' he mumbled and looked at the screen again to cover his discomfort. 'Let's see what we can find out about Eric Randall.'

The processor responded to his instructions and there, in front of him, appeared the details of his father:

> *Eric Randall: D.O.B. 23.11.2015.*
> *Breeder status commenced: N/A.*
> *Breeding commenced: 2035.*
> *Results: 27 breedings; 2 live off; 1 sp. ab.*
> *Breeding discontinued: 03.12.2041.*
> *Current address: Penthouse Suite; Riverside Apartments, S/E1*
> *   Providers' Zone.*
> *Current position: Barrister-at-Law; Leadlow Chambers, The Plaza.*

Monkey stared at the processor. Suddenly, in those few words on the screen, his father had gone from being an abstract figure, to a real person – with an address and a job.

'Why isn't it applicable when his breeder status started?' Monkey queried.

Angel looked at the screen. 'Think about it – he'd have been 16 in 2031. The Oil Wars didn't finish until 2032 and the revolution didn't happen until the following year.'

Monkey shot her a glance. 'Is there anything you *don't* know?'

Angel shrugged, modestly. 'Lots of things, I expect.'

'But even so,' Monkey went on. 'He didn't commence breeding until 2035. He'd have been 20.' Monkey shook his head in disbelief. 'Twenty years old before he…' He stopped, embarrassed. 'I don't understand. What was he doing?'

'Education?' Angel suggested. 'Or maybe, like Jordan said, he'd been with other pre-nurturers but it wasn't recorded?'

'I have to meet him,' Monkey muttered.

There was a whirring sound as the camera slowly turned in their direction.

'Quick!' Monkey said, grabbing an anti-static cloth and pretending to clean the screen. 'Look busy!'

Angel followed suit. The camera seemed to focus on them for several seconds before scanning the rest of the office and coming to a halt facing the far end.

'My turn, 'Angel said slipping in front of Monkey and addressing the processor.

But the results of her search were less successful. Her father, one Paul McFadden, was an accountant who had produced two live offspring: herself and Alex, but there was no record of his current address or position. Angel stared at the screen, disappointed. 'That's so unfair!'

Monkey checked the time on his new ring-cam. It was O-7:30. They'd got plenty of time, but the faster they got out of there, the better. 'Come on,' he said. 'We've got what we wanted.'

Angel shot him a look that said, *You might have got what you wanted, but I haven't.* Monkey shut down the machine and Angel sighed, puzzled. 'Why aren't his details up to date?'

'Dunno, but we need to split.'

Quickly, they gathered together the cleaning materials and left the Records Office, sealing the door behind them. Keeping their heads down in the lift, they exited on the ground floor and began wheeling the trolley towards the rear door. As Monkey raised his hand to press the release button, the younger of the guards looked up from the reception desk. 'Hey! I've been trying to call you two.'

Monkey went cold. He stopped and pretended to be looking for something on the trolley, allowing himself time to surreptitiously slip his new ring-cam from his finger and hide it beneath some wipes. 'Us?' he muttered, almost incoherently.

'Course you! Who d'ya think I'm talking to? Why aren't you answering your ring-cams?'

Angel shot Monkey a look of terror.

Monkey made a great show of holding out his naked hand, devoid of the new ring-cam, which was registered to *Ricky Kelly: student of education*, and not *Aston Holmes: cleaner*. 'Sorry,' he mumbled. 'We're new with the agency and they're not fully encrypted yet.'

'Useless!' The security guard tutted loudly. 'Well, anyway, some little pre-nurturer's been sick on the third floor. You'll need to go and clear it up. Must be her first time, eh?' he laughed, crudely.

'Er…' Monkey's mind was racing.

He glanced at Angel who was shaking her head, almost imperceptibly.

'We're just gonna take our break,' she said in the most artisan voice she could manage.

The guard began to walk round from the back of the reception desk. 'Break? I'll give you a break! What do you think this is – Vacation Village?' He approached the trolley and Monkey's mind was on overdrive: should he push the trolley at the guard and make a run for it? If he did, how far would they get before a whole squadron of Security was combing the town for them? 'Show me your ID,' demanded the guard.

Monkey's heart was racing. He pulled the small plasma card from the pocket of his overalls and handed it over, making sure to keep his face as obscured as possible. Angel did likewise. The guard scanned them on his ring-cam and seemed disappointed that they checked out.

'Now, get yourselves up to room 316 – pronto – and clear up that mess. You do a three-hour shift and you expect a break? Ha!' As an afterthought, he added, 'And I'll be telling the agency that we don't want you back here. Break, indeed!'

Monkey turned the trolley round and they headed back into the lift.

'What're we going to do?' Angel asked as the doors slid shut. 'We're supposed to have this lot back by nine.'

'I'm working on it,' Monkey answered obliquely.

As the doors opened at the third floor, one or two couples were beginning to emerge from their rooms. They all seemed much older than Monkey had expected. Tragic had been right again. This was another T.R.E.A.CL.E. lie exposed: they'd told them that they'd graduate and be selected for breeding immediately. '*It's not like they've told us it will be,*' Tragic had said, but Monkey hadn't believed him. He sighed. Had Tragic managed to escape the raid, he wondered? Or was he rotting on some Farm complex, chopping up turnips in all weathers? His train of thought was interrupted by an urgent nudge from Angel.

'Quick,' she whispered. 'I know her.'

Angel buried her head in a cleaning manual as a pre-nurturer, slightly older than her, walked past, arm in arm with a tall breeder who was probably about 20. They were smiling at each other coyly.

'She lives round the corner from me – well, from Sal,' she corrected herself with a note of sadness in her voice. 'Shanelle Pierce. She's at uni, studying politics. Hopes to be elected to The Assembly one day. Don't you remember her from school?' Monkey shook his head. 'She's about four years older than us. I don't recognise him, though,' she commented, watching the couple walk along the corridor, away from them.

Monkey watched the pair stop by the lift. The breeder put his arms round the pre-nurturer, pulled her to him, then kissed her. The pre-nurturer broke off, giggling.

A stern female voice sounded from the speakers that were dotted along the corridor: 'Couple Pierce and Holland report to check-out immediately. I repeat: Pierce and Holland to check-out immediately.'

'They're in for it,' Angel remarked, as they continued towards room 316. She knocked on the door and, when there was no reply, she pressed her eye to the scanner on the door and they went into the bedroom. The bed was unmade and the sour smell of vomit hit them as soon as they entered.

Angel put her hand over her mouth and opened the window to allow fresh air into the room.

Monkey, unaffected by the odour, looked bewildered. 'What d'ya mean, "in for it"?'

Angel had to check that his question was serious. '"No fraternising with breeders after copulation",' she quoted, matter of factly. 'Remember? *"Procreation not pleasure!"'* She looked at him and smiled. 'Didn't you learn anything at T.R.E.A.C.L.E.?'

'Not enough, apparently,' Monkey replied. 'What's wrong with a bit of *"fraternisation"*, anyway?'

'It encourages emotional attachment,' Angel went on, leaning out of the window and breathing deeply. 'It's OK for us to fraternise while we're choosing who we want to breed with but, afterwards, all contact is suppose to end until the next breeding. Think about it – the last thing The Assembly wants is nurturers attached to their providers. Society, as they've created it, would break down. Males might try to take back some of their power and females would be subservient again.' Then she added, facetiously, 'Because females are such fickle, weak-minded individuals who give away their power so easily!'

Monkey went over to the window and scanned the outside for an escape route. 'And what about you?' he asked, distractedly. 'What do you think?'

'Well, I don't think females are weak-minded, for a start.'

'No?' Monkey said, with a hint of sarcasm in his tone. Then added, 'Although maybe weak-stomached?'

Angel acknowledged his joke with a smile and gulped down more fresh air. 'I agree with Jane and Pat. I think strong bonds between nurturers and providers are essential so that kids grow up balanced and respectful of the opposite gender.' Monkey nodded. 'I'm not saying that parents should live together necessarily,' she went on. 'I mean, it must have been hell for children before the wars, if their nurturer and provider didn't get on and they were stuck between two warring parents. But I do think that having children carries responsibility and requires parents to work together as joint partners in their upbringing.'

Monkey pointed out of the window. 'Look, there's a fire escape over there. I wonder how we get to it from here.'

'You haven't been listening to a thing I've said, have you?' Angel asked, nevertheless, following the direction he was indicating.

Monkey drew his head back into the room and looked affronted. 'Have too! It's just that, I know we've been doing all this stuff for Tragic but, if I'm being honest, I hadn't really thought about the bigger picture.' He looked at Angel and thought again about breeding with her and raising offs together. Then, he thought of the couple they'd just witnessed kissing by the lift and having to wait another four years to consummate his feelings for her was more than he could bear. 'But what I don't understand… I mean, has that Shanelle already got children?' he asked.

Angel shook her head. 'No! I already told you, she's still at uni.'

'But then, why…' Monkey faltered. 'I mean… how… ' He was embarrassed talking to her about such things. With Tradge, it would've been different. But Angel was a … a what? A weak-minded female? No way! He smiled at the irony of the thought. What the hell. He took a deep breath and blurted out, 'Why didn't she just choose someone to breed with as soon as she graduated at 16? Why did Vivian and Eric wait until they were 20? Don't females have needs and urges and stuff like us?'

Angel stifled a smile. 'I don't know what they taught you at the pre-breeder T.R.E.A.C.L.E. sessions but, if they were the same as our pre-nurturer ones, you really weren't paying attention! Of course we have *urges*,' she explained, 'although probably not as intense as pre-breeders, but that's why the "*vitamins*" are provided for all breeders and pre-breeders – until they're on the breeding programme, of course.'

Monkey screwed up his face, recalling the tablets Vivian used to try to make him eat every breakfast before school and every evening when he got home. 'What've vitamins got to do with it?'

Angel looked surprised. 'They're not really vitamins: they're anti-androgens.'

'Huh?'

'Tablets to suppress testosterone and curb your *urges*,' she said. 'Why d'ya think The Assembly made them compulsory?'

Pieces began to fall into place; he'd taken his tablets regularly at first but, the deeper involved in the hood he'd become, and the nearer to graduation he'd got, the more he had rebelled against everything to do with Vivian – including refusing to take his vitamins. When he thought back, it was around that time that he'd begun to experience more *urges* but he'd just put it down to the fact that he was maturing. Although he'd liked Angel for ages, he'd only begun to feel *that* way about her a few months ago and, since he'd stopped taking his vitamins, the more attracted to her he'd become.

'How do you know all this stuff?' he asked, irritated, not only at her superior knowledge but also because he felt used by both Vivian and The Assembly. How dare anyone administer drugs without his consent?

Angel shrugged. 'While pre-breeders are out running the streets, most pre-nurturers are studying – and not just school lessons, either – studying life.' She shook her head. 'Honestly, males need to sort themselves out. There's no wonder Distaff have been in power for so long. And I'll tell you something else, too…'

'I can't wait,' Monkey said.

'The Assembly might go on and on about getting rid of the hoods and restoring law and order to the streets, but it's in their interest not to.'

Monkey shook his head. 'What're you on about?'

'Think about it: as long as the majority of voters are female and towing the party line, Distaff are assured of keeping their hold on The Assembly. As soon as you lot stop killing each other and start taking an interest in politics, Unity will be a credible challenge. '

'My lot?' he began, then stopped. 'You're right!' he conceded. Of course she was right, he thought, ruefully. She was usually right! 'United we stand: divided we fall and all that.' It became clear to Monkey what he had to do. 'Come on!' his mind was racing. 'We need to find Daz.'

'Daz? But, I thought…'

'Believe me,' Monkey reassured her, 'there is no way he's packing me off to The Ridings or anywhere else.' Seeing her dubious expression he added, 'Trust me – I'm more use to him right here.'

Chapter 18

Going Underground

MONKEY climbed out of the window and began to edge his way along the sill towards the corner of the building and the fire escape. The Centre was about 100 years old and the sills ran round the building as decorative stripes, becoming deeper with each window recess but narrowing to a little over foot-width in between.

Angel stepped out after him, very gingerly. 'I'm not sure about this. I've never been good with heights.'

'I thought you did gymnastics?' Monkey pressed his back against the wall and looked back to where Angel was standing on the ledge clutching the window frame, her eyes, wide as footballs; the sinews on her hands, taut with fear. 'Can't you just imagine you're on a balance beam?'

Angel shot him an irritated look. 'Have you ever been on a balance beam?' she snapped. 'For one thing; it's only 1.25 metres off the ground, whereas this is…' She looked down, gasped, then looked up again quickly, '…a good 30 metres. And, secondly – have you seen how many times people fall off?'

Monkey began to edge his way back along the sill towards her. She was beautiful and clever and fiercely independent – and he loved her for all those qualities – but, right now, he wanted her to focus on the independent part. The last thing he needed was for her to turn all nurtchie on him.

'Take my hand,' he said, offering her his outstretched palm. 'You can do this. Look straight ahead and slide one foot after the other,' he encouraged. 'It's not far.'

'What if…?'

'Don't even go there,' he cut in. 'Just stick with me – I've got you and I won't let anything happen.'

Angel straightened up and, with her back hard against the brickwork, did as Monkey said. He kept up his commentary of encouragement as they proceeded past three windows until the fire escape was almost within arm's length.

'Just a couple more steps,' he said, reaching out and grasping the metal balustrade with his free hand. He stepped onto the iron rungs of the fire escape but, at that moment, the blinds on the window that opened onto the emergency exit, rolled upwards and the breeder occupying the room looked straight at them.

Angel started, but Monkey was quick to grab her. 'Jump!' Monkey muttered to Angel, through half-closed lips, and he pulled her across on to the rickety ladder. 'You go down,' he ordered. 'I'll deal with this.'

As Angel made her descent, the window opened and the breeder narrowed his eyes at Monkey. 'Wozzapp'nin', cuz?'

Monkey recognised the speech of a former hood member and immediately relaxed into the same mode. 'Me and her's breedin'.' He tossed his head casually in the direction of Angel as she ran down the metal staircase, then grinned at the stranger, conspiratorially. 'But y'know what it's like, cuz. Two, three times a month max, just ain't enough.'

'Tell me about it,' the breeder said.

'So this is off the record – ya get me?' He gave a knowing wink.

The breeder nodded. 'Fridge! Go for it,' he said, turning back into the room.

Monkey ran down the fire escape, grabbed Angel's hand as she was waiting at the bottom. Tempting as it was to run the short distance back to de Beauvoir Tower, they walked it, so as not to arouse suspicion on any camera that happened to pick them up. When they arrived in the foyer, they went straight to the cupboard but there was no sign of Daz.

'Shiltz!' Monkey slapped his hand against his forehead. 'He's got our clothes and IDs and everything.'

'What are we going to do?' Angel asked.

'Maybe you should've thought about that before you trussed me up and went jaunting!' Daz appeared from round a corner, his face cut and grazed, his eye bruised and swollen.

'Daz! What on Earth happened?' Angel was shocked.

Monkey lowered his eyes, guiltily: he knew only too well what must have happened. 'Look, cuz, I'm sorry. I never meant for this…'

'Shut it!' Daz snapped. He tossed the duffle bag, unnecessarily hard, at Monkey's abdomen. 'Get changed!'

Monkey and Angel changed into the casual clothes of the street without speaking, then left the cleaners' uniforms in a tidy pile on the floor of the cupboard. They were supposed to have left the trolley of cleaning materials there too and Monkey bit his lip anxiously. Daz's injuries, no doubt at the hands – or feet – of the Broadwalk hood, had made him acutely aware that they were not alone in this: their actions had consequences for other people. He hoped Beth, and the unknown people who had helped her to gain them entry to the Breeding Centre, would not suffer as a result of their hasty and unplanned exit.

'Follow me.' Daz's tone was abrupt. 'And no more funny stuff.'

Monkey noticed that Daz was limping as he led them through Broadwalk. They took care to check every corner and alley for hoods as they made their way down to the river. Monkey and Angel followed, subdued and silent, until they reached the Water Turbine Plant.

'Pretend to be going down the bank,' said Daz. 'There's a drain cover a few metres to your right. Follow me.'

'What about cameras?' Monkey asked.

Daz shot him a look of contempt. 'You think we haven't checked that out? There are blind spots all over this town and we use them to our advantage – not everyone's as dumb as you, Monk.'

Daz rolled the heavy metal cover to one side and squeezed through the opening into an enormous concrete pipe. Monkey and Angel went in after him and he pulled the cover back to conceal the entrance. It was pitch-dark and Monkey felt a hand grab his arm then work its way down until it found his hand and held it tight. Even above the dank stench of the stagnant water around his feet, he could smell Angel's fresh, clean smell and he squeezed her hand reassuringly.

''S OK,' he whispered.

A sharp beam of light arced across the top of the pipe revealing it to be about three metres in diameter. Daz shone the torch along the tube until it petered into darkness.

'Come on,' he said.

'What is this?' Monkey asked.

'A storm drain,' Daz said, as they trudged, ankle deep through ice cold water. 'And keep your voice down – it amplifies everything.'

They walked for several hundred metres until Monkey could see a warm glow at one side of the tunnel. As they approached, they could hear muffled voices. A short metal ladder led them to a cavern cut out of the side of the storm drain. The walls were lined with rough bricks, and wooden props supported the roof. Monkey looked round the underground room, getting his bearings. It was illuminated by oil lamps and candles and, around the outside, were a number of mattresses. The centre of the space was occupied by a small furnace, with some cooking pots on the top and an enormous metal container to one side where water was being distilled. There were about 20 people, mainly of his own age, sitting on boxes or lying on the mattresses, some alone, others in couples. One or two of them were recognisable to Monkey: past Mooners, who, like Daz, had been supposedly sent to The Farm for cultivation therapy.

A pre-nurturer ran up to Daz and hugged him. 'Darren! What happened?'

Daz winced as she put her arms round him. 'Easy!' He pushed her away slightly and scowled at Monkey. 'Got done over by a posse from Broadwalk, but I'll be fine.' He turned to Monkey and Angel. 'Come and get something to eat, then you can explain what the hell you thought you were doing.'

The food was basic: flatbread and stew, but Monkey and Angel were grateful for it. The female who had embraced Daz was introduced as Mel, originally from Eldridge Way, a professional nurturing zone for teachers and office workers. Monkey was again struck by the unabashed affection she and Daz showed each other. He reached out and took Angel's hand, as much to bolster his own confidence as to reassure her.

As they ate, Mel left them to go and get more supplies and, when they had finished, by way of explanation for leaving him to get beaten up, Monkey gave a brief summary of their morning and their reasons for breaking into the Breeding Centre. Daz seemed unimpressed.

'We are truly sorry,' Angel said, aware of Daz's smouldering resentment. 'This place is pretty impressive.' She tried to engage him in conversation to ease the tension. 'What do you all do down here? Do you work, or what?'

'We plan and execute demonstrations of civil unrest,' Daz explained, relaxing a little. 'There are cells all over the country – at least half a dozen in every town. We're building up towards the election.'

'Civil unrest?' Monkey queried. 'I haven't seen any civil unrest.'

'Course not!' Daz said, sharply. 'You think The Assembly's gonna publicise anything that might make them look bad?'

'So what do you do?' Angel asked, trying to lighten his mood.

Daz turned his attention away from Monkey and addressed Angel. 'You know when you go into town and The Plaza's sealed off *"as a result of hood warfare"*?' Angel nodded. 'Well, sometimes it might be because a few hoods have got above themselves,' he glanced at Monkey, 'but more than likely it's a demo. I mean, think about it – do you really think they'd send out all that Security for a few pres?'

'But, what's the point of demonstrating if no one knows?' Monkey asked.

Daz shot him another irritated look. 'We're working on it. There's a whole series of camcasts waiting to be streamed onto ring-cams and info-cams countrywide.'

'So, what's stopping you?' Monkey pressed him.

Daz was clearly struggling with his patience. 'Our hacktivist cells can't get into The Assembly system yet. But, when they do…'

'It'll be too late!' Monkey interrupted.

Daz rolled his eyes. 'Oh, I forgot – you're such a genius, aren't you, Monk? I can't wait until you get to Burlington and start your training. Then you'll see what we're really up against.'

'I'm not going,' Monkey said, flatly.

Daz spoke very slowly, all the time holding Monkey's gaze. 'Listen up, and listen up good. Your transfer is already in place. People have put their necks on the line for you and antics like you pulled this morning are jeopardising people's lives. This isn't some little street-hood game, you know. This is real life and people have died for this cause.'

Monkey nodded. 'Appreciated, cuz, but I ain't goin' nowhere. I'm gonna make contact with my father and we're gonna go out there fighting this election for The Unity Party. We gonna chat with the hoods and tell 'em what's going down with Distaff so they'll bridge the turfs and unite against separatism and bring down The Assembly.'

'Yeah, right!' Daz jeered. 'For starters, your dad don't even know you – and second, you think you can bridge the turfs on your own – in time for the election?' He slapped his thigh mockingly. 'You's something else, Monk!' He dropped the street talk and turned serious. 'You either go to Burlington, or you're on your own.'

Monkey shook his head and sighed. 'When my father sees how families work, he'll want that for himself – and for every other father, believe me.'

'And how're you gonna show him a working family?' Daz challenged.

'Well, if he saw how Tragic's family get on and the others in the village…'

'*Used to* get on,' Daz corrected. Monkey stared at him, suspecting that he knew what was coming next but, nevertheless, hoping he was wrong. 'They were arrested on the night of the raid – almost all of them. Trevor's on remand on a Farm complex in the West Country, Jane's in The Sanctuary up north and Tom's been sent to a penal ship in The Channel. They'll come to trial for treason next month.'

Monkey could feel his chest constrict as he struggled to deal with his worst fear. 'How d'ya know?'

'Why didn't Professor Reed tell us while we were at his house?' Angel queried.

Daz shrugged. 'Everything's on a…'

'Need to know basis – I know!' Monkey snapped. 'Shiltz!' He stood up and began pacing the underground chamber. Some of the others looked up briefly, then resumed whatever it was they'd been doing. Monkey turned on Daz again. 'So, what does that mean, exactly?'

Daz took a deep breath. 'Legally: *High treason is the crime of disloyalty to The Assembly, amounting to an attempt to undermine their authority or the intention to attempt to do so,*' he quoted.

'Meaning?'

'Meaning, it's subject to special rules and penalties and, if Tragic and the others are found guilty, they'll get life imprisonment.' He looked from Monkey to Angel, then added, in a serious tone, 'Which also means they'll be sterilised… or worse.'

'Worse!' Monkey exclaimed. 'What could be worse?'

Daz took a deep breath. 'There've been rumours that breeders sent to The Farm are, shall we say, rendered incapable of breeding – ever again!'

Angel gasped. Monkey lowered his eyes.

'And some have even disappeared off the cam-nav completely,' Daz went on, soberly. 'That's why we can't afford anyone messing things up. After all…' He reached across and tipped Monkey's chin so that he was looking him straight in the eye, '…the community in Combe Magna had been operational for years until you decided to poke your nose in.'

Monkey sat down again digesting the enormity of everything he'd been told and his part in the downfall of his friend.

'OK,' he said. 'I'll go up north in three days on one condition.' Daz said nothing. 'You let me contact my father. He's a barrister and he might be willing to take on their case at the trial.' He waited for a response, but Daz was giving nothing away. 'If he's not interested, I'll go to Burlington and get trained up like the Prof said but, if he'll agree to defend them against The Assembly, I can stay here, work with him – and you – and try to make amends. Deal?'

Daz contemplated Monkey's offer. 'This isn't my call. I'll have to speak to people.' He stood up and indicated a mattress by the wall. 'Get some sleep, both of you. I'll be back later.'

And, with that, Daz made his way back down the metal ladder into the storm drain, leaving Monkey and Angel in the underground cavern. Angel dropped her head into her hands and began to weep.

'It was all our fault,' she said.

Monkey wrapped his arms round her and pulled her to him. 'Ssshh! We're gonna sort this. Trust me.'

He lowered his lips and kissed her gently on the top of her head. He wished he was as confident as he sounded.

Chapter 19

Arresting Developments

IT WAS dusk when Daz led Monkey and Angel along the old drainage system that ran under the town. Monkey was once more dressed in nurturers' clothing and Angel and Mel had spent the afternoon waxing the fine growth of beard that had begun to sprout along his top lip and under his chin. The community had an array of wigs and clothing to suit every disguise and Monkey had been kitted out so that, in the half-light of evening, he made a passable female.

To his relief, the ancient tunnels were dry and only the scurrying of rats remained as a reminder that they had once carried human waste to the treatment works. Since the Oil Wars, a more modern system had been constructed, directing the sewage across town to the Methane Processing Plant in the west; part of The Assembly's sustainable electricity-generation policy. But the crumbling subterranean network still existed and every street had a number of drains leading down into it. Although most had been sealed off, a couple had been reopened by the underground community. Their position in the middle of town deemed them too dangerous to use during daylight but the rebels often used them at night rather than risk walking through hood territories.

Daz came to a halt. 'This one'll bring you up in the service duct behind the leisure centre. You're about two minutes from The Plaza,' he said. 'You've got one hour. Be careful.'

Monkey nodded. 'Cheers, Daz. Appreciate this.'

Daz's face showed no emotion. 'The only reason you've been greened is 'cause of Eric Randall's rep. If he'll come on our side, it'll be a real coup.' He straightened Monkey's wig. 'Don't blow it!'

Monkey changed out of his now filthy trainers and into the court shoes that completed his disguise. He kissed Angel before stealthily climbing the metal ladder that led from the sewer, up a brick shaft, to street level. Lifting the heavy metal disk slightly, he peered into the dimly lit service area, checking for cameras, hoods, Security – anything that might jeopardise his mission. When he was sure it was clear, he pushed the lid away and stepped out into the alley.

'Shiltz!' he muttered, as he caught his leg on the edge of the drain-hole.

'What is it?' Angel hissed.

'Snagged my hose,' Monkey said.

'For...!' Daz began. 'Just get outta here.'

Monkey immediately did as he'd been told. Once out in the open, he gulped down a deep breath, relieved to be out of the fetid air below ground. He'd only been down there a few hours. There was no way he could stay down there for weeks – or even months – like some of the community.

He headed straight for The Plaza and Leadlow Chambers. He was using Angel's cleaner's ID – Roxanne Spall, and an appointment had been made for him to see Eric Randall at 18:00. He was on his own for the first time since the night of Fuse's murder and he felt alone and nervous. Without Angel by his side, he found it hard to muster the courageous front he put on for her. He wished she could've come with him. Then, another thought crossed his mind – he wished he'd given her some memento – just in case.... No! He stopped himself before his mind could complete the sentence. It was going to be all right. Everything was going to go just as planned: he was going to arrive for his appointment, Eric would take him into his office, he would reveal himself as Eric's son, Eric would be delighted and then Monkey would tell him about the rebels, ask for his help and Eric would agree. Sorted!

He felt ridiculous walking around town dressed as a nurturer. It was one thing to cycle out into the rurals like it, where no one was likely to see him, but to brazen it out in the middle of town was ranged! He kept his head lowered, partly to avoid the cameras but also so that he wouldn't be recognised by any marauding Mooners or passing pre-nurturers from school. The last thing he wanted was Moni Morrison to see him in a skirt and get Security on to him – apart from anything else, there was no way he'd be able to leg it in court shoes!

A pile of wilting flowers round the base of the clock tower brought him to an abrupt stop. They were in memory of Fuse and he paused for a moment, paying his respects to his mate. As he stood by the flowers, the interminable advertising screens flashed their slogans across The Plaza. Slogans that, a few weeks ago, he would never have thought to question: *RESPECT BREEDS RESPECT*. Respect? he thought, bitterly. What does The Assembly know about respect? Where was their respect for breeders and providers? He was on the point of turning away when one of the plasma-screens flashed up the next advert and Monkey stood frozen to the spot.

WANTED
FOR CONSPIRACY TO COMMIT
ACTS OF TREASON

Below the headline were two photographs, one of himself, the other of Angel. He went cold. His eyes darted around the people making their way home – females to their families, males to their segregated zones – checking that he hadn't been recognised. Monkey pulled up the collar of his nurturer's coat and dropped his head again, walking as quickly as he could to Leadlow Chambers.

Eric's practice was on the ground floor of a large office block at the north side of The Plaza but, when Monkey arrived, the building was in darkness. He pressed the entry-phone and rattled the doors. He checked his ring-cam – 18:05. He'd wasted time. It had taken him 10 minutes to walk there. But, even though he was late, the building was in darkness and the last thing he wanted was to be hanging around dressed as he was. Nervously, he pressed the buzzer by the door again.

If he didn't get any response this time, he told himself, he was getting out of there – pronto. A light flickered on and Monkey could just make out an elderly post-nurturer as she shuffled through to the front of the office and buzzed him in. Eric, she said, was still in court. He'd been due back an hour ago but Roxanne was welcome to wait.

'Erm…' Monkey's mind went blank. He hadn't planned for this. 'Fine,' he muttered in as high-pitched tone as he could manage.

He took a seat in the corner of the waiting room, relieved to be able to take the weight off his feet. How nurturers walked all day in those shoes was beyond him! He looked at his ring-cam again – 18:10. Idly, he scrolled through the plasma-journals on a low table in front of him but most of the news was of the election. He pressed the Sports button and saw an account of a pro-football exhibition. Any other time, it would have been interesting but, today, he couldn't focus. Time was running on. The elderly secretary was hovering, obviously keen to leave. Monkey was sure she was eyeing him suspiciously. Perhaps she'd recognised him from the wanted posters in town? He kept his head low, checking the time every few minutes.

Monkey had just decided to leave it and make another appointment when a tall male figure came through the door and spoke distractedly to Monkey and the secretary at once.

'Good evening, I'm sorry I'm late. Thank you, Frances, you can go now. Roxanne, if you'd follow me, I'll see you now.'

Monkey stared at the back of his head as he led him through to an office at the back of the building. Was this really his father? This brusque individual who hadn't even given him a second glance? Since seeing Tragic with Tom, Monkey had played through this moment 100 times; sometimes, Eric had recognised his son instantly and had clutched him to his chest, others it had taken a few moments to register. In none of his imaginings had Eric walked past him without even a hint of recognition. Monkey swallowed to hide his disappointment and began to wonder if this had been such a good idea after all.

The office was large and disorganised. Books, files and plasma-papers littered the desk. Eric poured himself a cup of coffee from a machine on the side, flicked on a large screen and indicated for Monkey to sit down.

'I understand,' he said, rubbing his head and staring at the screen, 'that you've been referred to me by...' His voice trailed away as he scoured the screen for the information he required. 'I'm afraid I don't appear to...'

Monkey's heart was racing. He could feel his cheeks flushed and hot. He pulled the wig from his head and said falteringly, 'P.A.R.E.N.T. I've been referred by Jane Patterson and some other members of P.A.R.E.N.T. who've been arrested for...'

Eric looked at him coldly. 'I'm aware of the circumstances of Jane Patterson's arrest. Now perhaps you can explain who you are and why you are wasting my time by entering my premises under false pretences. You have two minutes before I summon Security.'

Monkey felt his throat constrict. It wasn't supposed to be like this. 'It's me,' he faltered. 'Mickey – Michael Gibbon.' Eric remained expressionless. 'Your son!'

Eric nodded slowly. 'Are you aware that you are wanted for treason?'

Anger rumbled up from Monkey's guts. 'Is that it? Is that all you can manage after 15 years?'

'What did you expect?' Eric poured another cup of coffee and sighed. 'A sentimental male bonding experience, perhaps?'

Monkey rose to his feet. 'Yes, actually, that's exactly what I was expecting. Stupidly, I thought you might be happy to see the son you gave your genes to.'

Eric eyed him over the rim of his coffee cup. 'It was a business transaction; nothing more. I gave Vivian my...'

'I know what you gave her!' Monkey held out his arms as if to say: *here I am – look at me.* 'I just thought you might be a little more interested in what you got in return.'

'A son who's a dissident and a traitor,' Eric mused. 'Not a good investment, I'd say.'

'Cheers! So that's all I am to you is it? A bad investment?' Monkey shook his head in despair. 'So why did you *invest* in the first place? Because The Assembly required you to?'

Eric raised an eyebrow. 'You'll understand when your time comes.'

'Nice of you to keep track – but guess what? My time *has* come – and I *don't* understand. Perhaps you could explain why you chose to breed – three times – with the same nurturer and then walk away. You're clearly a bloke with a brain,' Monkey's voice was rising, 'but you're telling me that you've never questioned the system? Never wondered what happened to your children?'

'Vivian let me know when you and Penny were born – and I put two and two together when I saw the posters.'

'And that's it? That's the extent of your input? To know that I'd been born?'

Eric shrugged. 'It's for the best.'

Monkey slapped his hand to his head. 'Jeez! You sound just like Vivian! What is it with you people? You know, a month ago, I was buying into the whole Assembly thing too – but my excuse is that I was young and didn't know any better. Now, I may be only a few weeks older, but I've seen better – with my own eyes. I know there's an alternative. What's your excuse?'

Eric sighed and looked at his ring-cam – gold, flashy and obviously expensive. 'It's better to maintain the status quo. If it's not broken, don't fix it and the system works very well.'

'How?' Monkey was exasperated. 'Have you walked round town at night recently? You might get to sit in your nice penthouse with your flashy furniture but the movs can't cope! There are hoods running riot out there. My friend was shot – practically on your doorstep – because the pres are out of control and you big fat providers are happy just to sit back and *maintain the status quo*.' He sucked in air through his teeth in disgust. 'I really thought more highly of you than that.'

Eric remained impassive. 'If you can't be honest with me, at least be honest with yourself, Michael. Admit it: if you weren't in trouble with The Assembly, you wouldn't be here now. Amazing how you've shown not one iota of interest in who bred you until you're on the run. Then, hey presto, you come knocking at my door – wanting free legal representation I've no doubt. Well, let me tell you – I've worked hard to build up this practice and I will not jeopardise it for the likes of you and your little band of revolutionaries.'

Monkey slumped down in the chair again. 'For your information – *Dad* – I didn't even know I'd been accused of treason until I was on the way here. I've wanted to trace you since a friend of mine showed me how fathers and sons could work together, supporting each other, caring about one another...' He swallowed, determined not to let his bitter disappointment affect him. '...even love each other!' He leant forward in the chair and held Eric's gaze. 'I risked my own life, and the lives of other people, to find out who you were and where I could find you. It's got nothing to do with wanting anything from you – except a relationship.' He leant back, emotionally drained. 'But it seems that I was expecting too much. I was thinking I'd find a man with balls. Instead, I find someone too old, or too tired, or too selfish to care about anyone except himself. And,' he said, standing and pulling on his wig, 'traitor or no traitor, I'm ashamed to say I'm your offspring. I won't trouble you again.'

Eric rose. 'I'll show you to the door.'

'Don't bother.'

Eric followed him out of the office. 'You should be grateful – I really ought to have held you here and informed Security.'

'So, why don't you?' Monkey challenged. 'I'm clearly nothing to you so go ahead – don't do me any favours.'

As they reached the door Eric turned to his son. 'For what it's worth, it's been good to see you. I'm sorry about the circumstances. I had every intention of looking you up when you graduated, but there isn't any room for sentimentality in the Providers' Zone – you would've understood if you hadn't...'

Monkey ground his teeth. 'Save it.'

He made to open the glass door but stopped and stared at the scene of chaos outside in The Plaza. A stealth beamed its intermittent light around the square like a crimson strobe. Security officers had surrounded two females. The mov was shouting and being restrained; the younger pre was being arrested. Monkey recognised the nurturer first: it was Sally Ellison, Angel's nurturer. A cold shaft of dread filled his being. He looked towards the pre who was being dragged into the stealth – and his worst fear was realised. They'd got Angel.

Chapter 20

Parental Responsibility

A SCREAM froze in his throat. All rational thought deserted him. He wanted to run out there and save her. He'd be arrested, too, he knew that but, without Angel, what did it matter? His own life, Tragic's – they all meant nothing if she wasn't there with him.

Monkey turned on Eric. 'You bastard! You did this – didn't you?'

Eric's eyes flashed from his son to the scene outside. 'Don't be absurd.'

Sally Ellison's cries were blocked by the triple-glazed door but the anguish on her face howled volumes. Monkey watched as the Security officers tossed her to one side and the stealth, with Angel inside, crept slowly from The Plaza. He lashed out, catching Eric with his fist but Eric caught his wrist and held his son at arm's length.

In rage, Monkey kicked out. 'Satisfied?' he railed. 'Are they coming for me next? You got what you wanted?' Eric watched his son's grief and anger without comment. 'Well, there's more of us you know! Hundreds – thousands! All over the country!' Monkey shouted. 'And you won't beat us. You can arrest as many radicals as you want but you won't win because in the end there are more people like us who *are* interested in their offspring than the likes of you and my sad excuse of a nurturer.' He shook his hands free and glared at Eric. Calmer after his outburst, he looked his father in the eye. 'I knew it was a long shot coming here but I never dreamt you'd betray your own flesh and blood.'

'I didn't,' Eric said.

'Yeah, right!' From the corner of his eye Monkey caught a flash of movement in the glow of the street lights. He looked again. It couldn't be. The interior light of the foyer was turned off, making the office darker than outside. A figure was standing in a doorway, not 20 metres from Leadlow Chambers. And there was no mistaking her features. Moni Morrison was standing against a wall, arms folded, a look of smug satisfaction on her face. Then she turned and a second pre-nurturer came out of the shadows. It was his sister, Penny, and she, too, was grinning.

'Shiltz!' Monkey swore under his breath.

'Now, who's betraying their own flesh and blood?' Eric asked.

Monkey spun round. 'You recognise her!' It was an accusation rather than a question. 'You've seen her before, haven't you? How?'

'Come through to the back office,' Eric's tone was gentler.

'Why, so that you can keep me here 'till I'm arrested too? Forget it.' Monkey made to open the door but Eric blocked his way. 'You must be very proud of how your daughter's turned out. Ironic though – don't you think – that *I'm* the one wanted for treason? Nice work, *Dad*! Now, if you'll excuse me, I need to get back.' Monkey's voice was laden with contempt.

'Where will you go?' Eric asked.

'Like I'm gonna tell you,' Monkey sneered.

'Look, I didn't have Sally's girl arrested and I'm not going to hand you over, either.'

'Sally's girl?' So, Eric not only recognised his own daughter, but he also knew Angel's nurturer. Monkey didn't trust him. 'When are you gonna come clean and tell me what's going on?'

'Sit down,' Eric told him, but Monkey remained standing. Eric raised an eyebrow. 'Explain to me how you think the re-introduction of fathers into families will help?'

'Adolescent males need role models. It's that simple.'

'Need them, why?'

'To model how we're supposed to be!' Monkey clenched and unclenched his fists with exasperation. 'It's not rocket science.'

'Go on,' Eric encouraged.

'We've got no one to aspire to – except females; no one to teach us how to act; what we're supposed to do, what we're supposed to enjoy. That sort of thing.' He was expecting a response from his father, but none came. 'When I was at alpha-school I tried to sit in the urinals because I didn't know what they were for. You know, there're even some pres who can't piss standing up – because no one's ever taught them! No one can show us how to be adult males except adult males – and we don't see any until we graduate.' He began pacing the floor. 'It's too late by then. The damage is done. Have you been out on the streets lately? We're killing each other because there's no one to keep us in line. If this carries on, there won't be any breeders or providers – they'll have killed each other because the only training we've had is *"love conquers everything"* and *"respect breeds respect"*. And it's all horseshit!' His eyes scanned the room. 'And, if you've got this place bugged, I don't care that I've used profane language. That should be the least of The Assembly's worries. Kids need dads. There has to be a balance.'

Eric nodded, and Monkey thought he looked as though he was addressing the Court. 'You're supposed to be advocating fathers being involved in their families and appear to cite your main reason as being one of discipline – and yet you won't even sit down when I – *your* father – ask you to.'

He'd walked right into that, Monkey grudgingly conceded. 'What do you want?' he asked, sitting down. After all, what had he got to lose? Angel had gone. He was wanted for treason. In two days, he'd be packed off to The Ridings. What's the worst that could happen?

Eric paced the floor of the office. 'In the past, I have worked with Sally Ellison,' he explained. 'That's how I recognised her. As for your sister – yes, you're right – I have made it my business to follow her progress – and yours. From afar, you understand. I have never breached Assembly laws.'

'Perish the thought!'

Eric shot Monkey a look. 'I was a little older than you when I went off to fight in the Oil Wars. Of course I was only involved for a year or so…'

Monkey made to rise. 'This is hardly the time for a potted family history. In case you didn't notice, my…' He hesitated, unsure how to describe Angel. Friend? She was more than that. Girlfriend – as Tragic had described Zoë in the village? It sounded old-fashioned. The girl I love, he wanted to say. But he couldn't. Love wasn't allowed between genders: *procreation, not pleasure. No emotional attachment.* That was The Assembly's rule. But the reality was, he did love her. He ached inside and wanted to get out of there, find her and rescue her. 'I need to go,' he said, simply.

'I was in love once,' Eric said.

Monkey stopped, shocked. This was treasonable talk. He looked round, anxiously, checking that they weren't being filmed: that he wasn't being led into a trap.

'Long before Vivian came on the scene. She was called Juliet and, when I went off to the war and left her, it felt as though a hole had been cut out of my chest.' Something had changed. Eric's previous harsh demeanour had softened and he spoke quietly. 'I saw terrible things in the war and lost many friends but none of it compared to leaving Juliet.' Monkey wasn't sure where this was going. He hadn't even known that his provider had been in the war, and all this personal stuff was too much information. 'Sally's girl – the one who was arrested…'

'What about her?' Monkey said defensively.

'You love her, don't you?'

'Look, cheers for the overdue interest, but I'm outta here.'

'You'll need a good lawyer for her defence.'

'You offering?' Monkey challenged.

'Come and see me again tomorrow at 19:00. By then, I'll know where she's been taken and with what she's been charged. Now, you'd better go out the back way so that your sister doesn't see you.'

* * *

Monkey made his way back through the drain to the underground chamber, only to find the others packing up.

'What's going on?' he asked Daz.

Without stopping what he was doing, Daz replied, 'She knows where we are. We gotta move out.'

'Angel won't snake!' Monkey was offended.

'Course she will.' Daz's voice was cold and matter of fact. 'They all do.'

'Where're we going?' Monkey's breath was so shallow as to be barely perceptible. He rubbed his hands together anxiously. They couldn't move on – not now. Not when he'd got Eric to agree to defend Angel. And it would only be a matter of time before he took on the others' cases as well.

Daz turned to look at Monkey; his features heavy with contempt. 'Dunno where *you're* going, Monk. But *we're* outta here.'

'You *can't* go without me.' His eyes darted round the cavernous space. Bedrolls were being tied up, boxes and bags stacked in the centre of the underground room. But in the place where he and Angel had slept, nothing had been moved. 'I got him to agree,' he blurted, desperately. 'Eric's gonna take on the case.'

Daz shrugged. 'So?'

'It's what you wanted.'

'What I wanted,' Daz said, 'was to be safe – for all of us to be safe. But you and your little mate have put paid to that.'

'Why is that my fault?' Monkey gasped. 'What the fegg were you doing letting her go into The Plaza in the first place?'

'She was looking for you, you brickbrain!' Monkey felt his stomach lurch. He felt sick. 'One hour I said! One fegging hour! But you couldn't even manage that simple instruction, could you?'

'Eric was late,' Monkey offered, lamely.

'So you get outta there and make another appointment. You don't endanger everyone else with your self-indulgent fantasies about playing happy families. We're working for a bigger cause here.' He shook his head. 'You are bad news, man. Bad fegging news.'

'Let me come with you,' Monkey pleaded.

Daz dropped his voice and adopted the speech of the hood. 'It ain't happenin', cuz! All right? An' I get so much as a whiff of you stalkin' and you gonna wish you ain't never set eyes on me. Ya get me?' He turned his back on Monkey, indicating that the conversation was closed and that there would be no further discussion on the matter.

Monkey went over to the bedroll where he and Angel had rested. Their bags had not been touched. He changed out of the female clothes he'd been wearing and slumped on the mattress, watching as the rest of them filed down the metal ladder into the storm drain. Daz was the last to leave.

He pointed a finger in Monkey's direction. 'You listen up good, Monk. You stay here until 20:30 before you so much as move a muscle. Or, so help me…'

'Fegg off, Daz!' Monkey spat contemptuously. He lay down with his hands behind his head then rolled with his face to the wall. 'I ain't goin' nowhere,' he muttered, picking up the ring-cams that he and Angel had been issued and gazing at them with an air of despondency.

He listened to the receding footsteps of the group as they headed out of the storm drain in the direction of the river. When he could hear no sound other than the intermittent dripping of water, he sat up. The fire was still burning under the furnace, giving a soft glow to the chamber. Monkey shuffled across to it, rubbing his hands and holding them out to keep warm. It felt as though his entire being was filled with lead. He stared into the fire, trying to think of a plan but his brain wouldn't function. It was as though all the energy had been sucked from his body. He had never felt so desolate. Tragic, Fuse, now Angel – all gone from his life. There was no one left.

No one except… Of course! Why hadn't he thought of it earlier? Monkey had a variety of IDs and disguises to get him across town, now all he had to do was find his way to the Riverside Apartments, in Socio-economic Group One Providers' Zone, and locate Eric. His father had said he'd defend Angel, now he wanted to see if the great barrister was as good as his word.

* * *

Monkey was almost disappointed. For years, he'd craned to see over the walls of the Providers' Zone and catch a glimpse of the hallowed interior, when all he'd needed was the ID of an engineering student and the excuse of a game of squash!

'How come security's so crap in this place?' he asked as he wandered around Eric's penthouse apartment.

'The Assembly's not interested in who comes in here,' his father replied. 'It's *keeping* them in that's the problem.'

Monkey was standing before a plate glass window with views across the river and the town. He'd seen the building many times in the distance from Moonstone Park, never guessing that his own breeder lived there.

'So, what happens next?'

Eric looked him up and down and raised an eyebrow. 'Clearly, you can't stay here.' A shadow of disappointment passed across Monkey's face. 'You are quite obviously neither a provider nor SE One.' It was Monkey's turn to raise his eyebrows. 'I'll have to find you accommodation in the Breeders' Zone for the time being. You'll be fairly inconspicuous over there.'

While his father made several calls on his ring-cam, Monkey showered and changed into some of Eric's sweats. When he emerged from the bathroom, Eric had sent out to a restaurant in town for food to be delivered.

'I didn't know your taste,' Eric said, 'so I ordered English. I hope that's all right for you.'

He served the homemade pie, potatoes and beans onto two plates and handed one to Monkey. As Monkey went to sit down at the table, Eric took his food and sat on to the enormous settee that dominated the penthouse.

A grin spread across Monkey's face. 'We don't have to eat at the table? Fridge!' And he flopped down next to his father.

'Do you like sport?' Eric asked.

Monkey made a gesture as if to say, *who doesn't?*

'Football!' Eric ordered, and the enormous plasma-screen on the wall adjacent to the window flickered on.

'Whaled!'

They ate their food in silence as they watched the exhibition match until an election broadcast interrupted the game. Eric directed the laser-remote to the archives and brought up an old-fashioned boxing match for his son to watch. 'There are advantages to being a barrister,' he explained. 'Sometimes, one is required to defend a client who's been accused of illegally supplying contact sport vids.' He shot a wry smile at his son. 'And, occasionally, one forgets to delete them from one's system.'

Monkey nestled into the folds of the sumptuous sofa, replete and content. This wasn't as bad as Tom and those other escapees had made out. In fact, he could get used to this. All the tension of the past week began to ease from his shoulders. His eyelids were heavy, drooping under the weight of a full stomach and last night's lack of sleep. *'In the blue corner, the Light-middleweight Champion of Europe...'* Images of the boxers on the screen merged with Angel waving to him from under the loco bridge. Gradually, the match commentary, the lingering smell of the pie and the panoramic view across town, all faded from his consciousness and he sank into a deep, and long overdue, sleep.

* * *

Monkey awoke to an irresistible force pressing on his head. His face was being pushed into the fabric of the sofa. He tried to wriggle free. His hands were clasped tight by some unseen power. Suddenly, an agonising pain shot through his shoulder and his arms were wrenched backwards. Cold metal snapped round his wrists. He couldn't breathe. His chest was burning with the effort of trying to draw in breath. Wildly he lashed out with his feet but a solid weight landed hard across his knee. Monkey tried to scream but the force on the back of his head pressed him harder into the rough upholstery. He was struggling for air; suffocating.

The hand that had been at the back of his head, released its grip, grabbed a handful of hair and jerked his head up. He gulped in air, filling his lungs, trying to focus his mind and work out what was happening. Frantically, he looked round the flat. The front door was standing wide open. Where was Eric? Had they got him too? Or had he managed to escape?

Two male Security officers held him, one on each arm, while six others, mainly female, stood by watching as he was frogmarched out of the apartment into the lift.

'Where are you taking me?' Monkey asked, desperately. 'Eric!' he called over his shoulder. 'Dad! Where are you?'

There was no reply.

The interior of the elevator was mirrored and, as the Security officers bundled him inside, Monkey saw his own reflection – barely recognisable as the 15-year-old he'd been a few weeks ago, carefree and eager to graduate. Now, he was gaunt; his eyes dull and heavy. Eric's sweats hung off his slight frame. He was a bub in man's clothing. He stretched out his foot to try and stop the closing doors in a last bid to resist arrest. One of the officers kicked it away, hard. Not before the doors had opened again, though, allowing Monkey one last view of his father's home. The door of the apartment was still open and an election broadcast was playing on the screen – a repeat of the one Eric had turned off earlier. As the lift doors ground shut again, Monkey saw a reflection of someone in the enormous picture window. He craned his neck to try and make out the figure – was it a Security officer going through Eric's things for evidence that he'd harboured a wanted traitor? His mind raced trying to think of anything incriminating he might have left there. Daz was right – he brought disaster to everyone he met. He must have been spotted and followed. What an idiot he'd been. In the split second before the elevator closed on his liberty, Monkey saw the face of the person in the penthouse. It was Eric – and he was showing no sign of distress at the arrest of his son.

As the lift began to descend, the cold reality hit him: he'd been set up.

Chapter 21

Down on the Farm

THE FARM complex was stark. Kilometres from anywhere, it was equipped with only the bare minimum of requirements: hard beds, even harder food and no hot water. The uniform was coarse, pink serge and Monkey had had to make his own before he was even allowed to integrate with the other 'farmers'. The regime was harsh: up at O-5:00 hours, washed, dressed and in the refectory by O-5:15 and out into the fields by O-5:30. They worked a 12-hour day, had to cook their own meals, wash their own uniforms and every worker was electronically tagged around the ankle. Because he was not yet 16, Monkey was housed in the junior wing so, as a pre-breeder, he had to attend evening classes to keep up with his education – which, as far as he could make out, was little more than brainwashing with a heavy T.R.E.A.C.L.E. emphasis.

On his fourth day, Monkey had been assigned to a muck-spreading detail. He was one of two pres scattering the foul-smelling slurry from the back of a horse-drawn rulley while a provider drove two enormous shire horses. An officer walked with them back and forth across the furrowed field, ensuring that there was no talking and certainly no slacking off. Monkey's arms and back ached from the relentless shovelling. His head throbbed from the lack of food and the stench of the manure. And his knee still hurt from where the Security officer had hit him on the night of his arrest. He could think of nothing but trying to escape. The high razor-wire fences, however, were prohibitive.

He craved information about Angel but, when he had tried to ask for news, he had met a wall of silence. In what little time there was for socialising, he found he was ostracised – or worse – by the other pres. Monkey's reputation, it seemed, had gone before him; he was bad news, not to be trusted. Other than a cursory *'shove up'* in the refectory, no one spoke to him – not even the hoods – some of whom he recognised by face from his days on the street. The normal pushing and shoving of the shower room or the supper queue became noticeably more targeted when Monkey appeared and, twice in his first three days, his towel had gone missing only to turn up again stinking and caked in slurry. And the warders seemed blind to his plight: he was just another *'revolting misfit'* who didn't know what was good for him and deserved all he got. Monkey felt utterly alone.

The midday meal was a rock of bread with a finger of cheese brought out to the fields by one of the kitchen detail. And, on the fourth day, it was delivered by Tragic. Monkey could barely contain his jubilation.

'Tradge!' He leapt to his feet, the pain in his body momentarily forgotten.

Tragic nodded in silent recognition. 'Keep it down,' he said, under his breath as he rummaged around in his basket. 'We're not supposed to speak.'

'Quiet!' yelled the guard.

Tragic held out a lump of grey bread. 'Meet me behind the education block at 18:30,' he mumbled, pulling out a sliver of cheese with an electronic key hidden under it. 'Use this to undo your tag and leave it somewhere you're supposed to be.' Then he added, 'Angel's OK.' Monkey's heart missed a beat. His mouth opened but Tragic gave an almost imperceptible shake of his head and handed him a paper cup of water from an enormous tank that was strapped to his back. 'I'll fill you in tonight. Don't forget to take off your tag.'

Monkey slipped the key into his pocket and fingered it frequently as he walked the field throughout the long afternoon, barely able to contain his excitement about the meet. Supper was from 18:15 and education began at 19:00, so Tragic's timing could not have been better. Monkey ate very little, washed up his dishes in the slimy cold water of the kitchen, left his tag under his pillow in the dormitory, then took advantage of two female guards chatting to sneak out in the direction of the education block.

True to his word, Tragic was waiting for him. Monkey flung his arms round his friend and hugged him to his chest, but backed off when it was clear that Tragic was not reciprocating.

'Wazzup, cuz?' Monkey tried to keep the hurt from his voice.

'Cut the street-speak, Mickey. And I'm Trevor now.'

Monkey swallowed back his irritation at being spoken to like a bub. 'OK – *Trevor*. What's happening?'

'Your rep's not good, Mickey,' Trevor explained. 'Word is, it's down to you that the village was raided.'

Monkey sighed, exasperated. 'I didn't… It wasn't…' His voice trailed off. What was the point?

'I don't care,' Trevor said. 'What's done is done. But I'm putting my neck on the line even talking to you, so let's just keep this brief.'

Monkey was taken aback at the turnabout in their relationship. Less than a month ago, he had been the one calling the shots: Tragic had been happy to tag along. Now it was reversed and it stuck in his craw. He lowered his eyes and listened as Trevor filled him in.

Angel, Trevor told him, was in a Sanctuary in town and she was bearing up fine. Her nurturer, Sally Ellison, was the solicitor representing all of the rebels and a special court had been convened to hear their cases. They had been fast-tracked through the legal system to get them safely out of the way before the election: citizens being re-educated were denied the vote, so the hearing would be in two weeks' time.

'Sally will be in to interview you either tomorrow or the day after. And, Mickey…' Trevor slapped him on the arm and Monkey was grateful for the first semblance of friendship he'd had since arriving. '…keep your nose clean and try not to do anything stupid.' Monkey opened his mouth to protest but Trevor went on, 'Darren Bates and some of the others from the underground community are in.' Monkey's shoulders slumped. That was all he needed, Daz and his cronies bad-mouthing him all round The Farm. 'Believe me, you are not their favourite person. So, just lay low until the trial – OK? I'll arrange to be on your lunch detail tomorrow – you can give me the key back then.'

With that, Trevor left and Monkey sank to the ground. He'd wanted to know more about Angel – where she was, how she was doing, whether or not she'd asked about him. But, before he could wallow in the mire of self-pity that was threatening to overwhelm him, the siren sounded for the start of education followed by an announcement: *'Michael Gibbon to the interview hall immediately.'*

Monkey started to panic. He wasn't wearing his tag and this sounded as though Sally Ellison was here to speak to him already. He knew that if he entered the interview hall without his electronic ID, the alarm would go off, so he quickly returned to the dormitory, slipping a lie to the warder, that he'd forgotten his plasma-pen. The female officer was either too distracted or too lazy to check and Monkey replaced the tag on his ankle without incident. But, when he was shown to the small interview booth where Farm detainees spoke to their visitors and legal representatives, it was not Sally Ellison who greeted him; it was Eric Randall.

'You proud of yourself?' Monkey almost spat through the unbreakable glass screen.

'Sit down, Michael. I owe you an explanation.'

Monkey indicated his pink jumpsuit, with a facetious expression. 'You think?'

'You made quite an impression on me the other evening.'

'So I see,' Monkey's hostility was palpable.

'And here we are again,' Eric spoke quietly but with authority. 'A father asking his son to be seated, yet his son – the one who is trying to convince The Assembly that the re-introduction of fathers into families will return some sort of intrinsic discipline to society – refusing.'

'You're no father of mine! *Fathers* don't dob in their own!'

'First of all, how would you know what fathers do or don't do? And secondly, would you have felt differently had I ensured that you were placed in a safe house where I could have access to you whenever I wanted?'

'What do you think?'

Eric shrugged. 'Well, this seems pretty safe to me. You're off the streets and I know where you are. And, as your legal counsel, I can come and see you whenever I deem it necessary to speak to my client.'

Monkey held him with a look of incredulity. 'You're trying to tell me you did this for my own good?'

Eric shrugged. 'Where better to express your views, than the platform of a show trial?' He scrolled through the portable plasma-file in front of him and indicated for his son to sit on the chair at the opposite side of the glass. 'You can thank me later,' Eric said, the smallest suggestion of a smile on his lips.

With an air of resignation, Monkey sat down opposite his father. 'You'd better be as good as your rep!'

'Let's hope you're better than yours,' Eric said, dryly. He stopped scrolling and looked his son in the eye. 'You will be tried on three charges: the first being treason, for which you will be tried along with 43 others. On that charge, as everyone has agreed to a united front, there is no conflict of interest, so there will be just the one defence team – led by myself, of course. I shall apply for an adjournment, but I think it unlikely it will be granted.' Monkey sighed, heavily.

'The other charges are: that you and one other did attempt to murder and then kidnap one Monica Morrison.'

Monkey groaned. *One other*! That meant Angel was in as much trouble as he was. He eyed Eric and said with resignation, 'You've forgotten murder. Aren't they gonna do me for shooting Fuse while they're at it?' Seeing Eric's confused expression, he added, 'Mark Watts – you know – my mate who got shot in The Plaza.'

Eric raised an eyebrow. 'An arrest has been made for the murder of Mark Watts but, if you would like me suggest that the DPP add *handling a stolen firearm* to your retinue of crimes, I can do so. They certainly have enough evidence from the CCTV footage of that night. Personally, I think you are in quite enough trouble as it is.' Monkey felt a momentary sense of relief at hearing that he was not going to be made a scapegoat over his friend's death, but it was only momentary.

'So, let's look at the attempted murder and kidnap: starting with the witness statement of the victim of those two charges, Monica Morrison – known to you, I believe, as Moni…'

Monkey slumped in his seat – it was going to be a long night.

'And, by the way,' Eric said, once more looking at the screen. 'I've contacted Vivian. She's agreed to speak for you at the trial.'

Monkey rolled his eyes. He was well and truly stuffed!

Chapter 22

Courting Trouble

TWO WEEKS, and several visits from his father later, Monkey took his first trip in a motorised vehicle. In other circumstances, he would have been excited. As the heavily armoured State coach drove into The Farm, he was reminded of the old football vids he'd watched with Trevor and the way the players had been transported around the country in the old days. This was a beast of a vehicle, by far the largest Monkey had ever seen and, with its security grilles at every window, it made him think of a gigantic metal fly's head.

As the only pre-breeder involved in the rebel trial, Monkey was walked in chains to the adult wing before being cuffed to a female officer. The trial was scheduled for 10:00 but it was not yet daylight and the last remnants of a late-spring frost nipped at his nose. Unlike the electric stealths that rumbled their way round town, the enormous coach ran on biofuel and the throbbing engine made the vehicle seem even more intimidating. He shivered.

The guard hauled him up the steps of the coach and chained him to the seat in front. He stared out of the window onto the grey landscape just as the first detail of 'farmers' was heading out to the fields. If he had any glimmer of hope that his trial would be successful, he might have felt relief at leaving The Farm complex, but Eric had been non-committal when asked about the possible outcome.

Monkey watched as other males from the breeders' and providers' wings were marched from their blocks and herded onto the coach, each one accompanied by a guard. He gave a shudder, partly from the cold but also the enormity of what awaited him. Darren Bates was in the seat behind him and made sure Monkey received an 'accidental' clock around the ear with his chains as he sat down. Monkey rested his head against the window and wondered if Angel would be in court. Then, with a sinking heart, realised that she'd probably bought into the whole *let's-blame-it-all-on-Mickey* like everyone else! He closed his eyes and took the opportunity to snatch an extra couple of hours' sleep on the journey to blank out the fears that were beginning to germinate in his head.

When he woke, the first thing he noticed, as they drove through the suburbs of the capital, was how different everything was – how much busier. The roads thronged with bikes and carts; stealths cruised the streets and the people all looked as though they were late. Even young nurturers with bubs were rushing. No one took any notice of the armoured coach as it rumbled its way towards the Courts of The Assembly, suggesting to Monkey that it was not an uncommon sight.

Monkey tried to take it all in. He'd been hearing about the capital since he was a bub but had never been there before and didn't know when, if ever, he'd get the chance to see it again. Everything about the place was big: the buildings, the roads, even the river was twice as wide as the one at home. Monkey fingered the scar on his palm and thought wistfully of the night he and Trevor had swum the river to escape the hood. If, that night, someone had told him that, in five-weeks' time, he'd be standing trial for treason, attempted murder and kidnap, he would have laughed in their face. At least he wasn't being tried for Fuse's murder as he'd feared.

He felt the bus reduce speed. As they progressed slowly, Monkey noticed more and more Security officers lining the streets. They were wearing helmets with visors down and many had riot shields in one hand and either a baton or gun in the other. His attention was drawn to the metal crush-barriers behind them, keeping the crowds at bay. It took him several minutes to realise that what he was seeing was not normal crowd control, even for the capital: something else was going on. The people behind the barriers carried placards and banners with the slogans: 'KIDS NEED DADS', 'P.A.R.E.N.T.' and 'VOTE UNITY: END THE SEGREGATION LAWS'. Through the thick glass windows of the coach, a muffled chant reached his ears, 'What do we want? Parenting together! When do we want it? NOW!'

'Look forwards!' ordered the female guard who was sitting next to Monkey.

He averted his gaze from the window and turned to face the front, slipping her a baleful glance. 'What's going on?'

Ignoring him, she called to the coach driver, 'Lower the shutters!'

Metal shutters descended on all the windows of the coach, plunging the interior into gloom. But, despite their best efforts, the guards could not keep their prisoners ignorant of the number of rebel supporters assembled in the capital. The front windscreen was unobscured and Monkey craned his neck to take in the scale of the protest. Thousands of demonstrators were lining the route as the coach crawled towards its destination. Placards were being thrust forward and a cheer, muted through the triple-glazed and shuttered windows, followed their progress like a Mexican wave.

'Eyes down!' commanded the guard and, grudgingly, he obeyed.

Monkey was confused. He knew that Daz had said the organisation was huge, but they were supposed to be living in secret communes around the country, not all together in the capital and out in the open, on show for every camera in the city to register their faces. A seed of dread began to germinate. He'd put his trust in Eric, hoping against hope that he'd be able to get him and Angel – and preferably, all of the rebels – off the charges. He was now beginning to realise the enormity of the movement and what he'd got involved with. He hoped this demonstration wasn't going to give the authorities an excuse to make an example of them and send them down for even longer.

Eventually, the brakes of the coach hissed as they came to a standstill and were unlocked from their seats.

'Stand!' barked an officer. They all complied. 'Keep your eyes on the ground!'

As the doors sighed open, a deafening din hit his ears. One by one, shackles clanking as they walked, the prisoners filed down the steps and along a narrow corridor of National Guard. Hordes of people were pushing forwards, thrusting their placards over the shoulders of the soldiers. Occasionally, Monkey could make out a phrase or word from the cacophony; 'We want Unity!' or 'End segregation now!'

'Keep moving!' The prison guards were pushing them forwards.

Monkey dared to raise his head slightly. They were heading towards an imposing building with a gothic façade. Scales of justice dominated the front of the building and Monkey wondered with a sense of irony, how much justice he – or any of them – were going to see. A whack to the back of his head sent him stumbling into the provider in front of him. On seeing the incident, nurturers, providers and even pres in the crowd, all surged forwards. With a roar of protest, the wall of National Guard was breached. Hands grabbed at Monkey's clothing and hair, then batons were brought down sharply on his shoulders and head. He was jostled and barged as guards, soldiers and Security officers quickly formed a cordon around the prisoners. Shields raised to protect themselves and their charges, the officers shuffled the group along an alley at the side of the courthouse and down into the holding cells.

The cell, into which he and a dozen others were crammed, was in the bowels of the building and obviously dated back to the last century. It was small, windowless and possessed only one toilet in the corner. He slumped down onto the long bench, with a sense of bewilderment.

'You see!' Daz said, with a sense of triumph, the minute the door slammed shut.

'See what?' Monkey felt dazed.

'That this thing isn't about *you*! It's massive.'

It was true, Daz had told him that the movement was huge and had infiltrated the entire country, but Monkey had never imagined anything like this. All those people out there – with one uniform aim: to end the Segregation Laws and allow parents to work together to give their offspring a balanced and supportive upbringing.

'What do you want me to say, Daz? I told you I was sorry I messed up. I misjudged the situation – OK?' Monkey was getting tired of Darren's blame.

'It's a bit feggin' late for apologies.'

Monkey stood up thrusting his chest forward and the two confronted each other like rutting stags. 'I'm sick of you trying to dump this on me, Daz. You talk about Unity but where was *your* unity, eh? I was actually doing something positive. I had a plan to unite the hoods but, the minute Angel got arrested, you just bottled it!'

'Bottled it?' Darren repeated, threateningly.

'You never gave me a chance.'

'A chance to what? Mess up again?'

'You…'

'Leave it!' Trevor, pushed the two apart. 'We're supposed to be united.'

'Tell *him* that,' Monkey snarled at Daz.

'You OK?' Trevor asked.

Monkey nodded. There was an awkward silence between them and Monkey was aware that the tension of the day was getting to everyone. 'Sorry, mate. I'm just sick of being his whipping boy.'

Trevor started speaking again, gabbling to try and ease his nerves. 'Mum and Dad are going to be on trial today, too. I don't know when they're arriving.' Monkey didn't respond. He didn't know what to say. Did they blame him for their arrests too? 'And Angel, of course,' Trevor added.

A flurry of excitement shot across Monkey's chest and he felt his face flush at the thought of seeing her.

When the cell door opened again, silence descended. The pulsating drone from outside was still audible. A male guard read out a list of their names in alphabetical order, before they were led along the corridor, up the stairs and into an enormous chamber.

At one end, there was an impressive, elevated desk. In front and below it, sat two teams of lawyers, each occupying an entire side of the room and making sure to keep well away from the opposition. The whole of one side of the courtroom was sectioned off to form a makeshift dock with metal bars and it was into this enormous cage that the rebels were herded. A door at the other end opened and a dozen females emerged into the cage – amongst them Jane and Angel. Monkey felt a surge of emotion rush through him. He was standing at the front of the batch of male prisoners but, by leaning back, he could see her clearly. She looked pale and drawn but as beautiful as ever. Her eyes flashed a sideways glance but she looked away again quickly.

A torrent of elation shot through Monkey's whole being. His spirits soared, restoring his resolve and fortifying his determination. Any fears he might have allowed to creep into his mind were banished the instant he saw her. He knew then, beyond any shadow of a doubt, that he wanted to spend the rest of his life with her; he wanted to live with her, to make love to her and raise children with her. He wanted it more than he wanted his own life and he knew that the only way to achieve it was to bring an end to the Segregation Laws. He turned his gaze to where Eric's team of lawyers had huddled together, Sally Ellison amongst them. As though sensing his son's eyes on him, Eric looked up, the merest hint of a smile twitching at the corners of his lips. Monkey felt his mouth dry as nerves constricted his throat. He nodded acknowledgement of the gesture.

Suddenly, the sound of a gavel on wood echoed round the court.

'All stand!' ordered the usher, raising her voice over the noise of the demonstration outside.

Two females and a male entered from a door at the front of the courtroom and took their places behind the elevated bench. All were wearing black robes with white cravats at their necks. Their attention was immediately drawn to the back of the court, from where the noise of the protest could be heard. A sombre, irritated look passed between them and a chill of premonition ran the length of Monkey's spine.

The judges flipped plasma-screens up from the desk and immediately began making notes. Without looking up, the sinister-looking female in the centre instructed the usher to read out the charges. The officer stood and opened her mouth to read from her own screen but, before she could speak, Eric rose.

'With all due respect, Madam…' The three judges stopped and looked at him with disdain. 'Far be it for me to remind your honours of the Laws of The Assembly, but the jury has not, as yet, been selected or sworn in.'

The judges resumed their writing.

'Nor will it be, Provider Randall,' said the central judge. 'And you are quite correct – it is *not* for you to remind us of the law. Continue.'

The official stood again. 'Karl Appleton – on the charge of conspiracy to commit treason how do you…'

'Your Honours!' As Eric stood up, the official sat down again. 'As citizens of this country, my clients have the right to a fair trial.'

The sinister judge looked over the top of her spectacles. 'Which they will get. But, as I hope you are aware, Provider Randall, under the Treason Bill that was passed amending the Criminal Justice Act – as traitors…' She looked at the Security officers at the back of the court. 'Can't anything be done about that racket?' The guard nodded and left the room. She went on, 'As *traitors*…' she emphasised the word. '… your clients have *no* right to trial by jury – and *habeas corpus* has also been suspended.' She held Eric with a steely glare and Monkey felt a swell of pride that Eric didn't flinch or break eye contact. 'You will be allowed to present their cases to the three of us and we will decide their guilt – or otherwise. Please continue!'

The official stood up and, as though on a seesaw, sat down immediately as Eric would not be silenced. 'Madam, if I may draw your attention to Section B, paragraph 82, item three of the Constitution of The Assembly…'

'Provider Randall…' The judge placed her spectacles on top of her head and said, in a weary tone, '…I am well aware of the Constitution of The Assembly – section, paragraph, chapter and verse! As, I hope are you.'

'Indeed, Madam.'

'Then you will be aware that, *"where there is a danger that jurors could be undercover members of an insidious, illegal or treacherous organisation, trial shall be by three members of the Higher Assembly and* not *by jury".*' She replaced her glasses. 'So, if you were hoping for a show trial, I'm afraid you are going to be disappointed. Now, let us have no further discussion on this matter.' She waved a hand towards the official who, once again, took to her feet. 'Continue.'

As the usher addressed each of the rebels, reading out the charges against them, Eric sat down, looked at Monkey and gave a slight shrug as if to say, *it was worth a try.* The female officer went down the list in alphabetical order. Monkey heard Karl from the village and Darren Bates both speak out confidently, proclaiming their innocence. There were others whom Monkey didn't know. He waited anxiously for his turn.

'Angelina Hope Ellison…' Monkey leant back and tried to catch her eye but she was staring straight ahead. 'On the charge of conspiracy to commit treason, how do you plead?'

He held his breath.

'Not guilty.' Angel spoke clearly, if a little faint. His heart skipped a beat at the sound of her voice.

'On the charge of attempted murder, how do you plead?

Monkey closed his eyes, appalled at the consequences of having involved her in his activities and trying to shut out the enormity of the situation. Again, Angel's voice was soft but firm.

'Not guilty.'

'On the charge of kidnap, how do you plead?'

'Not guilty.'

Monkey released the breath he'd been holding throughout and was so racked with guilt about the charges brought against Angel and the danger he had put her in, that he was startled when his own name was read out.

'Michael Eric Gibbon. On the charge of conspiracy to commit treason, how do you plead?'

Monkey opened his mouth to plead, then hesitated. He rubbed the scar on his palm nervously, remembering the day he'd walked into Mov Felton's I.D.H.C. instruction trying to impress everyone with his injury; the day he'd seen the vid of the old man in the war crimes trial. Of course! This was his opportunity: he would show them that he wasn't the stupid idiot they took him for. He was going to be strong; he was going to be brave and be a part of the movement that was going to change the law so that he and Angel could breed together and raise children together and create a better future. He stepped forward from the rest of the rebels and steadied himself against the railing. He looked at his father, then glanced sideways at Angel and took a deep breath.

'I refuse to plead because I do not recognise this Court – or The Assembly.'

Chapter 23

Riotous Behaviour

THE NOISE from the crowd outside seemed to be getting louder, penetrating the tension of the courtroom like a swarm of angry bees whining through the sultry anticipation of a storm. All three judges stopped writing. They looked at Monkey in bemused condescension. The female in the centre removed her glasses, rubbed the bridge of her nose as though finding the whole business tedious, and spoke to Eric.

'Provider Randall, may I suggest you speak to your client and inform him that he is in contempt of court?'

Eric rose, inclined his head to the judges, then turned to the dock. 'You must plead guilty or not guilty to the charges against you. Do you understand, Michael?'

Monkey swallowed hard. He wasn't sure what to do. He'd wanted to take a stand; prove to the likes of Darren Bates that he was serious about the cause; show them that he wasn't some lamebrain, some immature hothead who messed things up. But it wasn't going the way he'd hoped.

'Yes, but…' he faltered.

Then, from the other end of the dock, a small but confident voice spoke out. 'He's right. I want to change my plea. I don't recognise this Court either.' It was Angel.

Monkey leant back and caught her eye. She smiled, reassuringly.

From behind him, another voice spoke, 'I don't recognise this Court.' Monkey swung round to see Trevor grinning at him.

Another voice, then another spoke up, all repeating Monkey's statement. Until, soon, all 44 defendants were chanting in unison: 'We don't recognise this Court! We DON'T recognise this Court!'

'Order! Order!' barked the usher.

'Silence in Court!' demanded the principal judge, banging her gavel on the bench.

But the chanting continued, drowning out the crowd outside, increasing in volume until no other sound could be heard. 'WE DON'T RECOGNISE THIS COURT!'

The half-dozen guards inside the dock began swiping at the rebels with their batons, bringing them down hard on their shoulders and necks. Monkey saw Tom Patterson sink to his knees. Karl, too, was cowering as blows rained down on his head. Monkey, incensed at the treatment of his friend's father, kneed a male guard in the groin and, as he buckled, he brought his chained fists up under the guard's chin. It was the sign the rebels needed. Like a shoal of fish with one universal consciousness, the prisoners turned on their captors. The guards, completely outnumbered within the confines of the dock, found themselves helpless to control their charges. Some of the older rebels kept the defeated guards at bay, disarming them of their weapons and then using them to control them. The captors were now captive.

A key was located on one of the officers and quickly passed around. Within minutes, handcuffs and shackles were unlocked and a sense of liberation began to fuel the rebels' determination.

In the courtroom, Eric undid his lawyer's cravat and threw it down on the desk. He walked over to the dock, held out a hand to Monkey through the bars and joined in the chanting. Sally Ellison followed him, clasping Angel's hands and, soon, the rest of the defence legal team also swelled the ranks of the rebels. The few security officers within the main court appeared confused, looking from one to another, unsure what to do in the circumstances. Monkey and his fellow dissidents grabbed the bars of the cage and began rattling them violently, never ceasing in their chanting. In panic, the usher spoke into her ring-cam, obviously summoning more

Security as the united voices of the prisoners increased in volume.

As the defendants rammed against the railings from within the dock, the legal team began to pull from the court side. Soon, the wooden supports that held the bars began to creak under the strain.

'All together!' cried Monkey above the chanting. 'Push! Push!'

He could feel movement in the bars. Again and again, the defendants crashed against the barrier until the wooden framework of the dock gave way, sending shafts of wood and metal bars across the floor. Monkey, Trevor and the others, liberated at last, fell out of their cage with a victorious roar. At the same time, the large, panelled doors at the back of the court were thrown open and dozens of back-up security officers spewed into the courtroom, visors down, stun guns at the ready. Almost unnoticed, the judges scuttled to safety through the door to their chambers.

Monkey grabbed a metal bar. Others wielded stakes of broken wood, lashing out at the guards as they descended on them with batons and stun guns. The courtroom was in chaos. Stormtroopers opened fire with wax bullets, forcing Monkey to take cover. He grabbed Trevor and the two of them crouched down behind the benches and desks.

Some were too slow. Monkey watched as two darts pierced Darren Bates' pink Farm fatigues and he fell to the ground, shocked and temporarily paralysed by the effects of a stun gun. Others followed and were dragged from the court. National Guard soldiers had taken up position on the balcony. At any other time, it would have been full of members of the public but, for this trial, the public had been barred. Instead, it had become an ideal vantage point from which the security forces could attack the rebels, raining down hundreds of wooden, rubber and wax projectiles from above.

'Have you seen Angel?' Monkey shouted into Trevor's ear. Trevor shook his head. Monkey peered out from under the desk, scouring the mayhem of the courtroom for a glimpse of her.

Then, above the din of the fighting, he heard the sound of double quick marching echoing along the corridors. With a sinking heart, he realised that reinforcements had arrived. It had been a brave attempt to break free, but a vain one. Before he was re-arrested, he needed to find Angel. If he was going to spend the rest of his life on The Farm, he wanted one last chance to tell her how he felt.

A security officer was lying unconscious on the ground in front of them.

'Help me!' he yelled in Trevor's ear and, together, they dragged her out of the aisle and into the space behind the desk.

Quickly, Monkey slipped the visor from her head and placed it over his own. Then, deftly removing her armoured vest, he strapped it over his pink jumpsuit. He pulled the tiny stunning-device, no bigger than a plasma-card, from the guard's hands and, crawling on all fours, groped his way along the aisle between the benches. All around him, screams and cries told him that his fellow rioters were falling victim to the hard projectiles that had been designed to hurt but not kill.

Carefully, he edged his way towards the front of the courtroom, hoping that Angel might still be at the end of the dock where the females had entered. A storm of bullets hailed down around him and he dodged back into the relative safety of the space under the defence team's seats. Carefully easing his head out from behind his shelter, he saw her: as he'd thought, still in the dock, crouching down at the very back, using a panel of splintered wood as a shield; her nurturer's unconscious body by her side.

'Angel!'

But his voice was lost in the din of the riot and the confines of the helmet. He stumbled forward, arms outstretched towards her. A sharp, stinging blow hit his hand, knocking the commandeered stun gun to the ground, forcing him to recoil in pain. He turned, coming mask to mask with a stormtrooper, his stun gun poised to render Monkey incapable of movement the minute the red light indicated it had recharged. Instinctively, he sprang forwards and grappled the trooper to the ground. Retrieving his own device from where it had fallen, he thrust the prongs into the leg of the trooper, who crumpled, limp and dribbling, unable to defend himself. More wax bullets fell around them, glancing against the broken dock as Monkey quickly removed the soldier's head protection and weapon, and tossed them to Angel.

'Put it on and follow me!' he shouted at her though the unbreakable visor. A heavy, rhythmical thud was now resounding from outside the courtroom.

Angel grabbed his hand and clasped it desperately. 'What about Sally?' Her voice was tremulous and distorted through the visor's mouthpiece.

Monkey hesitated. 'I'll come back for her,' he said, eager to appease Angel but aware that it was unlikely he would be able to do so. 'Keep low. We're going to get out of here.'

Using the wooden panel as a shield against the showers of bullets, he led her to the door where she'd entered. He knew it went down to the female holding cells and might be leading them to further danger, but anywhere was better than being in the fracas of the courtroom. He rattled the door, but it was securely locked from the other side.

'Don't worry,' he told her, not even knowing if she could hear above the screams and cries all around them. 'The judges' bench is only a few metres away. Once we're up there, we can head out of the door they used.'

Keeping low, Monkey guided Angel to the three steps that led up to the raised dais where the judges had been less than 10 minutes before, only to discover that that door had been barred from within as well. Frustrated, his eyes darted round the room, eager to locate a way out, other than the main door which was blocked by National Guard troopers.

'Get under here,' he said, indicating the judges' desk.

A rhythmic pounding penetrated the noise in the courtroom, rising above the screams and shouts of the riot.

It was coming from the outer doors and Monkey suspected it heralded the arrival of more troops. With a sense of urgency, he ducked down next to Angel. He took off his protective headgear and helped Angel to remove hers. Then, taking her face in his cupped hands, he kissed her.

'I want you to know, I am so sorry for everything,' he said.

Angel put a finger over his lips. 'Don't apologise. You've been brilliant, Mickey. I am so grateful to you. If you hadn't...'

The rhythmic banging suddenly stopped. A thunderous crash and a victorious roar told them that that the crowd from outside had successfully battered down the doors. Hundreds of supporters swept into the courtroom; males, females and children – all cheering and yelling; their placards becoming both protection from, and weapons against, the security forces. With the doors open to the outside, a blast of fresh air swept through the court and more rebel supporters poured up the stairs, into the gallery, their sheer numbers overpowering the State troopers. Monkey saw several uniformed officers topple helplessly from the balcony in the mêlée, landing with sickening thuds on the floor or across the wooden benches.

As the protesters took control of the courtroom, Monkey stood up and helped Angel to her feet.

He was shocked to see the extent of the damage. 'Shiltz! The place is wrecked!'

Bodies, both protesters and security forces, littered the once regal interior. The courtroom furniture, made of sturdy oak, lay broken and splintered. People were writhing and groaning, others lay unconscious. But what Monkey noticed more than anything, was the number of people in the room not in uniform far outnumbered those wearing it: the rebels had beaten the State forces. People began to cheer and give each other congratulatory hugs as though they'd won.

'Wow! Look what you've achieved, Mickey,' Angel turned to him with unabashed admiration in her eyes. 'All this is down to you. If you hadn't taken a stand...'

Monkey shook his head. 'It's not over yet. We might have won in here, but there's an entire country out there still under Assembly rule. The only way we can achieve anything significant is to get to The Assembly; show them that we mean business.' He climbed onto the elevated bench, behind which the judges had been sitting. Without realising, or intending it, Monkey's stand against The Assembly had elevated him to leader and he took on the mantle unselfconsciously. 'OK – listen up. We might have won the battle of the courtroom, but there's still a war going on out there. We need all the able-bodied adults to take the visors, guns and ring-cams from the security forces and then guard them up on the balcony! Anyone with any medical or nurturing experience, is to bring the injured and children into this courtroom and keep them safe. The rest of us…' he paused, suddenly aware that he was the focus of everyone's attention, '…will, er, make our way to The Assembly.'

A roar of approval went up and he felt Angel slip her hand into his. 'Quite the revolutionary, aren't you?' she teased.

`Come on,' he said, jumping down from the bench, then kissed her lightly on the lips before heading for the door.

From the foyer of the court, he looked out through the battered doors, down the steps to where thousands of protesters had gathered. But, the atmosphere was no longer that of the peaceful protest he'd seen when he'd arrived at Court that morning. Monkey was shocked at the scene before him. The crowd had become ugly. Pavements had been torn up and slabs of stone, smashed and bloodstained, littered the ground. Metal bins rolled across the streets where they had been wrenched up and used as weapons. Discarded placards and banners formed a carpet of debris over which the security forces charged in waves, wielding batons. The noise was deafening.

Monkey was momentarily confused. Faced with such an orgy of violence, his plan of going to The Assembly seemed naïve. He didn't even know how to get there! He hesitated, looking round for Eric who, he was sure, would know the way – preferably without having to negotiate the riot in front of him. He clutched Angel's hand and drew her back inside the foyer of the courthouse to give himself time to think.

But the scene inside was only marginally less intimidating than outside. Bodies lay all over the floor, many groaning in pain, others silent and unconscious. Monkey's attention was directed to where a nurturer was tending to the needs of the injured, speaking into her ring-cam, organising others and administering first aid from a medical bag. Instantly Eric went over to speak to her. And, when she looked up, Monkey was struck by a jolt of recognition. It was his own nurturer: Vivian.

He stormed across the forecourt; all the old bitterness he'd felt towards his nurturer rising like bile again. 'What the fegg do you think you're doing here?'

Vivian looked up. 'My job,' she said, matter of factly. And then, as she continued administering a pain killing injection to the leg of a wounded provider, 'You did well in there, Mickey – I was proud of you.'

'Yeah, right! I was born the wrong gender for you to be proud of anything I ever did.'

Vivian shrugged. 'People change. You've changed – or at least I thought that you had.'

Monkey felt his hackles rise as the old, familiar pattern of behaviour between them threatened to start up again. But, before he could come back with some sarcastic retort, an excited childlike yell echoed through the cavernous entrance lobby. It was Penny.

'Mickey!' She threw herself against his chest and hugged him. 'I'm so sorry! I should never have dobbed you in – or Angel. I'm really, really sorry.'

Monkey held her at arm's length and looked at her sternly. 'So, why d'ya do it?'

Before Penny could reply, Vivian's concern was of a more urgent nature. 'How the hell did you get here? Why aren't you at home with your grand-mov?'

Penny lowered her eyes and bit her lip. 'Moni brought me. On the train.'

'Moni?' Monkey shook his head in disbelief. 'And you expect me to believe you're sorry when you're still hanging with that squirrelling snake.'

Eric raised his eyebrow. 'Monica Morrison? But she's a witness for the Prosecution.'

'No, she isn't,' Penny said, eager to tell them the good news. 'She's changed sides.' Monkey raised a querying eyebrow. 'It's true,' Penny continued eager to convince him. 'After you got arrested, Eric... I mean, Dad,' she corrected, 'came round loads and was talking to Mum and explaining all the rebel stuff, about working together to make decisions about children. Anyway, I told Moni...'

'You told Monica what I'd been talking to you about?' Eric's jaw set.

'Yes – and she agrees with you and she said she was going to come here and tell you all before they could call her as a witness.'

'Yeah, right!' Monkey was sceptical.

'Where is she?' Eric asked.

'She's just over...' Penny turned round; then stopped. 'Oh!' Moni had disappeared. Monkey scoured the crowd for any sign of his former adversary. He had an uneasy feeling about her involvement.

Vivian looked at her daughter. 'Penny, I want you inside the court with the other children.'

'Aw, but...'

'No, buts – do as your mother tells you,' Eric interjected and Penny skulked off into the courtroom.

Vivian stood up and walked towards another injured protester. 'Now, Mickey – I'll do my job and you do yours: don't you have an Assembly to address?'

Chapter 24

Storming the Assembly

AS MONKEY headed for the door, he gave one last look round the courtroom. Of the original 44 prisoners, only 23 were still standing. Apart from Angel and Eric, Monkey knew only Trevor, his father, Tom, and Karl from the village. Darren Bates, having been rendered helpless by a stun gun, had received a blow to the head and lay unconscious in the foyer of the courthouse; Jane Patterson, like Sally Ellison, had been injured in the riot and had not, as yet, regained consciousness. Others had had limbs shattered in the fighting. A provider called Alan, whom Monkey had met on The Farm, had been knocked to the ground and trampled on when the stormtroopers had arrived: his body lay on the ornate marble floor of the foyer covered in coats.

Casting a look around the dead and injured, Monkey took a deep breath and focused his mind.

'Right then!' He squeezed Angel's hand – he knew better than even to suggest that she stay behind with the nurturers and children – and they stepped outside once again.

The courthouse seemed to have become a focus for the protesters and security forces alike and the surrounding streets were chaotic. Monkey watched as a barrage of horses charged towards a group of protesters and they scattered, terrified, running for their lives. Others lobbed stones, bricks, scaffold poles – anything they could lay their hands on – at the security forces. Some of the protesters were lighting homemade incendiary devices and throwing them into the sea of security. One or two could be seen holding up ring-cams, recording the scenes of violence and brutality on both sides.

'The Assembly Building is about a kilometre that way,' Eric said, pointing to the road directly in front of the court. 'And I suspect that, whichever way you choose to go, the roads will be much the same. This isn't some isolated little protest, you know.'

Monkey thought for a second then looked round. 'If we can't go to The Assembly, let's see if The Assembly will come to us. Is there a PA system anywhere?'

Trevor ducked back into the building and returned with an old-fashioned megaphone.

Monkey put it to his lips. 'Stop it! All of you!' There was no discernable hesitation in the affray. The faces of the security officers were concealed behind visors, but the universal expression of the protesters was anger. The wail of sirens drowned out anything he might have hoped to say and Monkey saw a wall of stealths trundling towards him from the direction of The Assembly. They were three wide and several deep, taking up the whole width of the road.

'They're here!' he said, grinning at Angel and the others with a degree of satisfaction. 'The Assembly's coming to talk. We've done it.'

But as the battalion of armoured vehicles moved closer, Monkey's confidence faltered and, finally, died. This, he realised, was no delegation for conciliation; this was an invasion force. The armoured vehicles rumbled down the street, showing no respect for the people in their path, ploughing on relentlessly, with no regard for human life. Providers, nurturers and even children fell under the caterpillar tracks, their screams of fear and pain inaudible above the din. Monkey saw a young breeder, not much older than he was, try to climb up one of the vehicles but an officer appeared from the turret of the stealth and brought a baton down on the side of his head. He lost his balance, caught his belt on the side of the vehicle and was dragged screaming along the road until the fabric finally snapped and he tumbled, helpless, under the tracks of the first vehicle and then the one following it.

Angel gasped and buried her head against Monkey's shoulder. 'This is awful. You have to stop it.'

Monkey put the loud hailer to his lips again but what could he do? He looked around at the scene of mayhem before him and realised he was impotent. Nothing he could say could have any impact on what was happening. He lowered the speaker and shook his head.

'All that crap we used to be taught about sowing the seeds of love and reaping the harvest of compassion. Look at them…' His voice tailed off.

Angel took his hand and squeezed it. 'Come on, you can't give up now. You were a hero in there.'

Monkey raised the loud hailer again. 'Put down your weapons now. This is not respect…'

A crush barrier was hurled through the air and landed at his feet.

'It's no use,' he said to Angel. 'We've got to get to The Assembly. We've got to speak to the Premier. Get her to see reason. Repeal the Segregation Laws, otherwise, it's going to escalate.' He looked round for a way round the back of the courthouse or down a side street but, everywhere he looked, there was rioting.

Placards and banners were now being set alight and tossed at the security forces. Anything flammable was burning. Suddenly, everything happened so fast. A building that was under refurbishment burst into flames, sending shards of glass like needles into the crowd. Security regrouped and, with arms linked behind their backs to form an impenetrable wall, they systematically began penning protesters into small groups down the side roads.

One group managed to burst through and surged forwards, attacking one of the stealths and rocking it so violently that it toppled and fell onto its side, blocking the road and sending a wave of triumphant cries through the crowd.

Instantly, there was a deafening report, as though a gun had been fired and Monkey saw a white vapour trail arcing through the air as tear gas grenades were fired into the midst of the protesters filling the streets with biting chemical vapour.

'Cover your eyes!' Monkey called out as he squinted, to try and lessen the effects of the chemical. People were panicking as cartridge after cartridge of gas exploded into the streets of the capital. 'Keep calm!' he yelled, frantically looking for the protective helmet he'd put down to address the crowd. But to no avail.

A burning, tearing sensation ripped at his throat as though he was choking on acid. He sank to his knees, weak with the shock. Angel! He had to make sure she was OK. He tried to call out her name but spluttered and collapsed, coughing as the gas burnt his lips and choked in his throat. Tears streamed down his cheeks as though a thousand onions had been rubbed into his eyes. The scenes of mayhem blurred before him. Staggering forwards through the fog, he reached out into the thick corrosive cloud, trying to feel his way out of the chaos; desperate to ease the burning in his eyes, nose – anywhere that had been exposed to the gas. He needed to breathe: if he could only get some clean air into his lungs. He stumbled against a wall and slithered down to the ground.

Then, through the confusion and chaos he heard a voice, 'That's him. That's Michael Gibbon. He's the ringleader.'

Painfully, he wrenched open his eyes – just enough to recognise the speaker. Even through her headgear she was unmistakeable: Moni Morrison was standing in front of a platoon of stormtroopers and she was pointing straight at him.

She was the last thing Monkey saw before a blow to the head rendered him unconscious.

Chapter 25

Gone Fishing

A KLAXON sounded, followed by a metal door being battered from outside. Monkey's head pounded. His throat felt as though he'd swallowed something caustic. His eyes were raw. He was aware of a rolling sensation beneath him, as though the whole world was being rocked. An electric light flickered on overhead and he raised his head tentatively from the rough pillow. Nothing was familiar. The room was small and stark with metal walls painted dark grey. He swung his legs over the side of the bed and felt rivets beneath his feet, like rows of cold carbuncles running along the floor.

He was at sea, of that, he was in no doubt. Monkey had never been on a ship before, but he'd heard about them – and seen them in I.D.H.C. at school. School! It seemed like a lifetime away.

The rolling of the waves, the ache in his head and the nauseated feeling that he'd ingested something toxic made him stagger back against the bunk. Where was he? Was he being transported? If so, to where? He looked round the tiny cabin. There were no windows: nothing to give him any indication as to where he was, or even whether it was day or night. He felt sick.

'Stand!' The door burst open and a female wearing a security uniform strode in.

Monkey straightened up, but a sudden lurch sent him staggering forwards and he threw up down the front of the guard, before collapsing on the floor. She turned, without speaking, and the door clunked shut behind her. Monkey remained on all fours surrounded by his own vomit. He closed his eyes to try and curb the hideous swimming sensation in his head. Could his life get any worse? The door opened and the guard reappeared with a bucket and mop.

'Clear it up!' she barked. 'I'll be back for you to report to the Governor's cabin in 15 minutes. And make sure you're properly attired.' She indicated a familiar pink jumpsuit on the end of the bunk before, once more, leaving him alone.

If Monkey had been in any doubt before, this confirmed that he was, once again, imprisoned. Only, this time, it would appear he'd been upgraded from The Farm to one of the penal ships anchored off the coast. Great – solitary confinement *and* seasickness!

Fifteen minutes later, he walked the narrow corridors of the penal ship, cuffed and shackled, until they came to a cabin at the fore. The guard accompanying him opened the door and ushered him inside to where a female, small-built with a face like a terrier, sat behind a gargantuan desk.

'Ever been fishing?' she asked, without looking up.

Monkey thought back to the days when he and Trevor would take their rods and sit on the banks of the river for hours on end in the hopes of catching the barbel that was rumoured to be the size of a porpoise. They seldom caught so much as a tiddler, but the memory brought a nostalgic lump to his throat. He nodded; frightened to open his mouth and speak, in case it triggered a rush of emotion.

'Good. You'll be on fishing detail from O-4:00 hours tomorrow.'

*   *   *

By four o'clock the following morning, Monkey was glad of any reprieve from the boredom of his solitary cabin. He had neither spoken to, nor seen, anyone since his meeting with the Governor the previous morning. His meals had been delivered to his cabin, as had his all-weather gear. But, if he had any illusion that the fishing that had been referred to bore any resemblance to the gentle angling he and Tragic used to enjoy, it was shattered the second he was led on board the boat. This was fishing of an altogether more arduous nature.

He was assigned to the small fishing vessel – his fluorescent pink oilskins the only thing to identify him from the normal crew – that and the ever-present guard who accompanied him to prevent any attempt at escape. Although, how anyone was supposed to escape when they were miles from land with swells sometimes several metres high, Monkey didn't know.

The work was hard – harder than he had ever imagined; setting the drift nets, hauling in the catch, drenched by waves that often crashed over the bows threatening to knock him overboard. Monkey ached in muscles he never knew existed. He would return to the penal ship every evening, exhausted. The days and weeks passed in a haze of sea spray and fish. Sometimes on the boat, they would drop anchor for an hour or two once the nets were set and the others, a provider and his son, would invite him into the galley for a mug of tea, but his guard invariably shook his head to warn them off – fraternisation with the prisoner was not allowed.

Each day was exactly like the last – perhaps the haul would be bigger or the weather better, but the routine was the same. Get up at four, back at 20:00, asleep by 21:00. Except for Sundays. Sundays were rest days – and he made the most of them, spending every Sunday in an exhausted stupor, trying to recoup enough energy to face the week ahead. There was nothing to do in his cabin – he wasn't allowed books or a plasma-screen. All he had were his memories and he lay on his bunk, hands behind his head, reflecting on his life before he knew anything about P.A.R.E.N.T.

He'd heard nothing from his father about any sort of re-trial – he'd just been dumped here and left. He was drifting through his life, much like the nets drifted in the ocean.

One night, about a month after his arrival on the penal ship, he crashed onto his bunk too tired to undress. It came as a shock to him to realise that he had forgotten his own 16th birthday. It had come and gone the previous week with no celebration; no cards or gifts and no graduation party. He felt numb. When he thought of the plans he'd had – he'd been going to have a massive send-off. Angel would have been invited – and the others from the hood. He'd have been bought gifts for his new breeder pad and talked about his plans for the future as a pro-footballer. He allowed himself an ironic smile as he thought about how he would have been trying to impress Angel, hoping against hope that she would choose him for breeding later on. He sighed, wondering where she was now. Had she been arrested, too? Was he responsible for ruining her life as well as his own? He did a mental checklist of the other people in his life: Trevor, Eric, Tom and Jane – Vivian! Now there was a surprise: Vivian with all her male-hating, Distaff-supporting, pro-revolutionary fervour, suddenly changing her tune.

Had it all been worth it? he wondered. Would they ever change the system and, if so, could co-parenting really work in practice? Could males and females truly work together to raise children like in the olden days? If so, why had there been a revolution in the first place? All these questions went round and round his head until, finally, he fell into a deep, dreamless sleep.

He woke the next morning to a clattering of feet along the metal corridors. Although his cabin had no porthole, he sensed it was much later than he was normally woken. Slipping out of bed, he put on the light and banged on the door.

'Hey! What's happening?' he called. 'Let me out!'

After a few moments, the door opened and a male guard entered holding a large paper bag. 'Here you are, mate. Get dressed.'

Monkey looked in the bag. It contained Eric's sweats, the clothes he'd been wearing before he'd been arrested. 'What's going on?'

'It's over, mate,' the guard said, grinning. 'Unity's only bleedin' well won the election. And the new Premier's offered an amnesty to all political prisoners.' He punched Monkey on the arm, playfully. 'We done it, mate! It's over. And you? You're a feggin' hero, you are.'

Monkey was carried along the corridor in a rush of released prisoners, all cheering and jostling to get to the recreation area. An enormous info-screen was showing streams of civil unrest from Wessex to Deira; from Anglia to Mercia. The news item stated that the entire country had erupted into scrupulously timed and synchronised riots immediately prior to the election, forcing the resignation of the Premier and the dissolution of The Assembly. The Unity Party had won a landslide victory. Pictures of the civil unrest and subsequent national celebrations were flashed onto the screen, including an image of Monkey on the steps of the courthouse, rallying the rioters through a loud hailer – judiciously edited, he noticed, so as to omit his somewhat less than glorious collapse and arrest. But, what wasn't seen didn't matter, and a roar of whoops and hollers went up from his fellow freed prisoners. Monkey felt himself being lifted up into the air and propelled around the room on a sea of raised hands to chants of '*for he's a jolly good fellow.*' Someone yelled, 'Three cheers for Mickey Gibbon!' and the entire penal ship reverberated with cries of appreciation.

Monkey felt confused; bemused even, by such hero-worship. He was as accidental a hero as ever there was and, regardless of how the media portrayed him, he knew the truth. And there was someone else who knew the truth too. As he was carried round the crowd on a wave of adulation, Monkey craned his neck to see the screen and try to catch a glimpse of her. The newsreel was on a continuous loop and he waited until his part came around again, scouring the screen for any sign that Angel had survived unhurt. But there was nothing to appease his anxiety. When the celebrations had subsided, he was left feeling flat and fearful. He just wanted to see Angel but he had no idea if she was alive or dead.

A fleet of luxury State coaches came to collect the released prisoners and there was a sense of camaraderie as the men said their goodbyes, each wishing the others well. An air of expectation hung amongst them with the talk of the New Assembly and the changes that would be made. Everyone was excited to be going home. Monkey stared bleakly out of the coach window as they neared the capital, ready to be transferred to the locos for the last leg of their journey. He was 16 now: a breeder in the old regime. But who and what was he now? And did he even have a home any more?

Chapter 26

Aftermath

MONKEY idly tossed pebbles into the river as he waited. The September evening was heavy and humid. From time to time, he rubbed the scar on his palm, remembering how he and Trevor had narrowly escaped from the hood across the same stretch of water: it seemed a lifetime ago. The music from the Lunar Park behind him was incongruously jolly and the reflected lights from its rides danced on the water. He sent another stone skimming across the surface. He turned on his ring-cam and checked the time: 20:00. She should have been here by now.

Hands slid across his eyes from behind and he felt a delicate kiss planted on the side of his neck. 'Guess who?' she giggled.

He turned within the confines of Angel's arms and held her tightly. 'God! I missed you.'

She laughed and pulled away. 'You only saw me yesterday!' Then, looking more serious, 'I've been trying to get hold of you ever since I left. Why was your ring-cam turned off? '

Monkey felt himself start to well up when he looked at her: how frail she was these days! Her hair, once cascading down her back, was cropped and stubbly, like a newly hatched chick. And her scars glared angrily from the tufts. The first time he'd seen her, she'd worn a headscarf to save him from the shock. She'd still been in hospital, but he'd told her to take it off. 'I love you, however you look,' he'd told her. 'I wouldn't care if you had no head – I'd still love you!' They'd laughed together – then cried as she'd told him about her head injuries at the hands of a stormtrooper. She'd required brain surgery and been in an artificially induced coma for weeks. Monkey had held himself responsible but she'd had none of it. 'I told you then, and I'm telling you now – it was *my* choice.' She slipped into a teasing imitation of street-talk, 'Don't big up your part, Monk! I do have a brain of my own you know – however battered up it might be! Now, I don't want to hear another word about it being your fault – OK?' Love and compassion and desire had overwhelmed him and he'd thought he might explode with the intensity of his emotions.

He looked into her eyes now, even more beautiful framed by her fragile features and wispy hair. He shook his head. 'You first: how was your interview?'

She shrugged. 'OK – I think. I still find it hard to concentrate for long but they said they'd take that into consideration and let me know. And, by the time I start, I should be back to normal, so – who knows? Fingers crossed, eh?'

'You'll get in, no probs. Star student like you? You'll be able to have your pick of unis.'

'We'll see. Anyway, tell me how you got on. What did the doctors say?' Angel asked him.

Monkey slipped his hand in hers and sat down on one of the new benches facing the river, pulling her down onto his lap. He sighed. 'Not good.' He looked out across the water so as not to meet her eye. He didn't want her to see his sadness. 'Looks like I won't be able to play professionally.'

'Oh, Mickey!' Angel dropped her head on his shoulder.

'No, it's fridge – really. I knew what they were going to say, so it's no big deal.' Monkey put on a brave face, determined not to let her see his disappointment. The severity of the knee injury sustained at the time of his arrest had come to light at his trial for the Pro-academy when he'd failed the physical. But he'd still held out hope that he'd be given the OK in the end. He'd told no one the devastating news, not even Eric who'd arranged the appointment for him at one of the top clinics.

They sat in silence for some time, the kaleidoscopic lights flickering on the water and the discordant tunes and squeals of laughter behind them in stark contrast to their mood.

It was Angel who broke the silence. 'You could get a second opinion. We could go up to the capital to one of the teaching hospitals and…'

Monkey squeezed her hand. 'Thanks, but there's no point. It's been playing me up since that bastard arrested me so I knew what was coming. Said I'd never be fit enough to ref professionally either.' He took a deep breath, forced his mouth into a smile and turned his face to hers. 'But they said I could probably train as a manager or coach if I wanted – and I could play social football.' He tried to make light of it, 'But, hey, it's not like it's the end of a dream or anything – I've still got you.' He looked away so that Angel wouldn't see his sadness.

'And will you? Train as a manager?' she asked gently, aware of the finality of the news he'd received.

Monkey shrugged. 'Dunno what I'll do. It was all I'd ever wanted for as long as I can remember. I need to rethink my whole life plan.'

'Well, not the *whole* of it – I hope.'

She bent forward and kissed him on the lips. Monkey responded, pulling her to him and feeling her lips parting under his. He ran his tongue across hers and felt an involuntary pulse stir in his loins, as he so often did since the 'vitamins' had been withdrawn under The Unity Party. He pulled back and grinned sheepishly. Although he and Angel had often talked about breeding in the future, the legislation was still going through that would allow them to consummate their friendship and Monkey felt embarrassed that his body was such a giveaway.

'You can't get rid of me that easily,' he laughed to try and divert her attention. 'I love you so much, you're gonna be in my life forever – like it or not!' He pushed her forwards playfully. 'Hey, who knows, now I'm never going to be a pro-footballer, maybe I'll even go to uni with you?'

Angel stood up laughing. 'Why not? You are an urban legend, Michael Gibbon! I think that qualifies you to study Politics with the best of them!'

He put his arm around her shoulder and they walked along the riverbank, towards the town. 'Maybe I could study Law,' he ventured. 'Eric was talking about me going and working with him one day. We could be: Randall and Gibbon – Attorneys-at-law! Or, better still: Randall and *Son*!' He ran ahead slightly then turned around and walked backwards, so that he was facing her. 'You remember when we were in court and there were all those people in cravats – that could be me, eh?' He pretended to be flicking a cravat between his fingers. 'Actually, I think I'd suit a cravat. I'm sure Eric's got one I could borrow.'

'You're such an idiot, Mickey!' Angel laughed at him affectionately, then her face adopted a more serious expression. 'How is it living with your Dad?'

'Aw, it's fridge! He's all right, you know, old Eric. And he's been seeing this nurturer recently, so he's hardly ever at home – which means that I get his massive plasma-screen all to myself most nights, *and* he leaves me his card details to order in takeaways. Trevor comes round now and then but he's heavily into that Zoë he met in the village. They're going to go to uni together.'

Tom and Jane were now living together openly, as were many other couples – whether they had bred together or not. Since the repeal of the Segregation Laws, cohabitation was being positively encouraged, especially where there were children in the household. Trevor's girlfriend, Zoë, had had no compunction about moving in with him and his parents.

Angel nodded and smiled. 'And Penny? How's she doing since Moni left?'

Monkey took up his place by her side once more as they strolled along the towpath, holding hands. 'Doesn't say much. She comes over to Dad's every few days but I think it hit her hard. She idolised Moni – God knows why!'

'Moni was my friend, too, you know,' Angel feigned offence.

Monkey shook his head. 'Do you hear from her?' Not that he cared, but he thought he should ask out of politeness.

'No. I doubt we'll see her again. I was in hospital when she left but Sal said her nurturer moved them out under false IDs the day after the election. I felt a bit sad that she didn't even come to say goodbye.'

'All I can say is: you need to pick your friends more carefully!'

'Hey! I picked you, didn't I?'

They continued with their easy banter as they walked back to town, stopping occasionally to kiss – as passionately as Monkey could bear without losing control. They kept a watchful eye out for marauding hoods. Although the opening up of the zones and the encouragement of co-parenting and discipline was being re-introduced, change did not happen quickly, and there was still a nucleus of pre-breeders who were out of control; roaming the streets causing trouble, albeit more vandalism than violence since the election.

When they reached the Upper Bridge, Monkey began to guide Angel away from the river towards Moonstone Park where she still lived with Sally and her brother, Alex. Although Sally Ellison had traced the father of her children, Paul McFadden, an activist with P.A.R.E.N.T. in Wessex, he was now living with a different nurturer and had bred a new family. Angel and Alex were planning to visit mid-term in the autumn, if Angel was strong enough by then.

'Where are we going?' Angel asked.

'You look knackered. I'm walking you home.'

Angel looked disappointed. 'I still haven't seen where you live these days.'

Monkey pointed to the large tower blocks at the other side of the river. 'You see that block on the right? Well, Eric's is right at the top.'

'I meant from the inside,' she smiled.

'Oh – OK.' Monkey looked uneasy. Although curfew had been abolished and there was free passage for anyone to enter any zone at any time of day or night, he'd never thought to invite her up to the penthouse as he did Trevor. 'I don't know if Eric will be in or not,' he warned.

'He won't.' Angel winked at him. 'You know that nurturer he's seeing? Well, she works with Sal and it's all arranged.' A knowing look spread across her face. 'In fact, he's likely to be out all night – if you get my drift.'

Monkey swept her up into his arms and kissed her again. 'You are one amazing woman, you know!'

She pulled a packet of the newly available contraceptives from her pocket and shook them in Monkey's face. 'I thought, with the coast clear, it was about time we practised some *pleasure not procreation!* What d'you think?'

'I think,' he said with a huge grin, 'I love you very much.'

Acknowledgements

I would like to thank the following people for their advice, patience, expertise, time and all-round support while I was writing *Toxic Treacle*:

My long suffering agent, Caroline Montgomery of Rupert Crew Ltd, for having faith in me and this book through its many, many re-writes; my fellow authors: Michelle Lovric and Nick Green for their help with a number of specific difficulties I encountered, as well as Diana Kimpton for her book 'Cracking Codes'; Craig Orr Q.C. for his advice on the legal system, Lynda Sinclair and Kameran Dhillon for painstakingly proofreading the manuscript for me, Claudia Pelligrini for her insight, Fiona Shoop at GGP for her objectivity during the editorial process and, finally, my husband Frank and children, Imogen, Verien and Jacob for their unswerving support through the rough and the smooth.